# PLASTIC GIRL

# EXTINCTION

## JESSICA MAISON

Published by Wicked Tree Press in 2022.

Author: Jessica Maison
Copy Editor: Trisha Alcisto Crabtree
Proofreader: Katrina Roets
Cover Artist: Leraynne

This is a work of fiction. The characters, incidents, and dialogues are products of the author's imagination and not to be construed as real. The author's use of names of actual persons, living or dead, and actual places is incidental to the purposes of plot and is not intended to change the entirely fictional characters in the work.

Submit inquiries through www.wickedtreepress.com.

*To Michael, the being lodged deep in my heart*

"Those who see all creatures in themselves
And themselves in all creatures know no fear.
Those who see all creatures in themselves
And themselves in all creatures know no grief.
How can the multiplicity of life
Delude the one who sees its unity."

*Īśā Upaniṣad*

# Prologue

*Light, the kind where no shadows are possible. The light into which the dead release themselves. The light that consumes all souls and makes us one. The light that draws the seed up through the dirt and dries up the plant in the end. The light that pushes us into our mothers' wombs, and the light we burn through with our first breaths. The light we spend a lifetime longing to return to, especially when we stare at the sun too long. The light that takes away our fear at the end. The light that leads to many paths, all necessary, all meaningless.*

*Some believe the light to be a place of salvation, but this wasn't that kind of light. This light was already full. This light didn't need but would take, nonetheless. This was the light that burned and churned souls all day and all night. This light was relentless.*

*Slurp. Squish. Slurp. Squish.*

*Millions of fusion reactions happened in a second, every second, every minute, every day, every month, every year, always, blasting hydrogen atoms together to form helium, over and over and over again. This light was energy, and it was life, and it was creation, and it was hungry, and it only cared to keep reacting and fusing and bursting out, radiating everything it slammed into. It did not have time for plans— only action, only creation and destruction. It blasted out into the universe and collided with galaxies, stars, and planets. Everything it contacted was transformed in one way or another, including Earth.*

*In the beginning there was light, and whether it was named goddess or god, it began creating and destroying in a never-ending cycle, and would continue to do so until the energy ran out and the reactions and fusions ceased. Many would harness this light, grow gardens with it, make life with it, create worlds with it, even expand universes with it, but no one could overpower it, not until they returned to darkness. Only the dark could stop the light, and only the light could stop the dark.*

*In this light, creatures had lost themselves completely and found themselves born anew.*

*Slurp. Squish. Slurp. Squish.*

*Iris squeezed her eyes shut, but no matter how tightly she closed them, darkness would not come, only blazing golden light, tinted with red. She opened her eyes, and the full power of the light blasted into her. She floated, feet dangling, lost in the all-consuming light radiating from the creature above her. The light stole her sense of time and space. She felt like a globular being, like one of the bright pulsing amoebas floating around her, slightly less golden than the light itself. She reached for the floating dark spots interrupting the ceaselessly bright light shining into her eyes, into her pores, and into her flesh, tearing into her spirit. She yearned for darkness in this light. It felt like a star had collided with her and wanted to inhabit her body. The nape of her neck burned as she felt it split open, her flesh sizzling around the edges.*

*Slurp. Squish. Slurp. Squish.*

*She felt the light pull something out of her neck as it tried to slip her molten flesh off her skeleton and discard it at her feet like folds of cooling lava at the edge of a volcano. Her insides tugged, and her throat pulled inward as that something reached out of the back of her neck, fusing with the light. Iris tossed her head back, snapping that something inside. She looked down at her hands and could see nothing but blazing light. She was burning. She wanted to stay and finish what had started within and around her, but something else rose inside her, rejecting this return. It was also hot and powerful. It was rage, and it replaced her desire for what was being offered. It pushed her to run blindly away. She ran, feeling something tear as she did—rip out of her—something small and powerful, something that was her and was not her, something more than her.*

*She tumbled off a slippery edge, and the light no longer scorched her skin. Her flesh cooled as it splashed into water. Her body returned to the refreshing underground pool below, thrashing and kicking away from the light, which glared down after her. She dove as deep as she could until she couldn't feel the light anymore, but still she needed to be farther away, needed to find the darkness, a place she might put herself back together again.*

# Day 2,411 – Labyrinth

A petite figure jogged through the dark, dank tunnel, splashing murky water up her leg with each step. The water glowed green as she disrupted it. The thundering of rocks crashing and wet soil plopping to the ground echoed behind her and through the wall to her left.

A faint blue glow radiated atop Iris's flesh, outlining her frame like a spirit. The algae in the damp tunnels created a vibrant bioluminescence which intensified with her every movement. She shook her arms, trying to get the organisms off her. The water smelled astringent, felt sticky and thicker, salty, not like the water above or in the cave.

The tunnel system was being ripped apart by a few—maybe many—rather large *somethings*. Iris had been running around for days trying to locate these creatures while simultaneously avoiding a direct confrontation with one. Their purpose and motivation were unclear to her.

Iris slowed her pace as the tunnel became very quiet. The constant rumbling ceased for the first time in days. Several moments passed and then—

*Crunch. Crinch. Click. Click. Crunch. Crinch. Click. Click.*

The creature moved slowly and methodically on the other side of the dirt wall. It was big and scuttled in a patterned rhythmic motion. Dirt shifted, hard parts clicked together over and over, and many pairs of feet shuffled—all slowly moving away from Iris. This went on for several minutes until the creature travelled so far away that Iris strained to hear even the occasional pile of earth plopping into the water.

She took a few steps, dragging her feet in the ankle-deep stream that filled the entire tunnel system. She was soggy and hot. A muggy steam rose off her body just as the earthy fauna and fishy rot emanated from the ground. She missed feeling dry. This place was brimming with birth and death, beginnings and endings, constant consumption, so different from the surface of the island where most of the creatures simply lived without the eating and dying—except for the humans. Down here was different. Down here, she feared becoming part of the cycle.

A loud swooshing resounded through the tunnel, followed by a gust of air. A clicking and clacking reverberated, increasing in speed and volume as the source came closer. Iris spotted a green flash racing in the shallow waters and silvery reflective eyes bigger than her head shooting toward her through the dark tunnel, large mandibles digging in front, soil shifting and falling around it. Rock and water shot out in front of it. With every splash and thump, the underground monster revealed more of its terrifying form. The bioluminescence and sludgy water gave this giant's white shell segments a ghoulish shine. The creature was completely white with silver eyes speckled with mud. Its form felt familiar to Iris. She had created smaller versions with Dee months ago. It was a giant isopod. They had read about them in one of Eva's books. Children used to affectionately call the smaller ones they found in gardens roly-polies. Iris liked the ones they had made to mimic those garden dwellers. The one charging her was not cute or likeable but formidable and terrifying, barreling toward her like a ghostly freight train with claws.

The beast was now close enough for Iris to see her own reflection in its eyes. Her face emitted an eerie blue glow around her piercing teal eyes. She looked like a ghost of an alien. She turned and ran for her life as the hairy feelers tickled her neck, dirt and rock raining down on her. The creature crawled faster than expected on its pleopods, feet that also function as gills, but Iris was just a little faster. The tunnel began to slope downward which tangled up the creature's feet, slowing it down. The distance between her and the creature was growing until the giant did something entirely unexpected. It huffed and slammed to the ground, dousing her with a small tidal wave. She shot a look over her shoulder as the beast rolled up into a ball and hurtled down the slant. At its new speed, it was going to plow her over and crush her under its hard exoskeleton in a matter of seconds. Iris feared she wouldn't survive being completely flattened. She pushed herself harder and shot down the seemingly never-ending tunnel with one last burst of energy. A shell hit her left heel and almost pulled her leg under. She stumbled into the left wall. Managing to keep her balance, she tripped forward into a running hop, just avoiding behind sucked underneath the living boulder. The slope steepened with each step. Iris was no longer controlling her own locomotion but was falling forward with increasing and frightening speed, barely keeping her legs under her. The soles of her feet barely touched the squishy mud floor of the tunnel. The mass behind her released a squeal as it bounced against the walls. It too had lost control of its trajectory and was simply rolling toward a collision.

The incline was now so steep that Iris was basically running down a wall. The water was rushing downward with a swift current pushing the mud and algae along its bottom. She clawed her hands into the muddy sides of the tunnel, which slowed her down but not nearly enough. She realized she was screaming along with the creature, both at the whims of gravity. A wall where the tunnel made a sharp turn was coming fast. She prayed she could turn before that creature crushed her against the wall. Iris kicked her legs out and held on as tight as she could to the side of the cave as she came to the turn, attempting to swing left to avoid a direct impact. She slammed into the dirt wall with her shoulder, momentarily blinding herself as she rolled to the left. She could hardly breath as she struggled to push herself up.

Above her, the creature screeched. Its shell segments opened, and its feet clawed frantically at the sides of the tunnel. Iris used every bit of her strength to drag the rest of her body out of the way, right before the clicking and clacking creature slammed into the rock, splashing everything around it with water, dirt, shell, and guts. Shards of shell sliced her skin like daggers. Slimy entrails splattered all over her body. Eyesight still blurry, she could just make out the creature's legs twitching as the life within began to fade. Pieces of white shell stuck to the walls. The green glow subsided with the creature's movement, its body curling in on itself.

As Iris examined the creatures' lifeless carcass, her teal eyes shone eerily. The rest of her skin emitted a darker greenish blue glow like the creature. The glow faded as the tiny creatures releasing it calmed and slid down her body. Iris pulled her knees to her chest and stared down at her foot. She wiggled the stump where her big toe used to be, the toe that the queen had taken from her. Leaving the queen had been the hardest thing she had ever done, and even deep in this cave, days after having escaped the cavern with the intricate icosahedron, leaving her friends—really, her children—encapsulated in their individual hexagonal chambers, she felt a powerful tug back toward that cavern, back toward a creator that wanted to dismantle her. Iris had spent many years making creatures out of plastic marine flatworms. She never intended to tear any of them apart and remake them. It seemed perverse and counterproductive. Still, she sensed that was what this queen wanted to do with her, but to what ends she could not piece together. She already felt the creatures that had made up her toe becoming part of something else, and it felt like an invasion to feel this other entity inside of her.

Iris was pretty certain that the tunnel system she found herself lost in was a giant spiral like a snail's shell. It seemed to shift and turn, causing confusion about which way was up or down, left or right. Iris realized that she may remain stuck below the island for many years unless she followed the tug of the queen, the tug that would unravel who she understood herself to be. No, she wouldn't return to the Source. She would keep searching for a way out. She hoped Eva had not followed her down here. Eva was too delicate a species to survive this type of expedition in these conditions. At the same time, Iris hoped that Eva had followed her. If Eva wasn't searching for her in the caves, it would mean she was still trapped with Adam or worse, dead. Iris shook off the despair that chased her through these tunnels, a predator far more dangerous than the broken monster beside her. She had to keep moving, stay ahead of it, and not lose hope. She grunted and pulled herself off the ground. The life around her hummed, but it was not speaking a language she understood, and she could not control it, not like she controlled life on the surface. It was alien, possibly another species that had evolved in this cave alongside hers, but entirely separate and, most likely, a competitor.

# Day 2,411 – Island - Lake

The wind whistled as it spun through the woods, whirling fallen petals into mini cyclones, then dropping them back to the ground. One petal kept hold of a gust and blasted through the trees, swatting against tiny branches heavy with leaves, barely holding its delicate form together as it raced toward the drifts that separated the beach from woods. The light pink petal skimmed the coarse sand as it slid across the shore toward the large waves slapping against the rocks. A cool morning fog billowed out over the breakers. The roars of the quickly moving waves were small compared to an ocean's, but for the little island it signaled troubled waters, the kind you should not be on. The delicate petal landed on the water, buoyed up by surface tension. It rode the waves, traveling down troughs and up crests, miraculously remaining afloat. The wind swept it off the top of a wave, over the rocky waters, and out toward the sandbar where it collided with a wooden oar.

Several small boats, dipping up and down over gentler waves, approached the island in the early morning light. Gabi's small, brown, calloused hand clutched a white piece of translucent plastic. It was one of the many Adam had brought back to the cabin where he had ordered Eva to transform the pieces into a goat. She instead turned its brothers and sisters into a beautiful dove, a koi, and a poison dart frog. Eva was the first person who had beaten Adam. She had done it quietly and cleverly, not by her brawn but with her brain. Gabi smiled at the memory as he stroked the lifeless creature with his index finger, his protective gloves resting on his wader-pant-clad thigh. He was wrapped head to toe in gear except for his naked hands. The nail on the finger that touched the plastic had been chewed down so much it bled a bit at the corner. Gabi glanced at Mari who sat up near the bow of the small vessel, squinting toward the island, searching for movement, searching for their protector, still hoping to find their captor. Gabi scowled at his sister. She fidgeted with her slick black braid, turned, and caught him glaring at her. She frowned back at him.

"Gabi, put your gloves back on."

"But—"

"It's not safe. Now."

Mari scowled over her little brother's head to address Matt, their jumpy and wiry ferryman. She softened when her gaze landed on his kind features. Mari had found Matt alone in a warehouse, beaten and nearly starving. Helping him was the only thing she had ever asked of Adam. She was both drawn to and repelled by his insecure yet kind nature.

"Matt, do you see him?"

"No, but if Adam doesn't want us to see him, we won't."

The boat jerked, and the motor sputtered. The rudder blades had just rammed into the sandbar. Mari flopped backwards, and her back slammed against the bow of the boat with an oomph. Gabi's weight jerked, but he shifted his feet when his body lifted and flopped back onto his seat with a thud, tightening a fist around the white plastic in his hand. Matt moved his hand across the tiller and shot a look over at the other boat about one-hundred yards starboard. Jake, Lena, and Dezi rode in that boat, all stronger and meaner than him. He yelled back as he shut off the motor and pulled it up, examining it for damage.

"Turn of your motor! There's a sandbar!"

Jake snickered as he switched off his motor. "We saw that." His face was completely concealed by a ski mask and goggles, and a bright orange hunting beanie covered his head. The other kids laughed, equally hidden beneath protective layers, shifting the weight of their guns as they chuckled. Lena sat facing Jake, holding his rifle, her knee touching his, her gaze always on his face unless she was scowling at another kid for something they did that she deemed stupid. In this moment, she aimed her gaze at Matt, eyes narrowed through her protective face shield, smirking, both her and Jake's guns leaning on her left shoulder.

Mari watched Matt, waiting for him to stand up for himself, but he only frowned as he wiped some of the sludge off the motor's last blade. He spoke softly to Gabi and Mari.

"The motor's fine. Gabi, switch places so I can row us in."

Gabi didn't respond. His eyes were wide as Mari glared at his still-gloveless hand.

"Gabi, come on, move," Mari snapped. The boat was being thrust around by the choppy waves, and Mari was looking green in the gills, her cheeks puffing up, hand clutching the edge of the craft, knuckles white. It was taking more and more of her focus to keep her small breakfast in her belly.

Gabi didn't move right away, but when he finally did, he raised his bare hand, eyes full of wonder at the magic trick materializing on his palm. A flat white worm wriggled, its body mimicking the waves in the lake as it rolled across Gabi's fingers. His voice could barely be heard over the water slapping against their vessel.

"It came alive."

"Gabi, speak up—" Mari started to scold Gabi, but then her eyes locked on the ebbing and flowing creature cupped in both his hands. As a sliver of sun peeked out from behind the gray clouds and warmed their boat, the rays reflected off the creature's skin, some of the light penetrating its translucent form, revealing shades of purple, teal, and blue just beneath its surface, its veins.

Mari's face softened. The light reflecting off the creature brightened her features.

"It's so—"

"It's beautiful." Matt finished her thought, also gazing at the creature in Gabi's hand, unable to look away from it.

Mari scowled at Matt, the magic broken for her. The creature was beautiful, but she needed him to be harder, tougher, more like Adam. If Adam really was dead, Matt and Gabi would determine her chance of survival. She needed them to be stronger than they were if they were to have any chance against Dezi and the others.

Mari glanced over at the other boat. Dezi and Adam had known each other the longest. Mari had heard Dezi say only a handful of sentences since she joined the group, and they weren't that memorable or coherent. Mari thought there was something wrong with her brain but couldn't be sure because Dezi kept her cards very close to her chest. Nobody but Adam really knew anything about her. Dezi had let Adam do most of the talking, but she was his co-pilot and was a better hand-to-hand fighter than Adam.

Mari sighed. She knew she might be in the wrong boat, but Matt was the only one she could trust to look after Gabi if anything happened to her, and that had to matter more than strength.

Gabi peeked over the edge, hundreds of the creatures like the one in his hand swarmed around the boat, some glomming onto the hull. The little worm in his hand flopped around, frantically. Gabi switched his gaze from the white worm he held to the swarm in the water, all seeming desperate to get to the other. Gabi lowered his hand close to the water.

"Don't touch them, Gabi!" Mari grabbed his shoulder, jerking him back. The white flat worm in his palm slid off as Gabi's hand tilted. It plopped into the swarm below. The other creatures fell back into the water and swam a bit deeper below the surface.

"They missed him, Mari."

"That's ridiculous. . ."

Mari released his shoulder as she watched the creatures swim in circles around their friend, other worms taking turns squeezing their returned brother.

"They do seem to be happy he's back." Matt kept his eyes on the swimming creatures.

Suddenly, a flash of scales, a gill, and a wide mouth darted through the school of multi-colored worms.

"Oh my god! It's a fish! An actual fish!" Matt jumped to his feet, pointing.

The fish was followed by another and another as an entire school darted past their boat. Matt couldn't help himself. He was whooping and jumping, rocking their small boat along with the larger waves, nearly stumbling over the edge. He grabbed the two sides of the boat and lowered himself down. Gabi leaned so far over the edge to see the fish a wave smacked him in the face. He pulled back, sputtering and cackling as he wiped his face. This was the first time any of them had ever seen a living animal.

Mari watched the two with a mix of disgust and amusement, wanting to feel happy but too worried to allow it. Out of the corner of her eye, she caught Lena's stare lingering on her.

"What are you all freaking out about over there?" Lena shouted across the lake, clutching her gun, shooting the water a suspicious glance.

Mari responded, just loud enough for her voice to reach the other boat. "There are fish in the water."

Jake and Dezi jumped to their feet. Dezi was thick—not fat, none of them were fat—but she was big-boned. Her waist was short and thick, while her legs were skinny and long. When she put her arms up like she did right then, her figure took on the strange shape of a cactus. Her hazelnut skin was always a shade of pink underneath from too much sun. She wore her coarse black hair shaved into a single spike down the center of her scalp. Dezi refused to wear gear on her face, said it was too itchy. She needed the sun on her face, always had. Mari liked the way she looked—hearty, sun-kissed, like a rough succulent that thrived in the extreme elements much better than the prettier trees.

"Dez, Mari's staring at you again." Lena shot Mari a cruel smirk. Dezi put her arms down, blushing and scowling. Mari reddened, but simply turned back toward Gabi.

"Don't let Lena get under your skin—"

"Shut up, Matt." Mari hissed. Tears welled up in her eyes for a moment, a rare moment of vulnerability for her. The beautiful moment on the lake had shattered, and the last thing she wanted was Matt to be nice to her. Several rougher waves slapped against their boat, drenching them. Matt rose to his feet quickly and stepped toward Gabi. "Gabi, move. I got to get us into shore before it gets any rougher out here."

Gabi leapt up and scurried around Matt, plopping on the bench in front of the motor, though he kept his eyes glued to the water, waiting for more life to swim by. Even his sister's sharp barbs and reprimands couldn't chip away at the smile plastered on his face.

"Eva's plan worked." Gabi straightened up and filled with pride. Mari looked stricken, paler, more upset.

"I hope you haven't done anything we can't fix. Did you even think what might happen without Adam?" Mari's eyes shot daggers at her brother.

""I'm glad I helped. Adam can't hurt us anymore."

She nearly spat at him with contempt. "He protected us. Now what do you think's going to happen?"

Gabi stuck his chin up defiantly, jaw trembling, eyes on fire. "We will find Eva and start a new life. We'll be happy."

"Or you've signed our death warrants."

"I would rather die than become something terrible like Adam."

Mari clenched her jaw. Her brother was too young to really understand what this world had taken from them, what parts of her she had turned terrible so they could survive.

# Day 2,411 - Caves

*Crinch. Crunch. Crinch. Crunch.*

*Within the briar of dead trees, Margo hunched, creeping deeper through the fallen trunks, their branches twisting around each other forming this snarled shelter. As Margo lifted her foot over a branch and bent down to avoid yet another, the skeletons of these fallen warriors creaked, twisting tighter, pulled in further by the vined and thorny bushes that grew around them, enclosing the girl as she pushed toward their shared heart at the center of the bramble. Margo was tall for eleven, and the roof of the gnarled structure was getting lower the deeper she travelled into it. Soon, she would not be able to stand comfortably.*

*The bramble was a dark place, one Margo's mom had warned her to avoid. Every year, a couple of children entered that part of the woods and never came back. In the old days, many of the townsfolk wanted to burn it down, but too many believed that the children were still alive in there, or that their spirits were forever attached, so it was never burned. Even though it was made of dead things, it seemed to expand in girth and height each year. As time passed, people just forgot about it, a haunted place deep in the forest that only children and teenagers visited. Still, a few of the adults swore they heard wails coming from the bramble but only for the briefest moments on the darkest nights.*

*The bramble had long, misshapen, yet razor-sharp thorns. Legend was that if they pierced your flesh and drew blood, you would become dizzy, your sight hazy, and you would stumble deeper toward the dark center until you entered the core and collapsed onto the soft dirt. No one ever said what happened after you collapsed. You just never came back.*

*Margo had been walking toward what she thought was the center of the bramble for hours. She didn't believe any of the stories about the place, not the supernatural components anyway, the parts with ghosts, entities, or monsters. Those parts were meant to keep children from entering a dangerous area of the woods, scaring them to keep them safe. Margo did avoid the thorns though. They had a toxin at their tip that made a person disoriented, distorted their eyesight, and in rare and severe cases caused blindness. Margo didn't grow more scared the deeper she ventured, even as the bramble around her became more enclosed, leaving her very little space to walk forward. If it got any tighter, she was going to have to crawl—*

"This really happened?" Jacob's voice bellowed through the darkness of the cave, startling Eva out of her story. The words vibrated through his chest across her back, his arms wrapped around her to keep them both warm.

"Stop interrupting! I was getting to the best part. And yes, it really happened." She elbowed him in the ribs.

"Ow. Well, where? Out here on the island?"

"No, weren't you listening to the beginning? On the mainland, out by the tip of the peninsula."

"So, you've been there? You've seen this bramble?"

"No, I haven't been there. I've been all over the peninsula and never found any evidence of a giant bramble, but the winds could have blown it away over the years for sure. Or it just slowly rotted to dust. Also, I could have missed it. It's a lot of dead forest area to cover. Don't you want to hear what happens to Margo?"

Jacob shifted his weight and pulled her closer to him. Eva's breath caught in her throat. She was still uncomfortable with so much human contact after years without it, and Jacob had kept her pretty close since they reunited on the beach several days ago. It was hard to stay apart since they were trapped on a tiny fishing boat floating deeper and deeper into a dark, creepy cave system.

Still, her feelings for Jacob weren't like her feelings for her parents or her feelings for Iris and the others. They were raw and static, ready to shock her if he rubbed his arm just right against hers or if his breath hit her ear just so, like right now.

"Does she get out of the bramble?"

"If I tell you, it will ruin the story."

"I don't want to hear it if she doesn't get out of the bramble. I don't like stories with sad endings."

"Some of the best stories have sad endings." Eva shoved him as she rose, peering deep into the cave, rubbing her neck where Jacob's breath had electrified her entire system.

"I will listen to the rest of this story on one condition. You first tell me if Margo lives or dies."

"I will tell the rest of the story the way it was meant to be told or not at all."

Jacob pulled her back against his chest. His lips brushed her ear. "She better live."

Eva's breath caught in her throat as another bolt of electricity sent her heart racing. Jacob's touch made it hard for her to think, let alone tell a story. Her mind was calmer and more focused when she was alone or talking things out with her sister. She had so much to tell Iris. She needed her more than ever after what she did to Adam out on the lake, and with how things had changed with Jacob. They had searched for Iris and the others in the dark, seemingly endless cave system for days with no luck. The fear of never finding them crept into Eva's mind and threatened to swallow her up. Better to focus on Margo's story then think those dark thoughts before they rested. She closed her eyes and took several deep breaths before she trusted herself to speak again.

*Margo lowered to her knees and crawled through a tunnel of woven dead vines. She moved very slowly to avoid the thorns, arms scrunched firmly below her chest as she inched forward. The passageway narrowed further, as though some invisible weaver pulled a central vine, tightening the tunnel. Margo's stomach sank. She felt nauseated. She had gone too far, just as she promised herself she wouldn't. There was no way to turn back. She could only wriggle forward and hope the path would open up again. The ground beneath her was a rough bed of leaves, sharp twigs, and dirt. It scraped against her covered arms. She had worn appropriate clothes for the adventure, but she feared the thorns would successfully search out any vulnerability in the tough canvas material that made up her overalls, jacket, and gloves.*

"Come on, was Margo really that prepared? This sounds more like you entering the bramble." Jacob chuckled.

Eva ignored him. She wasn't the only well-prepared adventurer. Smart girls don't enter a dangerous forest unprepared, and the world used to be filled with smart girls. Her foot touched her knapsack on the floor of the boat. She and Jacob had run out of food today. They had tried to fish but hadn't caught anything yet. At this point, Eva was almost certain that there weren't fish in this water. They should have brought more food, but the intensity of Iris's distress call had left little time for preparedness. "Stop interrupting."

Eva pushed away from Jacob and moved to the front of the boat, her back to him as she continued her story.

*Margo's jacket tugged her backward. A large thorn had snagged her coat's tail. She squirmed but couldn't reach it. It seemed impossible that she couldn't tear it free. Finally, in desperation, she used her teeth to pull off one of her thick gloves, hoping that without the cumbersome material she could get her coat loose. She slid her arm down her leg and slowly reached it up and over toward the back of her jacket, feeling for the snare that trapped her, hating that the skin on her hand was naked, unprotected.*

*She felt a jab like the fang of a snake stabbing into the flesh between her index finger and thumb. She screamed and tried to tear her hand free but whatever had stuck into her was still holding on. She screamed some more as she ripped her flesh free from the sharp object. She felt something hefty fling off to the side and shake the vines, dust falling to the ground and getting in her eyes and mouth. She coughed as she pulled her bare hand under her body and in front of her face. Bright red blood dripped down her arm.*

*A wave of intense vertigo slammed her senses. The tunnel began spinning, slowly at first but accelerating more and more with each moment. Her hand became fuzzy before her, and soon all she could see was a white circle way in the distance. Clutching her punctured hand, she dragged herself toward that light. The branch that had held her captive released her jacket when it stabbed her hand, so her body was now free to move forward, but her mind was reeling; her vision, blurring. She kicked her feet to push herself forward and pulled with her elbows, keeping her head low, hoping that the white target ahead was a way out rather than a forest spirit leading her the way of so many missing children.*

*Margo blinked her eyes. She had fallen asleep. She stared up through the dry vines, small slivers of sun peeking through. At first the branches were hazy, but after a lot of blinking and tears rolling down her cheeks, they snapped into clear focus. Margo rolled to the side and her cheek hit loose, warm soil. The dirt felt softer than any bed she had ever snuggled in, and she was so very tired. She let her bare hand, caked in rust-colored blood dig its fingers into the soil. A wet wound gushed in the center of the dried blood, something beneath its surface twitching with the movement of her hand.*

*Margo still couldn't lift her head. She felt the full crushing weight of gravity amplified ten times over, pinning her to the floor. She glanced around her surroundings, a small clearing. There was no evidence of the tunnel that had led her to this spot. Her body was curled up, knees bent toward her belly, head reaching toward her knees, like a fetus in a womb. The bramble had woven her into a wooden cocoon. A pulsing moved through the warm seed-like space, a beat that Margo couldn't escape, a rhythm that she soon realized was coming from within her.*

*Her body convulsed, and she reached for her injured hand. Something small and pointy stuck its head out of her bloody wound. A flash of green emerged from the fresh blood oozing out of the back of her hand. Margo moaned, struggling to rise off the ground to no avail. A soapy film slipped over her eyes right before they locked permanently into place. A green sprout reached up, pulling out Margo's red veins along with it toward the sun, growing rapidly, the two lifeforms twisting together to Margo's screams as she became the new growth of the bramble, just like the children who had come before her.*

The lapping of the water against the fishing boat was the only sound for several moments after Eva finished her story. Jacob exhaled loudly.

"Just wait, Eva. I am going to get you later, gonna tell you the scariest story I know. You will never sleep again, just like I will never sleep tonight after that one."

"You can sleep through anything. I find that story hopeful, not scary."

"You're more messed up than I thought."

Eva laughed. "I mean, it is scary, obviously, but the forest was dying, and somehow found a way to survive. That's the part I like."

"What about Margo? What a horrible way to die."

"She didn't die."

"Her veins were ripped out of her body. The bramble is consuming her. Of course, she died."

"I always thought of it like she was becoming part of the bramble."

"No way! I have a little firsthand knowledge about this type of thing. Like when Abel jumped into my body, he didn't tear me apart. He healed me, made me stronger, made me able to create life. That's becoming something new together. That bramble is destroying Margo."

Eva's mood plummeted. The story suddenly didn't fill her with any hope. Suddenly, she saw it more the way Jacob did. Suddenly, she worried about Abel being inside of Jacob, and if there was something inside of her like Abel, she worried about the creature inside of her. Were they content to live as passive participants? Was that their biological imperative? Their end game? Would she be content if the roles were reversed?

"Hey! There's a light!" Jacob shot up, rocking the boat. Eva leaned forward and spotted a dim blue glow flickering from around a large rocky wall, the river veering to the right toward it, leading to a new cavern. As she listened to Jacob pick up the oars, knock them against the inside edges of the boat, and slap the water with their ends, she tried to push Margo out of her mind along with all the stories she had read about parasitic organisms. As Jacob pumped the oars with a steady rhythm, the cavern filled with imaginary dangers, chasing her and Jacob deeper into a tunnel with no way out in sight. She didn't want to regret going after Iris and the others or realize too late that there was never any hope of saving them.

# Day 2,411 – Island - Woods

Gabi and Matt slunk through the overgrown part of the forest, mesmerized by the many shades of green and forms of life. Neither of them could keep their hands off the tall grass, the leaves, the bushes, and the flowers. Gabi had never seen anything green besides maybe a few soggy pine needles that had been frozen in the ice, preserved. Now, he was strolling through a botanical paradise. He heard tweets, chirps, and singing from up in the canopies and glimpsed an occasional flutter of feathers and beak across the sky. He still hadn't got a good look at any of the birds that soared above them. Buzzing and croaking rose from the undergrowth, a cacophony of forest sounds. His senses were overloaded. Usually, the only sounds around him were the others, and mostly unpleasant. The sounds on this island were strange, beautiful, and mysterious in a way that filled him with exhilaration instead of fear. This island was full of more miracles than he could process in one short walk. This island was not of this world, it couldn't be. Maybe he had been killed, and this was the heaven he'd heard about from those weird kids living in an abandoned church in a crumbling city. Those kids had tried to kill and eat them, so their spiritual ideals were a bit suspect. Luckily, Adam and Dezi returned from a food run just in time and made quick work of them. If there was one thing Adam would never tolerate, it was cannibalism. It was probably his only good trait, standards being low in the wasteland. Despite the cannibals who told him about it, Gabi had always liked the idea of heaven. He had just not believed in it until now.

He gazed over at the pistol in Matt's hand. It seemed perverse in the middle of this paradise. After that day at the church, Adam insisted Matt carry a gun. He spent the day teaching Matt how to shoot in a dilapidated factory, mentoring him on how to avoid detection when sneaking up on a person. Matt had recalled that day to Gabi as a good one. Adam had been nice to him, treated him like a person he might care for, someone of value. Matt never had a father, but for one day, Adam acted like what Matt thought a father might act like. Adam quickly turned back to the real version of himself, the one who hits you hard when you make a mistake and takes pleasure in seeing the blood drip down your lip, but even more in your humiliation and fear. Gabi avoided looking at Matt's gun; its cold metal seemed an affront to the wilderness. He wanted Matt to drop it and bury it in the dirt, never think of using a gun again, but still, he was afraid for them not to have one. The gun had protected them on more than one occasion.

Gabi stabbed the earth with his makeshift walking stick and stopped to pick up an apple blossom that had fallen to the forest floor. He held the blossom in his palm, caressing its five pink petals one-by-one. He lifted it close to his face. Hints of sugar and pepper filled his nose, and then soil and mushrooms followed by the sound of snorting. His head jerked up, and his eyes widened.

"Matt, look!" Gabi spoke so quietly Matt hardly heard him. He was pointing to a light green shrub with tiny singular oval-shaped leaves. Beside it, stood one of Eva and Iris's stout brown and gray boars. Its large grayish-brown ears perked upward, its gentle black eyes peering curiously at them over a long snout and short white tusks. Its tassel tail twitched a few times before it strutted toward them.

"What is it?" Matt asked.

"Eva told me about these guys. They're wild pigs."

The boar snorted, sniffing the ground, inching toward the two boys. Gabi kneeled, watching the creature as it studied him with its small, intelligent eyes. Gabi held his breath and reached out toward the beast's snout. Matt crept over slowly and crouched down as well. The pig stopped when it was still just out of reach. It pushed its snout toward Gabi, sniffing. Its snout and Gabi's fingers were an inch apart. Gabi slowly moved his fingers forward and brushed the pig's rubbery snout. The pig jerked back and so did Gabi, but it quickly came at Gabi again, nudging his hand with its snout. Gabi opened his palm and pet its furry, brown face. The boar snorted and strutted so that the length of its entire body was caressed by Gabi's hand, and then it twirled around to do it again. Gabi giggled. Matt moved closer to him and put his hand out as well. The pig's coarse hair scratched his fingertips, its tough but soft flesh racing by them and flipping back around, clearly enjoying the sensation of their hands on its fur. Matt started laughing along with Gabi until they were both in happy hysterics as this pig pranced around them, nuzzling their backs, occasionally poking one of them with a tusk. The boys and the boar played for a very long time in the clearing.

*Boom!*

A gunshot snapped them out of their revelry, piercing the peace in the wild orchard. The pig's ears shot up, and its tail stopped wagging before it darted into the forest.

"Come back!" Gabi chased after the boar.

Matt frowned and rose quickly from the ground.

"Gabi! Wait!" Matt stalked after him, grumbling. "You're gonna get yourself shot."

Gabi dashed ahead through the trees, ignoring Matt. Another gunshot blasted, much closer than the last one. A yelp followed by a horrible high-pitched whine. Gabi flinched as the creature yowled and whimpered. Laughter and sneering rolled through the forest toward the spot where Matt and Gabi stood. Matt leaned up against a tree, putting the large trunk between him and the noise. Matt signaled for Gabi to join him. Gabi squeezed his hand around the apple blossom and rushed over to Matt.

A gray wolf blasted out of the long grass, landing with a thud several feet in front of Matt and Gabi. Gabi released a small yelp, and Matt's hand quickly covered his mouth, his other hand gripping his own gun. This creature was even more beautiful than the wild pig. Its coat was fluffy and soft. Its narrow nose bared razor-sharp teeth, its eyes frantic and ears perked. Gabi wiggled out of Matt's grasp, staring wide-eyed at the terrified predator. Matt pulled Gabi back as he reached toward the scared beast. It sniffed the air, growled, and snapped its teeth at the two boys before it dashed off into the brush. Two other wolves followed shortly after but didn't even give the boys a glance. Soon, three more sprinted by, a blur of gray, white, brown, and black fur.

"Come on, I just saw them!" Lena shouted. She sounded like she was about twenty yards off. Matt tensed.

"Let's go back! We can track the pig. It's injured and doesn't have big teeth and claws." Jake shouted back to her, even further off. He sounded winded and annoyed.

"You always do what's easy," Lena snapped, her voice closer yet.

"Hell yeah, I do. Everything's hard enough, already. Why would I make it harder? It's just common sense."

"You only talk about common sense when it suits you." Lena chuckled. "I never saw anything like those things. They were so strong and furry. God, I love this island!"

"Come on, let's double-back and see if we can find it."

"Fine." Lena and Jake's voices became more muffled as they walked off in the opposite direction.

Matt released a long breath and glanced back at Gabi whose fists were clenched.

"They're going to kill that pig." Gabi's jaw tightened and his lip trembled, eyes flashing as an angry storm brewed inside of him.

"I know, I don't like it either, but we have to kill some of these creatures, Gabi. We have to eat." Matt spoke softly.

"I know! I'm not stupid, but they're going to kill all of them!" Tears fell down Gabi's face.

Yet another gunshot sounded from behind Matt, followed by whooping and hollering. Gabi's heart sank, settling at the bottom of the lakebed that surrounded this magical island, accepting that they had to eat, but wishing deeply that there was another way. He had just met his first adorable pig and wasn't ready to consume the sort of life that he had been waiting his whole life to meet. Gabi ran off in the direction the wolves had gone, away from the others—even Matt—frustrated that every time he experienced something profound in this world, it was immediately followed by heartbreak.

# Day 2,411 - Labyrinth

*Drip. Plop. Drip. Plop.*

Water and mud fell from the ceiling in random never-ending patterns that contrasted with Cain's disciplined footsteps, the constant cadence that accompanied everything he did. Cain trudged through the shallow waters of the tunnels. He hadn't been able to be still since he fell down the waterfall after Iris. Cain stopped, listening. This was the first time he could hear his thoughts since he and Iris had entered the waterfall cavern. Since then, it had been water crashing, rushing, swooshing, pounding melded with rock and dirt thundering, an avalanche of sounds constantly crushing him. He had not been aware of a real thought since Iris was dragged over the ledge by that leviathan. That last thought had been of utter despair. He had no idea how he could defeat this beast.

He followed Iris as he always would but had yet to find her. He assumed that the leviathan had dragged her into a different cavern. It would not have fit down the narrow rocky shoot that Cain had been sucked down. The waterfall had shot him into an underwater tunnel system, one he had thought he was never going to escape. Gravity and current moved him around the cave system, a steep, tight, water-filled passageway. Cain travelled down it at breakneck speeds for minutes, and then the tunnel started to curve, and the current slowed as his path became less steep and treacherous. Eventually, he slid into a damp muddy tunnel system, plopping into the cool, damp clay, water-logged and disoriented. If he had been human, he would have also been dead. He'd been lost in this stinky marshy hellhole inhabited by large beasts he had yet to see. For the second time in his life, Cain wanted to sit down and rest. The first time had been when Adam had filled him with bullets and nearly ripped him in half. Iris saved him, just as deftly as she had created him. He loved her and didn't want to leave her down here alone. He just didn't know how he'd ever find her again. The cave system was vast, seemingly never-ending, filled with life foreign to Cain. In this system, he couldn't communicate with Iris. Their telepathy was blocked, or they were just too far apart. He couldn't hear the others either. He was totally alone, disconnected in a way he had never experienced.

He knew that if he did not find Iris soon, he would have to leave her. She would survive on her own until Cain could come back for her. He had to return to the surface to find Eva. She was still with that monster, Adam, and that was his fault. Cain reached into his pants' pocket and pulled out a small motor component with a few wires sticking out of it. There was no chance that Jacob had left the island and rescued Eva. Cain had made sure of that when he sabotaged the motor.

He cursed himself for not having trusted Iris. He shoved the motor part back into his pocket. He huffed out a blast of air and when he inhaled in again, he gagged, hunching over a bit. A pungent smell plowed up his nasal cavity and down his throat. He placed his arm over his face, grimacing, peering down the muddy corridor at a dimly lit splatter of white cracked shell and goo ahead of him. He staggered toward the foul odor, pulling the collar of his shirt over his mouth and nose, squinting toward what lay ahead . . . or below. Cain stumbled as the ground quickly steepened. Soon, he was struggling to keep his footing in the slippery mud as he slid toward the stench. Before long, he was falling.

*Plop!*

Cain held his arms up, now covered in the warm innards of a giant isopod. He grabbed one of the thing's white legs and pulled himself out of the mess, gagging. His coughing echoed down the passageway. He gazed back at the remains of this prehistoric creature before him. The innards glistening on his skin were hot. The beast hadn't been dead long. Cain imagined this was the creature he had heard scuttling and tearing the earth apart around him, creating this vast tunnel system. He splashed the water around the creature, and it glowed dimly at his touch. He moved his hand faster to agitate the bioluminescent creatures. Their light brightened in the beast's large eyes. Cain jumped a bit when he looked the giant in the face for the first time. Its face was upside down, and its many legs were flung in all directions around it, several bending up and then back in toward the creature's chest. Chunks of its large protective shell held the gushy insides like a large broken soup bowl.

Shell shards stuck out of the muddy walls and floated in the shallow water. Water from above streamed down on the creature, splashing water up from its midsection.

Cain peered up. It was way too steep and slippery to return in that direction. To his back and to his right, there were only clay walls. He peered down the only remaining path and started putting distance between himself and the gory corpse. There was a relief in not having to choose the way, having only one path.

Cain sloshed through the tunnel, his constant cadence returning. The water and mud continued its dripping and plopping. The tunnel rumbled. He placed a dirty hand on the wall to steady himself. The wall vibrated, and soil crumbled off it, some of it hitting his feet. Cain backed away from the dirt pushing toward him. He dodged out of the way as another beast crashed through the wall.

Cain stared into one of the new creature's giant eyes, his brown eyes reflecting back at him, his hair damp against his copper skin. He was surprised how terrified he looked as the isopod's legs pushed its body forward, shifting toward the other of its kind. Cain stood frozen, watching it move back and forth, knocking soil out of the walls to make room for its large oval shell. Cain leapt over the creature's flailing tail as it finally freed itself from the dirt. It scuttled over to the splattered remains. Its antennae and feet wiggled above the smashed shell as it lowered its mandibles.

A high-pitched, melodic moaning filled the space. The walls lit up brightly, red hot in response to the sound. Cain covered his ears and staggered back and hit another fleshy form.

"Ahh!" Cain shouted, jumping away instinctively. The creature's moaning stopped, and the sound of its legs brushing against shell and water as chunks of clay crashed to the ground filled the space between them.

A hand reached out and grabbed his arm. "Cain, it's me, you big dummy." Cain turned to face Iris who shot him a tense smile, her teal eyes reflecting the bioluminescence in a way that made them glow ghostly. He pulled her tightly to him. "I found you!"

"Technically, I found you." Iris hugged him back.

The familiar scuttling and plopping approached the two. Iris peeked over Cain's arm at the advancing creature, its mandibles pinching together, its eyes narrowing in on the two. Iris wiggled out of Cain's hug. "We need to run."

Cain and Iris sprinted away from the creature as it picked up speed. One of the creature's pincers brushed Iris's back as she pointed. "Look! There's a passage! Turn!"

Iris veered to the right and pushed Cain in front of her. As they turned, the floor disappeared from under their feet. Cain flailed forward, still trying to run. Below them was an immense cavern, filled with exotic flora and fauna, some glowing, some not. Time stood still for milliseconds while Iris and Cain hovered five hundred yards above a land that time forgot filled with life and wonder and a large underground lake. Cain inhaled sharply, and they plummeted toward all that life. Iris shifted her body and spread her arms and legs, attempting to slow her descent. She fixed her gaze on the large underground lake below them. "Land in the water!"

Cain also shifted his body and put out his arms and legs, staring down at the land and bushes next to the lake, incredulous. "I preferred the giant bug!"

# Day 2,411 – Island

*Creak. Thud. Creak. Thud.*

*Jezzie held her breath. Her cut-off denim shorts and hoodie were damp with sweat, and the old empty building smelled like sausage and sawdust. The floorboards were rotting, so each of her creeping steps was an exercise of misguided faith in their integrity. The other kids had put her up to entering the factory. They had put her up to it in the past, but she had always been sly enough to talk her way out of it. Not this time. This time, Dev, the oldest and meanest of the group, the one with a snaggle tooth and warts on his fingers, the one she hated the most had all but thrown her through the front door. He said it was her turn, had been her turn the last four times.*

*The few remaining kids living in the city squatted in old homes, ran in small packs, and were constantly hungry, constantly searching for food. Jezzie lived with five other kids. She was the middle kid, both in age and size. It helped her remain mostly invisible in the group, but there were days when Dev insisted on seeing her, insisted on her doing her share.*

*Creak. Thud. Creak. Thud.*

*Jezzie took a few more steps into the factory. Her right foot was flat and heavy, painful to put weight on it. Last year, she had jumped off a car, and felt something pop in her ankle. Connor had done his best to mend it, but she never walked right again, never walked without pain, without a thud.*

"Why do your stories always have some cripple in them, Mari?" Lena shouted.

"SHHH!" Dezi smacked her arm, frowning as flames flickered and painted shadows across their faces and the camp. The skinned boar was roasting over a large fire, its fat dripping into the hot embers, which crackled and spit out at the group gathered around it. Half the kids stared hungrily at the boar; the others at Mari, anticipating the next part of the story.

"This isn't my story. It's one someone told me long ago." Dezi always listened to Mari's stories. She never said much about them but hated when people interrupted. Maybe that gives Mari an advantage, maybe it doesn't. Mari locked eyes with Dezi for a beat and then back into the fire, conjuring the factory and Jezzie's lame foot.

*Creak. Thud. Creak. Thud.*

*Jezzie stopped and listened. There had been an extra thud, one that had not come from her foot on the wooden planks. Jezzie slowly looked to the ground. A shadow moved in and out of the cracks in the floorboards. Something or someone was underneath her.*

*Thud . . . thud . . . thud.*

*It was travelling away from her now, rushing deeper into the center of the factory. Jezzie turned back to the loading dock entrance she had come through. Dev and the others were tossing a ball back and forth in the parking lot. Dev kept one eye on the dock, making sure she returned, making sure she didn't return empty-handed.*

*Jezzie hadn't expected to be alone. She had just hoped. Drifters squatted in these factories on the outskirts of the city. Their pack patrolled this section. When new arrivals moved in, then they went to work. The pack sent in a scout, alone. One person could usually get close, undetected, see if the new arrivals had anything worth fighting for. If the scout was lucky, they might find supplies left unattended, then they became a thief, making things cleaner, easier.*

*Scratch. Screech. Scratch. Screech.*

*Jezzie's eyes widened, and her sweaty skin went cool.*

*What made that noise?*

*She had never heard anything like that before.*

*Scratch. Screech. Scratch. Screech.*

*ThudThudThudThudThudThudTHUMP!*

*Jezzie was breathing fast, and she was rushing back toward the loading dock. Under her, the sounds intensified and got closer. Something was tearing at the floorboards, snarling.*

*CRACK.*

*She felt two large pieces of wood fly up into the air and crash to the ground behind her. Tears and snot fell down her face. She tried to scream but nothing would come out but ragged breaths and gurgles.*

*Thud. Creak. Thud. Creak. Thud. Creak.*

*Hot breath seared the back of her neck, and an enormous hand with talon-sharp nails swiped her shoulder, slamming her to the ground. Jezzie struggled to catch her breath, reaching her hand toward ugly, horrible Dev, praying that he would come save her from whatever gripped her bad foot. She was being dragged across the dusty, creaky floorboards toward the stairway leading down into the subterranean floor of the old mill. Jezzie lifted her head so that it stopped banging against the floor, afraid to look at the monstrous thing dragging her. Her ankle was shooting hot lightning bolts of pain up her leg. She felt a wet, thick, warm river flowing up her shin to her knee from her ankle. She glanced down and saw a dark red spot soak through her denim pants. She followed the blood to the claw holding her ankle. The skin was dark, black, not brown like a person, but black like the paw of a dog. The claws were razor-sharp and long, one was cutting into her ankle over and over again as the hairy beast leapt down the stairs, dragging Jezzie along. Jezzie finally screamed and clutched the stair railing. She caught one last glance at Dev jerking his head toward the loading dock gate, eyes wide. He gestured to the others, and they ran away.*

*"Come back, please!" Jezzie lost her grip on the railing, and her head collided with the second metal stair, mercifully sending her to oblivion.*

"I hate that ending," Gabi said in between bites of his roasted pig. He handed Mari a piece of hot meat. She nodded at him and took the piece. Jake burnt himself cutting equal pieces off. He handed one to Lena, then Matt. He glanced over at Dezi.

"Dezi, you want one?"

Dezi raised her hand, indicating she would get it later. Dezi continued to stare into the fire. Jake then cut a piece off for himself, same size as everyone else's. No one in this group ever took more than their share. It was considered one of the bigger offenses. Adam's way wasn't all bad all the time. The strongest and the weakest flourished or starved together.

"That's the ending. At least the way it was told to me, and the way my Nani told it to my mother. Then they would tell you never to go to the industrial part of town unless you wanted to be taken by the mutants. It's always been the ending." Mari shrugged as she took a big bite of pork.

"What happened to Jezzie?" Matt asked, taking a seat on a log by Gabi.

Not too far off, one of the wolves howled. Gabi jumped and then giggled.

"Do you think it's true?" Dezi's voice was low as she walked toward the pig, her pocketknife out. She lowered her head, shot a quick glance at Mari out of the corner of her eye, and quickly returned it to the pig as she reached it.

"I don't know what I think." Mari took another bite and chewed it slowly, savoring the roasted flavor as she watched Dezi's strong hands tenderly cut a slice for herself, the juices dripping down her arm to her elbow. "But my mom said my Nani's brother had warts on his hand, and his name was Dev."

"You think there was a real Jezzie?" Matt chewed with his mouth open, excited to hear something new for once.

"Why didn't you ever tell that part before?" Gabi licked his fingers, raising a disapproving eyebrow at his sister.

"Oh, put that eyebrow away, Gabi. You were too little. Now, you are big enough." Mari returned her gaze to Dezi who watched her as she took a big bite of her pork. Mari knew that this was an important moment for her, the moment she might win Dezi over.

"There is a little bit more to the story. It's not a version that many people have heard. No one actually told it to me. I overheard Mom tell it to Dad one night, when they thought we were asleep."

"No fair."

Mari shook her head at Gabi. "You were asleep. Did you want me to wake you?"

"Yes," Gabi grumbled as he took the last bite of pork.

"It was the last story I heard Mom tell." Mari's voice quivered for a moment, but then she took a deep breath and lost herself in the dancing flames, watching the story come to life among them.

*Jezzie awoke that night. It was cold, but she felt warm. Her head throbbed where it had slammed into the stairs. She rubbed her fingers through her hair, still wet with blood, and felt several large bumps and a welt. Her ankle did not throb or ache. Her hands and ankles were bound, tied to two separate beams, but she could just reach her ankle with a hand. When she touched her ankle, she felt a gash, but the blood was gone. Someone had cleaned her up.*

*"You were going to steal from us?" A growl rumbled behind her and into her flesh, knotting her stomach, coming up her spine, buzzing her brain. The voice felt like it had entered her. Jezzie seized up; she did not turn toward the voice. She was too afraid to turn around, too afraid to see her captor.*

*"Answer me, girl." The growl grew more sinister. Jezzie almost peed herself.*

*"I didn't want to. They made me."*

*Jezzie looked down at her hands and they seemed ashen. She rubbed them and looked again. They were gray. She brought them closer to her face, and it just seemed they were getting darker by the moment.*

*"The 'they' that left you?"*

*Jezzie nodded, trembling as her hands blackened and their muscles tightened and bulged. "What's happening to me?"*

*"You're with us now."*

*"Us?" Jezzie watched as her legs and arms also began to gray and darken. Her stomach and breasts followed. She released a frightened yelp and then a whimper.*

*"We're a different kind of pack. We don't steal from others."*

*"But there's no food, what do you eat if you don't steal?" Jezzie's stomach seized up as the same claw dug into her shoulder.*

*"We eat meat."*

*Jezzie's eyes went wide, and she involuntarily licked her lips. She hadn't eaten in three days. "There isn't any meat, not anymore."*

*"There is if you're one of us."*

*"What are you?"*

*"You're turning. Your hunger will teach you what you are."*

*Jezzie screamed as razor sharp claws pushed their way through her fingers, blood dripping past her knuckles to her wrists.*

*"Why? Why me?" Jezzie screamed as her body writhed, cracking and breaking, and healing and bending as she transformed into something new, something deadly, something that didn't discriminate between animals when it fed. A primal hunger rose within her, growing stronger with each stage of her transformation, a hunger that was uncontrollable by the time her new friends untied her.*

*Her captor, her new father stepped around her carefully. His skin was dark but no longer black, and his fingernails were long, but no longer razor-sharp claws. "You're hungry. You need to eat."*

*Jezzie felt blind with hunger. She had no idea how many days she had been tied up, but it felt as if she had been turned inside out. "Well, to eat, you need to hunt."*

*The stout, middle-aged man untied her hands. She slashed the air in front of him, and he punched her in the face, dropping her to the ground.*

*"We don't attack our own."*

*Blood ran from Jezzie's blackened face. She nodded her head. The man walked over to the other rope and untied her feet. Jezzie crouched on the ground. She felt as strong as she felt hungry, otherworldly. Her insides had changed as much as her outsides. She touched her arms. They were covered in dark fur as were her legs, her stomach, her chest, and her face. She growled and touched her sharp incisors. She stood; her legs were strong.*

*Her ankle didn't land with a thud anymore. The pain was gone, replaced by hunger and strength.*

*"Go. Bring that boy who left you back here. Be back by morning."*

*Jezzie dashed toward the stairs and disappeared up them on all fours.*

Mari stopped and popped the rest of her meat in her mouth.

"Is that the real ending?" Jake snorted, putting on a bored look as he stared out across the lake.

"Did Jezzie kill Uncle Dev?" Gabi's eyes were wide as saucers.

"Mom said Uncle Dev disappeared. Same week a girl named Jezzie disappeared. Both down by the industrial part of town."

The wolf howled again. This time another and another joined in. Finally, the whole pack was howling.

"It's just a story to keep kids from going down by the warehouses, Gabi. They were dilapidated and dangerous, drifters hung out there."

"Drifters, huh?" Dezi stepped away from the fire, staring out into the woods toward the howls of the wolves.

"Yeah," Mari whispered. Dezi glanced back at her. They locked eyes. She saw tears well in Dezi's eyes, and then they were gone. She turned back toward the woods. "We need to stand watch tonight, keep the fire going. These wolves are not afraid and have sharp teeth."

Gabi snuggled up to Mari, and she placed an arm over his shoulder. Mari had never gone to the warehouses. Gabi either. No one went, not by choice, but near the end, before Gabi and Mari left, plenty had been taken there, and none of them returned. Matt ruffled Gabi's hair and jostled Mari's shoulder. "Good story, Mari. Maybe leave the extra bit off next time, so we can sleep."

Mari tried not to think badly of Matt for being so kind, so gentle, but she was scared. He reminded her too much of Gabi, too much of their father whose kindness got him and their mother killed.

# Day 2,411 - Caves

Eva steered the humming boat down the river, deeper into the cave, keeping a careful eye on the gas gauge, willing it not to dip below half a tank. She needed to reserve enough gas so they could zip out of the cave for a quick escape. She frowned, wishing she had brought more of the gas she had stowed in the other boat to get back to the mainland. Her eyes flitted from shadow to shadow as she reviewed all the possible scenarios in which this trip could go wrong and remembered all the things that had already gone wrong.

"You know, you're beautiful when you're contemplating all the ways we might die." Jacob nudged her playfully with his boot.

"You're annoying when you aren't contemplating any of them." She beamed. Eva took compliments very well. No one had trained her to pretend not to like them. She maneuvered the boat around a rocky, narrow turn.

"I'm officially getting very hungry."

"Me too. Starvation is at the top of the list of ways we may die in here."

"Starvation's always at the top, isn't it?"

"Yeah, it is." Eva killed the motor as they entered another cavernous room. She'd been saving something, waiting for the right moment. Now felt like the right moment. They were both alive and weren't in immediate danger.

She reached for her pocket but before she reached it, Jacob's hand touched her back, and he slid next to her. She started at his touch and pulled away a little. He slipped his hand around hers.

"I want to talk about what happened."

"A lot has happened."

"I want to talk about me leaving you before you found a new species out on this island."

"Oh." Eva glanced down at their hands, intertwined. "Okay."

"I was coming back, Eva. I swear it."

Her eyes shot up and met his, searching. "Don't lie. Not about that."

"It's the truth, and I need to say the rest of it before I chicken out. I left that day because I was scared. Scared about how much I cared for you. Scared for you to care that much about me. The very few people I ever loved died. I didn't want that to happen with you, so I left. There was no excuse for it no matter the reason, but I couldn't go through with it. I was coming back. I didn't want to abandon you and what we had. I promise, I was coming back... then a storm came in, and I'm terrible with boats. Well, you know the rest."

Eva remained silent. She had always wanted him to come back. Even when she had was maddest at him, she loved him.

Jacob placed his forehead on hers. "Eva, you have to believe I was coming back to you."

She squeezed his hand for a long time before she softly kissed his lips. She pulled away, smiling. "I do."

Eva reached into her pocket. "I also have something to confess."

She flipped her wrist to reveal two small apples. "I stole these from Adam. To be fair, he stole them from me first."

Jacob reached out and put his hands around hers, grinning.

"You've had these the whole time?" He shook her hands playfully. "I almost starved to death."

She untangled her hands from his and held back the apples, laughing. "This is the last food in the cave. We need to ration them."

"They're too little to ration." He reached toward the apples, leaning over her body, bringing his face to hers, and brushing his lips against hers as he clasped his hand around her hand, bringing her hand and the apples between them. There was that electric jolt again. The edges of Eva's world softened. Her skin felt like it wasn't part of her body anymore. She leaned in and fully kissed him. He brought his other hand up into her hair by her ear and kissed her back. They embraced passionately and awkwardly pressed together, trying to become experts at this new thing between them, each gulp of air a painful reminder that they couldn't always be this close.

Eva's mental doomsday clock began ticking—how long they had before they starved, how each bit of gas they used lowered their chances of getting out of the cave alive, and how every second they kissed decreased the chances of seeing her sister again—and it eventually pulled her away from him. His expression matched what she was thinking—they would never have enough time. She opened her hand, revealing their consolation prizes. "You pick."

He smiled and picked the smaller one. He took a big bite, almost finishing the whole thing in one go. Eva chuckled.

"I'm not sharing mine with you just because yours is gone."

"But I got the small one."

Eva laughed before taking a tiny bite of hers, savoring the tart juice as it dried up her mouth. Her lips felt swollen, and the crisp fruit soothed them. As she chewed the apple, a feeling that this moment could be one of their last crashed into her mind and darkened her spirits. She shook off the thought and took another bite, but the taste of the fruit had soured.

"Hey, what's wrong?"

"Besides everyone I care about being lost in this cave?"

"Bright side, we're all lost together."

Eva bit into the apple again, finishing off half of it. Jacob was never much of a bright side guy, so she knew he was playing a part for her right now. The gesture worked. Her apple tasted better again.

*Splash!*

From the deepest end of the cavern, the water rippled, and a faint light shimmered before disappearing beneath the water. "What is that?"

Jacob flipped around, peering deeper into the cave. The corner was filling with blue, green, and purple light.

"That doesn't feel right."

"You feel something?" Eva looked at him uncertain.

"Not Iris or the others . . . something else."

Eva nodded. She had felt it too. She hadn't felt Iris since they entered the cave three days ago. Three days ago, Iris's voice had been clear and crisp as it always was in her mind. Jacob had felt her too, and then after about a day, Iris went completely silent. The sudden void had given Eva a strange sense of vertigo and returned her to feeling the way she'd felt before Iris first opened her eyes out on the lake. She had built Iris out of the plastic worm species she had discovered, and the island's magic answered her prayers and breathed life into the sister she always wanted. Iris had been her salvation from loneliness. Eva would take her back to the cabin every night, needing her to be close. Iris would sleep until Eva returned her to the island, and its magic would revive her again. Even when Iris insisted on staying out on the island permanently, Eva could still hear whispers of her. Now, she heard nothing.

"We shouldn't go to it, Jacob."

"What choice do we have? It's the only sign of any life we've seen down here. We either find Iris today, or we will have to go back without her."

"I'm not leaving until we find her."

"You won't do her any good dead, some starved skeleton for someone else to discover one day."

Eva bit her lip and glared at Jacob. "Go really slow. I'll be ready to peel out of here if that thing tries anything, which I am pretty certain it will."

Jacob grabbed the oars and started rowing. "I'll just get us a little bit closer then wait for it to move. Maybe we can follow it."

Eva nodded but something inside her was screaming for her to turn back. Her hand trembled as she rested it on the tiller, peering toward the glowing water in the distance.

# Day 2,411 - Labyrinth

Gigantic flowers resembling stars on stems towered at heights between twenty and eighty feet creating a forest around the underground pool. Each flower's center was comprised of thousands of disk florets radiating a warm yellow light that shimmered across their translucent safflower-colored petals, illuminating the forest floor. The water leading to the mossy bank of the lake was filled with reeds and plants that resembled cattails. Iris kicked and paddled through the swampy waters, her eyes frantically searching this alien oasis in the middle of an underground tunnel system. She parted the bright green algae atop the surface with swift, precise strokes, careful that her legs avoided getting tangled in the vast network of underwater plants below.

"Cain!"

No answer for the hundredth time. She wasn't ready to give up her water search. If Cain hadn't landed in the water,

Iris was certain she could not put him back together, not after a fall from that height, not if he hit solid ground. She continued to maneuver her way through the swampy waters searching for her favorite person. When Iris thought things like that about Cain, she surprised herself. She believed she loved Eva most, but that didn't mean she liked her the best. No, Iris loved Eva, but Eva wasn't her favorite person. She had hurt Iris too much when she first came to life. Eva had insisted on always taking Iris back to the mainland with her even though she knew that Iris would fall into a little death the moment they crossed the sandbar just off the shore of their island. Eva let her die that death many, many times until Iris had made Cain, until she made Eva stop. Iris loved Eva with all her heart, but that initial cruelty caused a deep pain inside of her. Even if Eva hadn't fully understood it as a violence against her, the cuts of those little deaths would always stand between them. In contrast, as soon as Cain took his first breath, he had protected her. He had given her the strength to stand up to her sister, her creator. He was her first real friend. She supposed that since she had created him, he would seek independence from her one day like she had from Eva.

Near the center of the lake, Iris spotted an out-of-place lump in the red and green algae. She swam over and when she got closer, she could see that it was Cain. He was floating face down, motionless. Iris reached out and grabbed his arm. She rolled him over, so he lay on his back, face up. She held onto his shoulder and started dragging him toward the shore. As she moved through the water, his body became heavier, his legs slowly sinking.

"Cain! Wake up!" She spat at him, struggling against the drag of his sinking legs. She slapped him in the face several times, screaming, "WAKE UP!" She tugged and pulled at him as his chest began to follow his legs. She clawed at his hair and neck as she tried to keep him above water.

"Cain, I can't hold you. Wake up!" Cain's head slumped beneath the surface, but Iris kept tight hold of his neck. She sank into the murky water. The warm yellow light of the flowers did not penetrate the algae. The large spirogyra was tangled up like piles of tentacles with little round pods that looked like closed eyes, a resting monster waiting to rise and destroy the universe. Cain landed on top of it and began disappearing into its deadly coils. Iris desperately tugged him up. She lost her grip and her nails scratched across his face as he plummeted further. Iris kicked back toward the darkness to find Cain. Loose strands of the plant twisted around her legs and arms, holding her back. She was very sure she could never drown. The new terror of being trapped in this plant's clutches below the surface for the rest of her very long life crashed down on her. She began desperately ripping at the plant. One large strand had twisted tightly around her leg, and she could not get it off. As it tightened, it was tugging her closer to the larger pulsing plant mass. She stopped struggling and started sinking, hoping if she relaxed completely her binds would loosen naturally. She continued to sink, and the plant only tightened around her.

One small bubble and then another and another rose around her, followed by many more. A garbled shout came from below. A strong force slammed into her. She turned, and it was Cain, a gash on his face where she had scratched him. Iris yelped and bubbles travelled to the surface from her mouth. He tugged her upward, but the plant tugged back. He reached down and tore at the vine until it came apart. Iris kicked her leg free, very happy she had made Cain so strong.

Cain grabbed her hand, and they kicked their way to the surface.

Cain and Iris, drenched and exhausted, sprawled out on the rubbery grass near the mossy shoreline, both gazing up into the star-like tree flowers. Cain touched the scratches on his face. They were sealing up but not as naturally as they would if he had other plastic creatures to help heal him.

"Does it hurt?"

"Not much, better than being trapped in the center of some plant prison."

"Yeah, I think I was more scared of that idea than guns."

"Gonna call it a tie on those two."

Iris laughed. Cain sat up and glanced back at the star trees.

"How do you think they are creating that light?"

"What if they are more like stars than trees? Over millions of years down here, they've grown hotter and hotter until their heat finally produced mini nuclear reactions. That would allow them to emit that type of light. Gravity does feel different down here, heavier, capable of altering the dust and gas in this chamber. Maybe that isn't a plant at all, maybe it is just gas and dust reacting to the forces around it, getting smaller and hotter, finally burning bright after millions of years of pressure. It's light and that water making all this alien life possible."

"You may be on to something. The rules of life down here are clearly different from those on the surface. The air is heavier and tastes different. The pressure is intense, constantly pushing down on me. Maybe you are right, although it doesn't explain their stems. But I agree that those star plants are the source of life in here."

"Not our source of life though. I think this is something entirely different from the plastic worms. I can't communicate with it. I feel separate from it. Alien. It's another life source completely. It feels nothing like what I saw after I went over the waterfall."

"What did you see, Iris?"

"I found the Source, at least the one we've been looking for."

"What was it?"

"It was a large colony of the plastic worms we make life with, trillions of them and one of them all at once. They are so connected that they hardly feel like separate creatures where I was, probably the same way they feel once they become another creature or when they become us. Many acting as one."

"And this one, it was the leviathan that dragged you over the edge?"

"No, that was just more of the many. The one at the center was a giant golden being, a queen. The rest of us are extensions of her. She had Marin, Brigid, Rhea, and Dee, all trapped, transforming."

"Transforming into what?"

"I don't know, Cain. Maybe they weren't transforming, maybe they were returning."

"Returning?"

Iris bent her knee and touched the stub where her big toe once existed, her tears welling up.

"Like this. I left them unraveling, coming apart."

Iris lifted her hair and bent down revealing the nape of her neck to Cain.

"See for yourself."

Cain leaned over her neck. There was a gape, smooth edges revealing layers of her skin and flesh. He could see the bone of her neck. It wasn't gory. It was clean like a plastic model a professor would use in the classroom. He leaned in closer to see deeper. He thought he saw something glimmer within. He touched the wound gently. Iris flinched and dropped her hair over the wound.

"Does it hurt?"

"Not exactly. . . it aches."

"The queen, our mother—she tried to make me like the others. They were pupas like from the books in the cabin, their bodies no longer the ones we knew. I couldn't stop what was happening to them, it had gone too far for that."

"So, what happened?"

"Just being around the queen, you want to go to her. You want to give yourself to her. I started to do that."

Iris's lips trembled. She stood up and shook water from her hair and removed a bit of algae clumped on her temple.

"I sank into her warmth, into the light. It felt good, Cain, really good. I felt the promise of fulfilling a destiny I'd known nothing about."

"What made you come back?"

Iris's jaw clenched, and her teal eyes gleamed. She glared up at the star flowers.

"It wasn't the destiny I had planned for myself."

# Day 2,411 - Caves

The object beneath the surface grew bigger as Eva and Jacob closed the distance between them and it. Eva caught a gleam in Jacob's eyes as the beast's glow flashed across them. He looked mesmerized, maybe even affectionate as he stared at the leviathan ahead of them. The pace of his rowing was speeding up.

"Jacob, slow down," Eva hissed, nudging him with her boot. Jacob's back tensed, and he pulled the oars into the boat and set them down, dripping. He jumped his legs over his seat and turned so he was facing her. He leaned toward her.

"I think it wants to help us."

"Why would you think that?" Eva leaned back away from him, recoiling a bit. Her renewed trust in Jacob was still fragile, a delicate glass figurine she balanced in her palm, always moments away from one of his actions forcing her hand into a fist, an act that would shatter it and cut Eva deeply.

"You can't feel it at all?"

"No. What do you mean?"

The purple light in the cavern dimmed as it changed to indigo.

"I don't know exactly. I just feel safer since it arrived. Safer the closer we get to it."

"Well, I don't. I feel the opposite."

Jacob reached a hand toward Eva and placed it on her knee, trying to hold the hand she pulled away. The indigo light disappeared completely, and the cavern went dark.

"Eva, I'm not going to do anything you don't—"

"Where'd it go?"

Eva pulled out the flashlight from her pocket and flipped it on. It flickered on and off, the batteries almost depleted. She swore her mother's foulest phrase. She pointed the flashlight over the boat's edge, its dim light barely illuminating a small spot on the water by the boat.

A large shadow floated just below them, easily four times the size of their boat.

"It's right under us. We need to get out of here."

Eva reached for the motor's on switch.

"Wait! Maybe if we hold still, it will move on. We can follow it. It might lead us to the others." Jacob squeezed her arm tightly, holding it so she couldn't reach the switch.

"Let me go—"

*Thunk.*

The boat swayed back and forth, the lake's water sloshing around them. Eva grabbed onto the edge of the boat as Jacob released her arm to steady himself. He leaned over the boat, trying to get a closer look.

"I don't think it's trying to hurt us, Eva. I think it's trying to tell us something."

Eva shot Jacob an incredulous look and flipped on the motor. It roared to life, sending a cacophony of sound slamming off the rocky walls of the cave. It vibrated the boat and sent ripples through the water.

"I don't like how it's communicating."

Eva's small flashlight flickered against the water as the large shadow flickered back, glowing a faint teal then switching off, then on, then off, again and again.

"There it is." Eva revved the engine several times. The creatures glowed more intensely with each rev. The boat sped away from the creature, shooting a small wake toward it, jettisoning Eva and Jacob away from it.

"What's the plan, here?" Jacob darkened as he watched Eva steer the rapidly moving boat away from the beast.

"Not to become fish food, mainly." Eva's face flushed, her body boiling despite the chill of the cave.

"We can't just leave."

"I'm not leaving, I'm circling and then trying to get by this thing, get in front of it." Her heart was racing, and her vision was narrowing, chest tight, breath short. Jacob was right, she was panicking. She slowed the boat down a little and focused on breathing and keeping the boat from hitting rocks.

"I'm afraid of it, Jacob," she finally rasped.

"I'm afraid of it—"

"No, you're not."

Silence. Jacob didn't contradict or confirm her assessment. Eva stopped the motor, and the water lapped against the hull. She kept her eyes on the area of the water where they had last seen the beast. The teal flickering of the creature had stopped, or it had dived so deep it was no longer visible.

"You think we scared it off?" Jacob searched the dark cave, a sad yearning lacing the edge of his tone.

"I hope so. We should row around the far side, try to get out of this cavern as quietly as possible." Eva tilted the motor up out of the water.

"Do you think Cain would go after it?"

Eva focused on locking the motor in place, avoiding Jacob's gaze.

"I don't know for sure. What does it matter?"

"You trust Cain, right?"

Eva remained silent.

"If Cain was here saying we should follow this creature to Iris, you'd do it, right?"

"You don't know anything about Cain and me."

"Well, then tell me."

"It's complicated."

Jacob looked like he had been slapped in the face. "Yeah, I thought it might be." He coughed and lifted his legs over the seat, flipping himself around to face the bow. He pulled up the oars and dipped them in the water.

Eva felt anger rising from her stomach to her heart, shooting up toward her brain where she didn't want it. "This isn't about Cain or you. I don't like the way that thing makes me feel. That's it. Okay?"

"Yeah, okay." Jacob rowed along the edge of the shore, keeping the boat as far from where they last saw the creature as possible. For a long while, the only sound in the cave was the oars entering and exiting the water. Jacob's cadence was not as crisp and precise as Cain's, not quite as reassuring and stabilizing. Still, it lulled Eva to a peaceful place for long periods of time then disrupted her and then lulled her back, a calming force with a recurring hiccup. The hiccup was what kept Eva's focus on Jacob, what drew her to him over Cain.

"Eva, look, right there," Jacob whispered as he dropped the oars into the boat with a thunk-thunk-thunk. He pointed toward the corner where they had first spotted the sea monster. Just below the surface, a few figures darted through the waters. Those fleeting figures were soon joined by ten others, then a hundred, and then they became over a thousand strong. Eva's eyes widened as the smaller creatures swam toward them, glowing faintly, some green, some teal, some blue, some indigo, some purple. As they swam closer, their forms became more defined. It was a whole school of glowing—

"Fish!" Jacob whooped. "We're saved!" Jacob reached for the fishing pole, fidgeting with the line. "We have to catch some of these suckers."

"Where did they come from?" Eva watched the school of fish come together and then separate like electrons flying around a nucleus.

"The same place as that other thing. We found life in here. It's just new. Maybe it's that Source you are obsessed with. The start of all this, the start of what is healing our world. A good thing, right?"

"Yeah." Eva wasn't so sure. Jacob cast off, and the bait landed about twenty feet away with a plop, sinking into the center of a mess of glowing fish. Eva could only wonder, if there were fish and giant sea creatures, who was making them?

# Day 2,411 - Island

Embers blazed red as Dezi tossed another log on the fire. She kept one eye trained on the woods, homed in on a section of the dark forest with a fierce focus. Laying on the ground as close to the fire as she could get, one arm draped protectively around Gabi, Mari watched Dezi. Matt curled up next to them, creating a closed circle, all keeping tight for warmth, acting more like a pack than a group of human children. Mari still hadn't slept that night. She was restless, worried.

An hour earlier, Dezi's whole body tensed, and she rushed for her gun. She stood and crept toward the woods, weapon raised for a long time. Mari had quietly watched her since then, partially out of curiosity and partially because she always watched Dezi, liked to watch her. Mari couldn't see what Dezi was seeing from her position on the ground and didn't want her to know she was awake. Maybe one of the wolves Gabi and Matt had seen earlier was getting too close, but she didn't think so. Dezi looked like she had seen a ghost, not an animal she could wipe out with a single bullet.

"I know you're awake, Mari." Dezi didn't look away from the woods. Mari didn't answer. It was still so strange for Dezi to speak so much in one day. The pleasant shock of Dezi's voice made Mari want to remain quiet, to make space for more of it. Reluctantly, she lifted Gabi's head off her arm and gently placed it on Matt's chest, rising quietly and slowly.

"You need to get some rest. I can stand watch for a while." She sat on a nearby log and peered into the woods.

"I prefer sleeping in the day." Dezi always insisted on doing night watch when the group was staying somewhere new. Mari always wondered why but never asked. She felt it was a topic Dezi wouldn't appreciate being brought up. Mari picked up another log and placed it on the fire. She sat closer to the warm flames.

"I never thought a place like this existed."

"Me neither."

"How long do you think Adam was going to keep us from coming out here?"

Mari was silent. She wasn't yet comfortable saying anything negative about Adam. Her hope combined with fear of him returning prevented her from being honest in this moment.

"Maybe he was trying to make sure it was safe before bringing us all out."

"Is that what you really think?"

Dezi glanced back at her. Mari remained silent and lowered her eyes to avoid Dezi's.

"That's what I thought."

A twig cracked in the distance and Dezi jerked, grabbing her gun again and walking to the edge of the camp. Mari stood up and followed her.

"What do you think it is?"

"Not sure. Could be anything out here."

They both watched the twisted branches of the trees sway in the wind. The night was calmer than most. It would become more violent in nights to come. It always did by the water. Mari sighed and glanced up at a single cloud in the starry sky. She searched for the easiest to spot constellation, the two shaped like bears. She traced lines between the stars with her gaze, forming the shape, remembering the story of the bears, wishing some god would throw her and her brother into the sky to protect them from danger.

"What I think is that we are going to have to figure out shelter tomorrow before the weather turns. Do a search of the island."

"Yeah, that would be smart."

Mari looked away from Ursa Major and focused on the constellation of freckles on Dezi's cheeks. "Maybe you could suggest it in the morning?" Mari let her question linger while Dezi thought quietly. She knew that Lena and Jake were more likely to listen to an idea coming from Dezi.

Dezi didn't answer. Instead, she asked a question. "Do you think Eva could have killed Adam by herself?"

Mari glanced back into the wicked woods. It was so beautiful in the day but terrifying at night. Dezi answered Mari's unasked question with this one. She had seen something out there, and it was a human something. Or at least Dezi thought it was.

"She is clever." Mari glanced back at Gabi sleeping by the fire, fearful of his involvement in whatever befell Adam out here. She glanced back into the wood. "It's possible, I suppose. I just don't know how she would have done it."

"He would have killed her, you know?"

"What?"

"Adam. He would have killed her. She pushed his buttons."

"Yes, I think you are right."

"That seems stupid to me."

"Excuse me?"

"After seeing this island and all this life. This way of life that could be ours, and he would kill the person who could make it."

Mari nodded. Dezi was asking her something that she wasn't sure how to answer.

"I put up with a lot from Adam because I trusted he had the group's best interest at heart."

"Yes."

"I don't think that anymore."

"No." Mari spoke softly, her heart started racing as she studied Dezi's jaw clenching and unclenching.

Dezi turned and locked eyes with her. Mari's breath caught in her throat. "After your story . . . you and I have seen what happens when people run out of food. The true horror of it."

"Yes."

Dezi's hand was suddenly on hers. Mari started but did not pull away. She lifted her gaze to Dezi's. Dezi left her hand there for several moments, clutching her gun in the other. "I can't see that again, ever. Do you know what I mean?"

Mari placed a hand on top of Dezi's. She nodded. "I do."

Dezi slipped her hand away and turned back toward the forest. "You should get some sleep. We'll have a lot to do in the morning if we hope to have shelter by tomorrow night."

Dezi smiled at her, and her cheeks flushed. Mari smiled back, suddenly feeling shy and self-conscious, feeling Dezi might finally be letting her in, something she had long hoped for.

# Day 2,411 - Caves

A flopping fish with glimmering turquoise scales and a thick long body like a bass landed in the boat. Jacob hollered with excitement.

"Shhh!" Eva smiled as she kept an eye out for the leviathan. Jacob carefully removed the hook from the fish's lip. He squeezed the fish in one hand and thrust the pole toward her with another. "You give it a try. I caught three. You are the better fisher than me. You'll probably catch thirty."

Eva chuckled, taking the pole. "Maybe not thirty." She slipped a bit of rancid hot dog on the end of the hook and peered at the glowing fish darting under and around the boat. She spotted a large group clustered together about fifteen feet from their vessel. She let her arm with the pole fall off to the side and flicked the pole with her elbow and wrist. The line flew through the air with a whizz, and the bait landed near the glowing cluster. A few of the fish broke from the group and circled her bait. As one swam close by, it shoved its head toward the bait and took a quick nibble. Eva saw it before she felt it, the line pulling the rod a bit. Another fish went in more aggressively, and the rod bowed. With a quick tug up, she hooked the fish.

"Here, take the pole." She thrust the pole into Jacob's hand. With her gloved hands, she slowly pulled in the line, playing a game of tug of war with her catch. The bioluminescence made this one of the most exciting fishing excursions of her life. She had never seen what was happening underneath the surface so clearly. It also made her empathize more than she normally did with the fish, and that was already a lot. A tear escaped down her cheek. She shook it off as she pulled the fish closer to the boat. Eva smiled at Jacob again. "We should probably catch as many as we can and find a place to start a fire and smoke them."

Jacob grabbed her fish. It had purple glimmering scales and a thin long body like a perch. Eva shot a worried look into the water, keeping up her active search for the sea monster. "We should get to shore as soon as we can."

Jacob studied her out of the corner of his eye as he removed the hook from her fish's cheek. She could tell he wasn't worried about the larger creature but was holding back from arguing with her. "We have plenty of food now. We can keep looking for everyone. That's a good thing, isn't it?"

"Yes, but it, it's too easy, Jacob. It's not natural."

Jacob chuckled. "Coming from the girl who redefined what natural means."

"I'm serious, something is helping us. Isn't it obvious?"

"I think you're right. Don't we deserve a little help, Eva?" He gazed up at her with such a sincere expression, absent of any doubt or suspicion. She had never seen him look that trusting and hopeful. He gently set the fish in the bottom of the boat and put another piece of bait on her hook. She loved how he set the fish down, with reverence and care. She felt some of her fear dissipate and tried to enjoy this improbable and magical fishing trip.

"We do deserve that."

Except, one thought kept tugging at the spell.

*Why was something helping them?*

Eva bit into a charred fish with a loud crunch, the skin perfectly crisp, fatty oil dripping down her chin. As she tore into the pungent flesh, the scents of lake water, stone, and smoke made her eyes water. She said a silent prayer for the perch as she took another hungry bite. Jacob was on his second fish.

"I'll only eat two, I promise." He grinned as he chewed. A large pile of fish filets was roasting on the fire. They should last them a week, maybe two.

"Eat as much as you want." Eva took another big bite. She was on her second fish too. Her hunger was subsiding, and she felt stronger, more confident with each bite.

The rest of their fish were tied to the boat trapped in a makeshift container they had made from the netting and sticks Eva had in her kit. Eva hoped they would stay alive until they needed to cook more.

They had set up camp at the far corner of the cavern where they had first spotted the leviathan. There was a small flattish ledge just big enough for their boat and the fire and another tunnelway nearby.

"Which way do you think Iris went?" Jacob said after he swallowed a big bite.

"No idea."

"I think she would have followed the life."

Eva shot him a wary look.

"You said that everyone was hearing something you couldn't hear, something speaking to them, right?"

Eva nodded and took another bite of her fish.

"Well, that something must be alive, right? So, follow the life, that's what I think."

Eva peered into the dark tunnel. A green and indigo fish darted out of the entrance. Eva rolled the bits of cooked fish around in her mouth with her tongue. It tasted like the other fish, her fish, not exactly the same but close. They must be connected to the Source, connected to Abel, Abel who was inside of Jacob somewhere. She peered at Jacob's chest, the place where Abel, her flat plastic marine worm companion, had disappeared to save Jacob from dying. She wondered if he was still really Abel in there or just part of Jacob now, consumed by his cells or mutated by them.

Jacob felt her stare and touched his chest self-consciously.

"Sorry." Eva lowered her eyes. "I was just wondering . . . do you feel him?"

"Sometimes. Like when I tried to leave the island, I felt a tug that was very obviously not me, pulling me both toward you and back toward Iris and Cain at the same time."

"How do you know it wasn't just you?"

Jacob bit his lip and glanced into the water at the fish struggling in the netted cage. "I don't have a delicate way to put this."

Eva whacked him lightly on the arm. "You don't have to be delicate with me." He rubbed his arm.

"Maybe you could be a little more delicate," he joked. "I just wouldn't have been that conflicted on my own." He touched her fingers with his and moved a little closer to her. "I wouldn't have been struggling between going after them or going after you. I would have just gone after you."

Eva watched Jacob's hand on her fingers. His touch sent unsettling shockwaves through her system. When Eva had read fairytales and stories about love, they always ended with the one big romantic kiss at the end. That was the end of the story, the lesson. She now found herself in very unchartered territory after the initial kiss she'd shared with Jacob, a kiss she needed to ask him an awkward question about right now and had no idea how to ask it.

Jacob raised an eyebrow at her and moved his hand off hers. "Did I do something wrong?"

Eva's eyes shot up at him, startled by his sudden movement away from her. "No, why?"

"Because you just made the strangest face."

Eva blushed. She was thankful for the fire's heat disguising the deep red her cheeks must be at this moment.

"I have to ask you something, and it's weird."

"It's possible to get weirder?"

Eva chuckled and felt a little less anxious.

"When's the last time you felt Abel, like for sure felt him?"

Now Jacob's face contorted into a grimace. "A little before we entered the cave."

"Yeah, me too."

"Wait, you felt Abel?"

"I didn't feel Abel. I felt something want Abel. Does that make sense?"

"Yes. It does."

"There's something inside of me that is in love with Abel."

Jacob moved close to Eva and placed his hand on hers. They both were watching the flames jump and the fat and the skin of the fish sizzle. He leaned over and brushed his lips on her jaw by her neck and whispered. "Do you think it's just you being in love with me?"

She turned so her lips were very close to his and shook her head. A dark cloud crossed Jacob's face for a moment and then passed. He held still, unsure of the next move.

"I know it's not just me being in love with you because I've been in love with you since I met you. I tried to stop that, believe me, but it never went away, not all the way, even when I wanted to kill you. But, after Abel jumped inside of you, something changed, and I needed to know if it was the same—"

Jacob was kissing Eva. It was fishy and sloppy yet deep and overpowering. His hands were in her hair, then on her arms and around her back. She was laying on top of him before she realized she had flipped around. She was kissing him now, and she felt ablaze in the freezing cave. After a day of the leviathan chasing them and thoughts of starvation and death, Eva wanted Jacob and Abel to be as close to her as possible. Despite the fact that she was burning up inside, she shivered as she pulled away. He looked up toward her lovingly, his hand on her face. "I love you too, Eva."

She smiled, feeling truly seen and loved for the first time since her parents. She didn't make Jacob or create Abel. They found her, searched her out, and loved her, and she loved them, whatever that meant. A small nagging guilty thought about Cain interrupted her blissful feeling. She loved him too. She knew that was true, but it was different and complicated like she had told Jacob.

"Where'd you go?" Jacob touched her cheek. She pushed thoughts of Cain to the back of her mind as she placed her hand on Jacob's. "I'm right here." She leaned down and kissed him again, staying with only him for a very long time.

Eva's head lay on Jacob's chest. It rose and fell unevenly as he slept. She smiled as he softly snored, only partially awake, imagining that this was just the beginning of many such moments together. She couldn't sleep, not after everything they had shared that night.

A large splash echoed from across the dark pool and broke the spell. She pushed herself up, panicked. The chamber was glowing, the familiar green, purple, and blue light shimmering below the water. "Oh my god . . ."

"What? What is it?" Jacob scrambled up and turned around. They both stared, slack jawed as the leviathan emerged, twice the size it had been earlier, a giant manta ray covering half the surface of the water in the cavern. The cave lit up even brighter as it skimmed across the surface. "How did it even get in here?"

Eva glanced at the fish on the fire and then back to the ones struggling in the net, fighting to get back into the water. The other fish in the water swam toward the giant beast and disappeared beneath it. Eva watched closer and realized they weren't just disappearing under the creature but were molding into it. She pointed at several swimming toward it. "Look. They're becoming part of it."

Jacob and Eva gawked as the fish deconstructed at the periphery of the beast. They became flatworms like Abel and the others for a moment, and then they molded into the larger beast. Eva felt sick to her stomach, like the parts of the monster she had eaten were going to force their way out and go back to where they belonged.

"Do you think this is the Source we've been looking for?" Jacob whispered to Eva who could only shake her head in horrified wonderment as the fish continued to return to the leviathan, and it continued to expand.

Eva grabbed his arm. "What if it's trying to bring us back to it, just like those fish?"

"It's not trying—" Jacob sucked his breath back into his throat. The leviathan dipped completely under the surface and torpedoed toward them. Eva pushed him aside, rushing toward the motor. She tried to start it, but it only puttered then died. The leviathan halved the distance between them. She tried the motor again. This time, it roared to life. She put pressure on the throttle, and the small boat jerked forward, knocking Jacob back. "Not so fast!"

A large tentacle formed out of the leviathan's body, reaching out toward the boat. "Jacob! Look out!"

"I see it!" Jacob grabbed an oar and swung, connecting to the tentacle. It recoiled but quickly swiped at them again. Jacob dodged. The tentacle smacked against Eva. She fell over, losing her grip on the tiller. The boat slammed against a rocky edge. She dragged herself up and pulled the tiller in the other direction. Jacob regained his balance and grip on his oar. The creature whipped its tail around and hit the side of the boat, almost capsizing it. Jacob fell onto the middle seat. "I take it back! Get us out of here as fast as possible!"

The first tentacle collapsed back into the body of the leviathan, but another was sprouting out toward the boat as Eva swerved blindly through the cavern toward a narrow opening in the far corner.

# Day 2,412 - Labyrinth

Cain gazed up at one of the shortest star flowers. His hand rubbed the incredibly smooth white bark. Iris had shimmied a third of the way up the tree but was struggling.

"I can't hold on . . ." Iris slid back down the trunk and landed on her butt next to Cain. He held out his hand for her. She grabbed it, frowning up at the trunk and cursing under her breath.

"You've gotten really good at expletives." Cain raised an impressed eyebrow. "I was wrong. It is an artform."

"I just want to know what makes them work." Iris stomped a foot, arm akimbo, huffing as she kicked the tree's base.

"Well, we've both tried many times. We aren't climbing it. Hopefully, we can find something to climb near one."

"We need to get out of here." Iris gazed up at the way they had fallen in. Cain studied her for a moment and then returned to surveying the strange marshland. It was large, but he could still see rocky walls in all four directions.

"We should walk the perimeter, see if there's any other way out." Cain peered back to Iris to see if she agreed. She nodded but didn't move.

"Which way are we trying to go? Up? Down? Do we even know what those directions are anymore?"

"We don't know is the right answer. I do know we need to get out of this place as soon as possible."

"Yes, me too. Very much."

"So, you feel it too?"

"I feel tired, drained, unsatisfied here, like there's a void in my stomach that needs filling. All things I don't normally feel, all unpleasant."

"I think you feel hunger, maybe even decay. The air, the water, everything about this chamber is extremely different."

Iris glared up at the star trees. "It's those plants. They are creating conditions that we don't thrive in. Each moment we are here brings us closer to actual death, Cain."

Iris turned to him, eyes fearful and more childlike than she had ever appeared to him. Cain nodded and grabbed Iris's hand. "We'll work faster then." He shot her a tired smile as he lifted her onto his back. He charged through the reeds and cattails. The aching from the back of her neck intensified with each of his steps.

Cain trudged along through a variety of marshland flora, every leaf perfectly still unless they brushed against one. There was no wind in this chamber. Iris frowned at his labored breathing and dropped from his back.

"It's too still here."

"Yes. I haven't seen an insect, bird, any animal. We've almost travelled half the perimeter."

"Maybe animal life can't thrive here, not yet."

"That seems like a good assumption."

"I wonder if this chamber is connected to our ecosystem somehow, like it feeds into it at some level, whether the gases that rise or if the water systems are connected . . ."

"I really hope the way out of here isn't through that terrifying lake."

Iris paled and gagged a little. "Me too."

Small yellow flowers opened in tiny clusters growing out of stubby bunches of pale fleshy green leaves. This unfamiliar succulent covered most of the ground away from the shore.

Iris bent down and dug her fingers into the ground near one of the plants. She rubbed the bluish silt between her fingertips.

"Even the dirt is a different color."

Cain kicked the clay with his boot. He wheezed, constantly searching the rocky wall for an opening, a way out. His breathing was coming harder than usual like he was gulping in the air and still needed more.

"It's the air I'm worried about."

Iris nodded, shooting him a concerned look. She was short of breath too, but Cain was declining faster than her. She charged ahead, disappearing into the tall orangish wetland grass. Cain followed her dark hair bobbing just above the blades of grass. She started running. Cain began to jog but had to stop after several moments to catch his breath. He gazed over the grass, under a few of the taller star trees, and spotted a hole in the rocky surface where a cluster of white and green vines grew out and around like a braided mane. They reached for the glowing orb on the nearest tree, growing toward the light. Many of the thick vines had grown out until they reached the tree's trunk and clung to it, growing with the tree and over to the next one, and down to the ground toward the water. Small white flowers and a red fruit that resembled spiky sea urchins grew from the parts of the plant that were closest to the glowing star tree.

"I found something."

Cain walked slow and steady concentrating on his breathing. He held out his left hand, allowing the grass to brush his fingertips, the soft caress of the many blades calmed his breathing as he approached the trunk of a vine-covered tree.

"I can climb this one!" Cain followed Iris's voice up the tree. The vine plant wrapped around the trunk all the way up to the flower atop it. Cain followed the vine and saw that it grew from the hole in the rocky cliff above.

"It leads back into the cliff. That plant must lead somewhere."

Cain felt the tough green vines and their tougher white counterpart. He rubbed his hands against both for a moment.

"Iris, these are roots and vines intertwined together."

Iris reached out and touched a braid that contained both the white and the green twisting together. She followed the braid to where the two separated, the green growing toward the light and the white travelling down toward the soil and water.

"I wonder what is happening to the plant above. It must be a twisted mess."

Cain grabbed onto a large white root and gave it a good tug, testing if it would hold. It did. He lifted a leg and hoisted himself up onto the stalk and followed Iris. "We're going to have find out. If we wait much longer, I won't be able to climb."

Iris gazed down at Cain, frowning. Her chest burned hotter with each step and pull. A dull ache was forming in her lungs from the exertion. Cain was right. This was their only option. They didn't have time to search for a better way out or determine if the way they were headed was safe.

Iris shimmied across the vine bridge, hanging a few hundred feet above the marshland below. Cain crawled on all fours directly behind her, two-thirds of the way across. Swaying, she took a moment to survey the beauty of this chamber of alien life one last time before she crawled forward. As she moved further from the warmth of the star flowers atop their sturdy stems and her body cooled, she longed for the warmth she had felt when she stood in front of the golden creature, her mother, her queen. In that moment in front of the queen, she had felt on the verge of becoming what she was meant to be, but when she had reached out and touched the creature and felt her neck split open, she panicked. Instead of embracing it, she had ripped away and fled to the water, diving deep to the stony bottom. The golden light had radiated above the surface, beckoning her, but it did not chase after. She had seen the leviathan building back together on the surface, plastic glowing flatworms dodging around it until they found just the right spot and melded to it. Iris swam away from it to the far side of the cavern opposite the crashing waterfall. She spotted a darker spot in the water and propelled herself toward it. It was a hole. She reached her hand in it and felt around. The space was tight, but she would fit. She glanced behind her and saw the leviathan lazily floating toward her, growing as it approached. She crawled into the small nook, hoping to hide until she could make a plan or until Cain showed up. The leviathan had gotten closer and closer until part of its flowing body lay flush, sealing Iris into the tight space. A tentacle began growing from the creature and reaching out toward her. She glanced at her missing toe and pressed back further into the little tunnel. Right as the tentacle was about to wrap around her, the ground fell out from under her, and she started falling.

"AHHH!" Iris's foot slipped. She cursed under her breath, hanging tightly to a dangling root, now only five feet from the hole in the cliff. "Cain help!"

Cain crawled swiftly to her and grabbed her arm, pulling her back up on the vine. She held onto him, feeling his strength, but also hearing his haggard breaths. She hoped they would both return to their old selves when they left this horrid chamber.

"You okay?" Cain peered down at her.

"I hope so." Iris turned to face the vines and roots tangled within and around it. In the center, there seemed to be a tunnel big enough to crawl through, but she couldn't see in very far. The vines and roots tangled around each other leading into the giant mass reminded her of something else. She gasped when she remembered swimming in the lake earlier. She had seen the water plants piled on top of each other. Cain was lost in them, and they were pulling her to its murky depths.

"Cain . . ."

"We don't have any other choice."

"What if we get stuck in there? It's not like we are going to die, we're just going to be in there for eternity."

"Then, let's not get stuck."

Iris released a tense laugh and inched forward, pulling herself up a smaller vine toward the hole's entrance. She reached over to grab another root and sliced her hand on a sharp barb. She recoiled and shook her hand. A moldy musk of soil and metal invaded her nostrils. Blue blood dripped down her palm. She examined the gash on her palm. It wasn't that deep, but it stung and ached more than her usual cuts. Maybe they could die down here.

"Watch out, the vines are sharper up here." Iris pulled herself up and climbed into the hole's entrance. Cain quickly followed her, avoiding the barbed parts of the plant. They kneeled side-by-side staring into a tunnel created by twisted vines and roots on all sides.

"You should go first." Cain gestured for Iris to enter the tunnel.

She frowned at him. "I thought you liked going first."

"Yes, but you're smaller, and if we get to a point where I can't get through, I don't want to block the way out."

Iris hit him in the arm hard. "I'm not leaving you in here."

Still, she listened to him and led the way into the tunnel, crawling gracefully, carefully setting her hands and knees down to avoid getting cut or stuck, very happy to be able to see well in the dark as the last bit of the light from the star flowers disappeared.

# Day 2,412 - Caves

The boat zipped into a narrow passageway, scraping its sides along the stony edge, just barely escaping the chamber holding the rapidly growing leviathan. Jacob clutched both sides of the boat. "I think you can slow down now!"

"Not until we are safe!" Eva screamed back. She executed two hairpin turns in the narrower passage before she finally eased up on the gas. "Can you see it?"

"No, I don't think it's following us."

Eva maintained the slower pace while maneuvering the boat away from the larger chamber. The glowing leviathan and its tentacles still did not follow, neither did any of the fish. "You still think that thing wants to play nice?"

"I don't know what that thing wants." Jacob was out of breath, still clenching an oar, searching for signs of the stingray-shaped leviathan. The river's current picked up speed, bumping them into the rocky side from time to time. As Eva turned the motor off, the boat shifted, and they jerked downward. "You feel that? We're going down," Eva muttered.

"Do we want to go down?" Jacob shifted his weight and positioned the oars, getting ready to row if necessary.

The tunnel was pitch black. The glowing fish they had captured broke free from their makeshift net when the leviathan had entered, frenzied and emboldened by that creature. Despite having lost their living lanterns, they still had a week's worth of cooked fish. Eva hoped they wouldn't need more than that to find the others.

The boat jerked forward again, and they started rushing faster down into the cave.

"Ow!" Jacob crashed into the other side of the boat as it slammed into a rocky wall. He moaned as he dragged his body up and flopped back onto his seat. "Can you see anything?"

Eva shook her head. "I can't see a thing. I don't think we can do anything about this either way. Just hold on and hope this doesn't get any steeper."

The water sprayed them both, soaking their supplies. They hit the other side of the tunnel a few more times. Water sloshed into the vessel as the boat tipped from side to side.

"We're going to capsize!"

"Throw your body in the opposite direction, even it out!" Eva shouted back. She felt the current change below them. The boat jerked again. She prayed they wouldn't go faster. The water calmed slightly as the river flattened out. The boat swayed less violently, and they stopped hitting the rocky edges. By the time they glided into a small cavern with still waters, the boat wasn't rocking at all.

They were both quiet for a long time. Their rapid and ragged breathing slowing down in unison. Eva was the first to break the silence.

"Anything broken?"

"Nah, but my hands won't stop shaking."

Eva snorted. "I think my teeth are shaking the whole boat. I'm freezing."

"Are you hurt at all?" She felt him clumsily grabbing her leg, reaching out to her in the darkness.

"I'm okay. Are you?" She reached over and grabbed his hand.

"Yeah, got a bump on my head that hurts like hell, but I'm okay." He squeezed hers back.

Eva pulled out her flashlight from her damp parka. She flicked it several times. Nothing. "Flashlight's totally dead."

"I can light a match, but I'd rather wait until we are building a fire."

Eva felt around until she found the oars. She lifted them, slipped them in the water and rowed. Each movement caused an ache from a new bruise.

"You want me to row?"

Eva did want him to row. She was so tired, but she also wanted to warm up and rowing helped with that. "No, I'm okay."

"I can't believe it's possible, but it's even darker down here than it was at the beginning of the river."

"Yeah, it feels like it." The cold and dark of the caves were getting to her. During that sudden drop in the river, her internal compass broke, and she suddenly felt like a planet knocked out of orbit. Like that orphaned planet, they were floating further and further away from the things that brought them warmth and life into a cold abyss.

"I can't believe I'm saying this, but I want that thing to return and light up this place."

Jacob laughed. "Me—"

A large flapping echoed from the top of the cavern, quite a far distance above them. Eva stiffened. This sound was not their leviathan. It was something completely new. She couldn't hear Jacob's breath anymore. He must be holding it. She inhaled through her nose. The cave still smelled of water, stone, iron, and earth, but there was something new, something fresh that reminded her of dew-covered grass at dawn.

A buzzing sounded from the far end of the cave, opposite to where they had entered. Eva set the oars back inside the boat. She gazed upward, wondering if a light would appear and reveal the source of the sound. None did. The flapping and buzzing sounded and silenced several times. It became clear by the location and frequency that there were at least two creatures making the sound, two flying creatures.

Jacob leaned toward Eva and whispered, "They're big."

Eva nodded, knowing Jacob couldn't see her. She was too afraid to speak. When they departed on this mission to find the others, she had known there was something alive in the cave, but she had always imagined it to be something smaller like the worms, not a giant manta ray or a human-sized bat. She had once read about bats that were as big as children and had secretly been pleased they were extinct. She had never planned on making one. Now, she was about to come face-to-face with one or maybe even something bigger.

Jacob slid his foot next to hers. "We need to try to get to shore."

Her hands trembling, she reached for the oars again. The sounds ceased, and the cave went quiet. She slowly rotated the oars, out and into her body, dipping them stealthily into the water. There was a very small plop when they touched the surface, but it rang like a crack of thunder exploding through the cavern. Eva flinched but continued rowing, holding her breath.

The buzzing and flapping began again from both sides of the cavern, circling in, getting closer and closer until they could feel the air thrusting down upon them. The creatures hovered above them like owls ready to stoop. Eva crouched down, her eyes darting around, the field mouse. She froze.

A whooshing sound, then Jacob yelled. "Get off me!" The boat shook as Jacob's feet kicked the sides, fighting off whatever held onto him. Eva lunged toward the sound and her fingers grazed the tip of his boot which hovered above the boat. She shot up and reached up, but only found empty air, Jacob was just out of her reach. "Where are you?!"

"Way up here! There are two of them! Get out of reach! Jump in the water!" Jacob shouted, now even farther away from her. Eva squinted, fruitlessly searching for a shadow in the darkness. "I'm not leaving you!"

She heard a struggle in the air.

"Jacob!"

A fist pounded against flesh.

"Let me go!"

She stood in the complete darkness, mind racing. She couldn't leave Jacob. She couldn't jump in the water. She was frozen.

"Ow! He just hit me!" Another voice rang through the chamber, one that punched Eva in the gut. She recognized that voice. She heard the flapping and buzzing above her move in the direction of the voice.

"Get out of this cave, Ev—"

There was a thud, and the cavern went silent. Tears fell down her face, and she clamped a hand over her mouth, holding perfectly still. The beating sound of large wings travelled further and further away until it was gone.

Eva lowered slowly, taking a seat in a circling boat, dazed and completely alone. After several moments, she wiped the tears from her face with her parka sleeve. She put her hands on the wood of the oars. Her gaze hardened, determination replacing her fear and anguish. She did what she always did when she felt hopeless out on the lake, she started rowing. She turned the boat toward the direction she had last heard the flapping. She remembered a time when she was too cautious even to attempt taking her boat around the island, how meticulously she had planned the expedition that had eventually led her to these other creatures, her destiny, and eventually into the heart of this cave. That old Eva would never have travelled this deep without many shorter excursions, without studying the cave, without a clear risk evaluation, and several escape plans. She sighed. That Eva didn't exist anymore. This new Eva brought someone she loved deeply on a dangerous suicide mission. The new Eva scared her. She had to find Jacob before it was too late and before she again transformed into an even newer Eva. One thing she had learned on this island was that she was constantly changing from one day to the next, with each new experience or loss. She was never the same Eva as she had been the day before. She, and all the Evas before her, wanted to use the motor, but *they all* knew it was too dangerous. She couldn't see, and she didn't want whatever stole Jacob away to hear her coming. She had to go forward even though everything, including herself, had just shifted again. Everyone she had always cared about was in that direction.

# Day 2,412 - Labyrinth

The vines and roots twisted tighter together as Iris and Cain travelled further up. The tunnel, overgrown with vines had steepened dramatically. Without the bramble to hold onto, Iris and Cain would have plummeted back down to the cavern filled with glowing flowers and toxic air. Iris glanced down at Cain who wiggled upward.

"You still fit?"

"Yes, but if it gets any tighter. . ."

Iris squinted upward. It was difficult to determine if the passageway became narrower or if it just curved. The vines and roots entwined so tightly together, it was near impossible to tell which ones were closer and which ones were farther away. To add to the discomfort of the tight quarters, her whole body stung. She was covered in tiny scratches, and her raw skin burned. She wanted to rest which was extremely unsettling. She never wanted to rest. After all her little sleeps, she thought she had rested enough.

*What was this place doing to them?*

"Cain, are you tired?"

"Yes. And my body is on fire. This plant's thorns are toxic."

Iris squeezed and pulled her body a few inches higher.

"Wait there. You'll never get through."

Cain stopped as Iris kicked away at a vine. It took her sixteen hard thrusts and grunts until a chunk popped out and fell onto Cain. He shook it off, and it plummeted downward, hitting other parts of the plant on the way.

"You'll be able to make it now."

Cain gripped a root and lifted his left leg to find a bearing. He pushed up and forced his way through the tight spot as Iris pulled herself further up the tunnel. She continued to ascend, climbing a little more agilely through the bramble, her steps a little bit lighter than moments ago.

"It's getting a little wider. I think we just passed the middle. Maybe this is where this plant started as a seed, and it grew out from here?"

Cain felt around the tight space. "It's possible. I wish Dee was here. She would know for certain."

"I don't wish anyone else was here. This is awful."

Cain chuckled. "Yes, this is indeed the worst." He pulled on a vine as he struggled to rip himself through the narrowest part of the tunnel. "Iris, I need a little help."

Iris peered back down and lowered herself slowly, until she was squished against Cain's chest, standing on a root.

"Jump on that part." Cain gestured with his head at a section of the tunnel, holding himself up. "But hold on. I don't want us to drop and end up bottlenecked in here together."

"Got it. You ready?"

Cain nodded. "Keep jumping until I say stop. Go!"

Iris jumped on top of the protruding part of this monstrous plant. A few of its vines shifted. Cain grunted as he shimmied and elbowed upward.

"Your shoulders got through, the rest of you has to fit!" Iris held tightly to a thick root and allowed her body weight to drop down on a larger root blocking Cain's way, her bare feet landing with a thud. She jumped up and dropped again, over and over. She winced with each painful impact of her bare feet. Cain pulled up and yelled as loud as he could as his hips slid through the small area. "Stop!"

Iris kicked up and climbed upward to keep in front of him. Cain dragged himself toward her, just barely wriggling through the narrow passage. He huffed and remained silent for a long time but finally gazed up at her.

"Agree to never do this again?"

Iris smiled at him over her shoulder. "I don't know. I'm kind of getting the hang of it. Come on, I think I saw a light." She climbed further up, leaving a large distance between the two of them. Cain didn't move. "I think you are making this light up to make me feel better." Iris giggled and kept climbing. "You'll have to catch me to find out." He rested for several moments before he pulled a leg up, found a spot for his toe, and pushed upward. The tunnel or, more accurately, the hole, widened just enough so he could move his legs, at least for now.

The reach of the twisted roots and vines had ended abruptly twelve feet below a hole. Perhaps the plant couldn't thrive here any better than Iris and Cain could in the strange star-flower-lit world below. This hole was about five-feet wide, four-feet long, and just out of their reach. They stood breathless on the mass of root and vine, examining the cylindrical sheer rock walls surrounding and rising above them. Both were physically spent from the treacherous and thorny journey that led them to this entirely new and infuriating trap. A very small stream of water trickled down the rock. Cain stomped on the plant and laughed.

"You couldn't have just grown a few more feet?" He shook his head at the pile of thorns and vines. Iris pointed toward a dim teal light flickering from the other side of the hole.

"At least the light is real."

He peered up at the tunnel's exit. It was at least six feet higher than the top of his head. Cain rubbed his palm along the smooth rock wall. "Might be too high and steep to reach it."

Maybe if I crawl up on your shoulders?" Iris glanced back at Cain.

"Maybe." Cain didn't sound sure at all as he lowered himself and put his hands together to form a little step for Iris. She placed her foot in it, and he raised her above his head. Iris could feel his arms trembling beneath her, and it filled her with dread. Bearing her weight would usually be no problem for him, but now, he was struggling. She swallowed and stood as tall as she could, trying to reach the top. She was still two feet short.

"It's not enough. Bring me down."

Cain lowered her back to the ground, almost dropping her. He sank down onto the vines, careful not to fall into the hole below.

He was winded. She studied his slumped shoulders and the scratches on his face, neck, and arms, making sure none of them were too deep. She examined her own arms and legs that were covered in about the same number of scratches. They stung and burned less with each minute that passed. The wounds should only be a nuisance to him. Iris slid next to Cain and leaned on his arm. She lifted his hand and checked the gash on his palm. The two sides had sealed up so he wasn't bleeding anymore, but it wouldn't mend on its own. She would have to fix him once they got back. He pulled his hand away, wincing when he formed a fist. He forced a smile and joked, "We only have to wait until it grows taller."

Iris peered down at the plant. It was sharp and hard, brittle at times. It had gotten more so the higher they got. She placed her other hand gently on a vine. "It's not growing anymore. This part of it is dying."

"Yes, I believe it is."

"We should have never come down here." Iris was angry. She was also worried. They had come down here to find the others, save them if necessary, but also to get help. Eva needed them. They had left her trapped with horrible, dangerous, deadly Adam. She had tried to keep dark thoughts of him out of her mind while she searched for a way out of this labyrinth, but now that there was nowhere to go, all of it crashed through her mental dam and cascaded down, crushing her spirit.

"Do you think Jacob went after Eva? What if that monster boy came back to the island?"

"I hope he came back." Cain spoke softly. His face distorted into an expression Iris didn't recognize. She frowned at him.

"Why would you hope that?"

Cain shifted his weight, his hand falling heavily on his pocket.

"It's the only way Jacob would have been able to help Eva."

She followed his hand and spotted a lump in his pocket. Her eyebrow raised. "What did you do?"

He slipped his hand into his pocket and pulled out an item. He kept it concealed in his fist for several moments, his face frozen, lips a thin line. "No one is angrier about this than me."

Iris held out her hand. "If that's what I think it is, that statement is not correct."

He placed the small part of the boat's motor in her palm. He locked eyes with her. "I don't trust Jacob. I never did. I never will."

She turned the part over in her hand, a mixture of rage and despair twisting up inside her as she twirled the wires. She tightened her fist around the small part and released a scream as she kicked the wall.

"Why would you do this?" She glared back at him, the color of her eyes deepening to an indigo as her anger flared. He held her gaze but flinched, his cheeks singed by the heat of her rage. She smacked the wall. "Damn it, Cain. He was going to go back and help her. You could trust that. At least I could. You could have trusted me! Instead, you made it impossible for him to save her!"

"Eva doesn't need saving," Cain rasped. Iris shot him an incredulous look. "Unless you save her, is that what this is about?"

Cain looked like she had struck him. "No, of course not."

Iris backed up against the rock wall, eyes darting around for an escape, the hair on her neck and arms bristling like a cornered animal. She had convinced herself that Jacob had made it back to Eva's cabin, that he had used his awful gun and stopped Adam from hurting her. Now, holding the piece that made the boat work, buried deep beneath the island, she knew with certainty that none of that had happened. She was filled with disgust and terror. She couldn't look her dearest friend in the eyes, not without feeling sick.

"Why did you lie to me?"

Cain's head jerked and his defiance flashed across his eyes. "I did not lie to you. I just didn't listen to you. I thought you were wrong to trust Jacob, and you weren't hearing me."

Iris's head jerked up. This was the moment she had always dreaded, the moment when Cain would challenge her, like she had once challenged Eva. She felt her blood cool as anguish replaced her anger.

"Your choice may have killed her."

"My choice would have been to go after her first." He nodded his head toward the motor part. "That was a compromise."

"So, this is my fault?"

"No, but we all have made choices that have put members of the group in danger. My choice to take that part does feel like a mistake right now. Believe me, I understand the steep price of it but who knows what has happened on the surface. Maybe our choices are made the way they must be made, and the outcome will be what it must be."

"I don't believe in predetermination. If Eva was killed by Adam because Jacob could not cross the lake, it will be your fault," Iris snapped. Cain recoiled a bit at the accusation.

He peered back toward the jagged opening above them. "I know."

Simmering with nothing else to say, Iris turned away from him and tugged on a large white root, slowly untangling it from the vines it had entwined itself with as it grew through this tunnel system. Cain joined her, both remaining silent. With each one of their tugs, the vines tightened around the root, not wanting to release it from the bunch. Iris's eyes narrowed, and she pulled harder. She was not accustomed to the world around her being so defiant. She was used to it being obedient as a devotee to a goddess. She couldn't even rely on Cain's constant support anymore. She had lost the control she had become so reliant on. She hated how helpless she felt in this foreign ecosystem that had no true place for her, no need to heed her. As she continued to tug the roots and vines, unravelling them a foot at a time, she realized she also felt more alive down here with everything so fleeting and dangerous. She had only ever felt that way for Eva, not ever for herself. At least this new fear, this new drive to survive was fully her own. Hopefully, it would be enough.

# Day 2,409 – Island - Lake
## *Three Days Earlier*

*Dark. The kind where shadows are not possible. The dark the buried find themselves in, the dark that consumes us all and makes us one. The dark that swaddles a seed in the beginning, and the dark that breaks down flesh in the end. The dark of the canal we squeeze through right before taking our first breaths. The dark we spend a lifetime longing to return to every night when we close our eyes. The dark we fear as we near our end. The dark that leads to two paths, one good and one bad. The dark where we must travel alone, once in birth and once in death.*

*Some believed the dark to be a solitary place, but this wasn't that kind of dark. This darkness was full of life. In this dark, no being was ever alone.*

*Crunch. Crinch. Crunch. Crinch.*

*The dank smell of wet rotting leaves, a tinge of sulfur, that sting of rotting eggs, the unsettling earthy stank of mushrooms accompanied this dark. The microbial processes of decomposition created a warm, pungent heat that powered a steaming and thriving community beneath the cool waters above, glacial waters that formed this great lake thousands of years ago when a giant ice sheet pressed the earth down, forming basins and then filling them as it slowly ceased to exist and transformed into a different form. Beneath the remains of this ancient glacier, thin layers of plants melded together, pressing tighter, shifting as the clay-like sediment above shifted with the sandier layer above, which shifted with the motion of the water atop, which shifted with the air and the motion of the planet, which shifted because of a bang that went off long ago in the very beginning. And through all the motion, the constant sounds of consumption.*

*Crunch. Crunch. Crunch. Crunch.*

*Microbes gorged themselves on decomposing duckweed, bladderwort, and water meal just beneath the lakebed, about twenty feet from the sandy shore of Bear Island, or Rainbow Island as Eva had briefly renamed it before she brought the bears back from extinction. The byproduct of these tiny creatures' feast—methane—rose, creating a pathway through three feet of sediment, forming a small mound on the sandy floor until bubbles plopped through the wet sand, now racing other methane bubbles on the same journey through the eight feet of water toward fresh air, defying the hundreds of millions of gallons of water pushing back against them. The breakdown of the once-thriving aquatic plant-life trapped in the lake's sediment poisoned the planet more rapidly than ever.*

*A few hundred years ago, trees had grown close to the lakes. Their dead branches would fall into the water, and the byproducts of their decomposition would help trap the carbon, preventing it from joining with hydrogen to create methane. Their natural decay slowed the creation and release of methane, but most of those trees had been cut down and taken away long ago, leaving only the smaller plants to decay in the lake, leaving methane creation unchecked.*

*On top of the loss of trees, the glacial ice that had once covered vast swaths of the planet was almost completely gone, each having released more trapped carbon and methane from the decay of the prehistoric plants trapped below. Adding this to the current breakdown of organic materials in the Earth's lakes, the methane bubbles had become too many to harmlessly dissipate into the atmosphere, a silent and unfriendly gas army. The natural process was amplified and accelerated by man, the hastened breakdown of ecosystems a byproduct of lack of foresight.*

*The bubbles raced from beneath a submerged biofilm-covered branch, then by a hiking boot brushing against the slimy branch, a leg covered in denim, a ghostly white hand, and finally, a head concealed by long, straggly, black hair. The hair floated to the side to reveal part of a gruesome face that had once summoned fear along with fierce loyalty from those around him. The face now seemed at peace, bobbing in the water. The denim pant legs were lumpy, filled with rocks that kept his boots scraping against the slimy branch and his body below water, out of sight.*

*Darting around the body and between the bubbles and floating grains of sand were thousands of small flatworms and a few larger, cleverer ones interspersed. Many of the flatworms swarmed the log, pushing and tugging to get the best place on the slimy surface.*

*A large beige worm, edged with a bright blue margin and a central blue stripe along the length of its body, glided toward the floating boy. Its edges curling up and down, creating waves out of the stretched-out circumference of its oval frame. Two crests in the front of its body formed what looked like antennae as it slid up Adam's leg toward his torso. It slid around the bumpy curve of his thigh as it continued to propel itself upward, disappearing behind him, wrapping itself back up around his waist and toward his chest. Each movement frantic, growing more urgent the closer it got to the young man's lungs and heart. The creature sailed along the chest, twirling its crests and troughs like the tide, moving like a lazy misshapen wheel, and slipped beneath Adam's shirt. It slowly flattened the curves of its edges, part of its body poking out of the neckline. A loud sucking sounded, muffled by the water, followed by a large bubble rising out of the shirt toward the surface. Adam's shirt floated up around his arms, revealing the creature spread out across his hairy chest sinking into his heart and lungs. Its curves had completely flattened, and its form had shifted into something more like a strange bandage than a vibrant, living being. A flash of blue burst from the creature's edges and middle line as it sank into Adam's flesh and disappeared within.*

*Bubbles rose from within Adam's lungs, pushing up against the water. Trapped air travelled through the bronchi tubes toward the alveoli sacs. The air violently burst into the capillaries, driving oxygen into Adam's bloodstream and forcing a lifeline to his heart and brain. The bubbles rose and forced their way out of Adam's trachea, toward his mouth. Adam's still lips pushed out, forming a slight mound, and then air and water gushed out of his mouth, bubbles racing to the surface as his body convulsed. His arms and legs flung outward into an X. His eyes shot open and blue light flashed across the entire surface of his body. More bubbles erupted from his mouth, and he curled back inward into a ball. The fleshy ball trembled and jerked, jolted several times, and then stilled. His arms slowly floated up, but his legs dropped again, pulled by the rocks Jacob had shoved in his pants to sink his dead body. His boot tip touched the slime atop the dead branch on the sandy floor, and his entire body ceased moving.*

*Yet, bubbles continued to force their way out of his blue lips. One bubble after another plopped out and raced their brothers and sisters toward the surface of the lake, toward the oxygen in the air, beckoning the rest to follow, to return to others like them, return to a place of composition, not fall into a system with the complete opposite goal— decay.*

*Adam's eyelids twitched open again. He reached down and pulled his pant legs out of his socks and shook the stones from his pants. After several moments of struggling, his green eyes shot upward, and he kicked his way to the surface, chasing the bubbles toward the air he had missed so intensely. A trail of biofilm clung to his boot. Adam returned to the surface with part of the dark trailing after him, the life forces beneath the toxic lake more part of him than ever. He shot up toward the surface, out of the dark, a path chosen, a path he would make sure led him to Eva.*

*The log he had launched himself away from settled back into the sand, disturbing the sediment with a small thud. Sand mushroomed up and swirled before each piece settled back to its new place on the lakebed.*

*The surface broke above. The sound of a loud inhale, a splash against the water and wet hacking travelled back down to the sandy bottom.*

*The particles had settled back into place along with the branch, wisps of the slimy biofilm floating above it, a mound formed on the sand.*

*Plop.*

*A methane bubble rose and followed another dangerous element to the surface. Beneath the sand, the dark was busy doing what the dark does.*

*Crunch. Crinch. Crunch. Crinch.*

# Day 2,409 – Island - Lake
## *Three Days Earlier*

A pile of white plastic flatworms twisted, writhed, and flopped on the wet sand about a foot from the shore and a few inches from the dry sand the water hadn't touched yet that day. Tiny waves lapped over the rocks, licked the sand, and rolled back. Behind the pile of flatworms was a large brown boot next to a white animal figure, gleaming as the sun bounced off its plastic surface. "Not again!"

A wriggling plastic flatworm fell next to the boot and a large dirty hand scooped it back up. The animal figure was a baby goat like the one Adam had tried to make back in Eva's cabin, the misshapen goat that came to life and then melted in the bottom of his boat. This time, the goat was holding its form. Its eyes weren't drooping. They were straight and centered with its nose, mouth, and ears. Adam's twisted black hair hung over one of his eyes. His other eye focused intensely on the wiggling plastic piece pinched between his thumb and pointy finger. He bent it in half and placed it over the last opening on the back of his goat's hindquarters. He linked then folded it into the neighboring piece that reached out toward it. "Stay, stay . . ." The surface locked together as the final piece flattened and melded into the rest. A ray of sunlight reflected off the goat's back and flashed into Adam's eyes. He lifted his arm over his eyes and squinted, holding his breath while listening for a sound other than the water hitting the shore. *Baa-bleat. Baa-bleat.*

Adam gazed down as the baby goat timidly testing out its hooves on the squishy sand, bleating with each wobbling step. The remaining flatworms stretched and pulled away from the goat toward the tiny waves lapping over the rocks.

Adam whooped and jumped up, prancing around the baby goat as it bleated and attempted to follow him in circles. Adam bent down and scratched the white fur on the top of the goat's head. It nuzzled into him and bleated again.

Adam scooped it up and held the little creature under his arm. He checked its head, neck, and body. Everything seemed to be in place. He ran his fingers through its fur, feeling the skin underneath. It was soft. When he poked it, it was squishy just like flesh should feel. Adam smiled. He checked the creature's legs. They were floppy but strong. He frowned when he reached the hooves. They were deformed. They looked more like a soft foot with a large black fingernail on them, not like the hoof they should be. Adam tucked the creature's toes underneath his arm, out of sight.

*Baa-bleat. Baa-bleat. Baa-bleat.*

Wearing a pleased smirk, Adam trudged through the sand toward the house that Eva and the others had built, carrying his imperfect bleating goat.

# Day 2,412 – Island - Lake

Mari and Dezi strolled along the island's shore. It was easily the most beautiful place either of them had ever been. Matt and Gabi followed about twenty yards behind them, stopping to examine every rock and creature that popped its head out of the water. Their laughter came in bursts, and the gentle winds carried it across the lake. Mari walked beside Dezi, shifting her gaze between a white bird flying low, nearly brushing the small waves with its wings, and Dezi. Mari opened her mouth several times to say something, but stopped, shutting it again. She had a hard time finding the right thing to say to anyone, but with Dezi, it was near impossible. Everything she thought she might say sounded incredibly stupid or inconsequential when she rehearsed it in her mind.

Dezi kicked a rock and shot Mari a neutral stare.

"What?" Mari's cheeks flushed, and her heart raced.

"Really? You're staring at me."

"I'm not staring at you." Mari glanced back to the water and found her white bird, now floating, bobbing up and down on a wave. Mari pointed at it. "I was watching that bird for your information."

Dezi looked out onto the water and found the bird. She smiled when she spotted it. Mari peeked over at her and smiled at Dezi smiling, but quickly returned her gaze to the bird. Dezi held a rock out to Mari. "Have you ever seen anything like this?" Mari peered down at the gray, black, and tan rock with a sunburst pattern on it. She reached out and touched it. She didn't move her hand, not even when Dezi brushed her palm with the side of her finger, sending a jolt up her arm to her neck, leaving her body buzzing. "No, it's beautiful."

Dezi held the rock out for a few more beats then pocketed it. "Want to try to find some more?"

Mari glanced back at Matt and Gabi who were chasing another bird in the opposite direction. They should keep looking for shelter like they had all agreed at breakfast, but she wanted something for herself today, something happy and free. Mari turned back and nodded at Dezi.

"I would."

Mari and Dezi laughed. Mari held her shirt up to form a makeshift satchel. It bulged with the fossils and rocks the girls had spent the afternoon collecting. Gabi and Matt had disappeared after a butterfly into the woods a while back. Mari heard their laughter and used it to track her brother, but not quite as obsessively as normal. They had walked a long section of the island and were coming up on a turn.

"Do you think we need to keep all of these rocks?"

"Which one would you give away?"

Mari studied the collection. Each rock was unique in size or shape. She couldn't pick one to discard. Each one reminded her of a different moment with Dezi, carefree moments she had only dreamed of before today.

"That's what I thought. We're keeping them all, Mari. All of them." Dezi laughed and landed in the sand. She flung her arms and legs out and moved them around. She stood up and admired her sand angel.

"Here, hand me the rocks, and you make one." Dezi lifted her shirt. Mari caught a glimpse of her soft stomach. She lifted her shirt and dumped the rocks into Dezi's. Their hands brushed again during the exchange. Mari's cheeks were aflame.

Mari sat down a few feet from Dezi's sand angel. She leaned back and put her arms and legs out. In stark contrast to Dezi's style, she methodically moved her legs back and forth. She closed her eyes as the sun peeked out from behind a cloud. She heard the rocks drop softly on the sand and then against each other. She felt the pressure of a knee sinking in the sand next to her and felt a shadow block the sun. A face moved in close to her ear, and lips whispered something very softly.

Mari smiled and opened her eyes. Dezi was grinning down at her. And then another larger shadow appeared.

"Well, isn't this sweet?" An all too familiar voice snarled. Dezi's eyes went wide as she scrambled to her feet.

Mari didn't move for a moment, wanting to remember each pattern in each rock, the feeling of the sun and sand, and the sound of Dezi's voice when she whispered that she didn't mind if she looked at her.

"Well, come on, Mari, get up. Let's go get the others. I want to show you all something truly amazing." Mari rose to her feet and glanced at Adam. His hair was more tangled than normal. His clothes were dirty, but he looked stronger, rejuvenated, different. Only Adam could die and be stronger because of it. He kicked over the pile of their rocks and stalked past them. "Then after, I need to sit down with Gabi, have a man-to-man talk."

Dezi touched Mari's arm and scooped up one of their rocks and slipped it in her pocket. Mari leaned down and did the same. Dezi smiled shyly at her before jogging off after Adam. Mari stared at Dezi's back and then Adam's before her gaze shifted into the woods. She searched desperately through the new growth, trying to catch a glimpse of her brother or Matt so she could signal for Gabi to stay far away.

She took a few slow steps through the sand and found her white bird flying above the water. She cursed herself for imagining a world without Adam. The imagining had made each step back toward him heavier than the last.

Matt clamped his hand tightly over Gabi's mouth as they watched Mari and Dezi follow Adam. Matt glanced down at Gabi who was struggling against his grip, eyes flashing, ready for a fight. The sight of Adam, still alive, brought out a new fire in Gabi, a dangerous one.

Matt's mouth was close to Gabi's ear.

"I'll let you go, but you have to be quiet and not run after them."

Gabi nodded, and Matt slid his hand off his face and let him drop to the ground.

"We have to go after them."

"What if Adam knows you helped Eva?"

"I want him to know." Gabi stuck out his chest, but there was fear in his eyes.

"Don't be stupid." Matt kept his gaze trained on Adam and the girls.

"You need a hiding place, a good one."

"I'm not hiding."

"What else, Gabi? Go back to camp, hope Lena and Jake will take your side?"

"Maybe. I don't think Jake really wants to go back to the way things were."

Matt scoffed. "And Lena?"

"I don't know. I can never figure her out. She'll go along with Jake."

"You mean, he'll go along with her. They'll stick with Adam, you know that as well as I do."

Gabi watched Mari disappear over the bank. "Yeah . . . unless they think we can beat him." He turned back to the woods. "There's a way we can."

For the rest of the afternoon, Gabi and Matt kept close to the beach, just within the woods for cover. The sun was now low in the sky, sinking behind the trees on the mainland. Matt trailed behind Gabi, keeping an eye out for the wolves and the others. A gunshot fired further inland. Lena and Jake's muffled shouts travelled through the trees.

"We're still too exposed out here."

Gabi crept toward a gnarled, dead tree. "I need to show you what I found, just in case."

Matt shot him a questioning look. "Just in case, what?"

"In case Adam finds me."

Gabi climbed up the trunk of the tree with a stick under his arm. Once perched where the trunk forked into two larger branches, he gestured for Matt to climb up next to him. Matt scurried up and peered into the hollowed-out branch that ended a little after the fork. He saw nothing but a pile of leaves and sticks at the bottom.

"There's nothing there."

Gabi jabbed the stick down into the hole and brushed some leaves aside to reveal Adam's duffle bag.

"I found it buried in the woods by that cave."

"Why didn't you tell me?"

"I wasn't going to tell anyone."

"Why?"

"We don't need any more guns. They're gonna run out of ammo at some point, right? Then they'll stop killing everything in sight."

Matt smiled at him. "I'm sure they'll figure out other ways to kill everything in sight."

"It'll slow them down at least."

Gabi covered the duffle back up with leaves and pulled the stick out.

"You need to hide." Matt shot Gabi a fierce look before he climbed down the tree.

Gabi dropped the stick and jumped out of the tree, landing gracefully. "No way. I'm coming with you."

Matt grabbed Gabi's shirt and shook him harder than he had ever shaken him. "You can't, you hear me? Not right now, not until I know what Adam thinks happened with Eva."

"I'm not leaving my sister alone."

Matt pulled Gabi up to his face level, leaving his toes just touching the ground. He growled, "You aren't. I'll be there. Dezi too. Mari can handle Adam a lot better if she knows you're safe. You'll get her killed if you come back now. You get me?"

Matt released Gabi, dropping him to the ground. Gabi fell back on his butt. A look of remorse crossed Matt's face, but he quickly toughed his expression. "Keep out of sight. Find Eva and Jacob if you can. Let's pray they're alive. Meet here at sunrise, tomorrow. If I don't show, come again at sunset. Keep coming at sunrise and sunset until I make it back. Okay?"

Matt reached his hand down, offering to help Gabi up. Gabi swatted it away, tears welling up. He wiped his face and scrambled to his feet, glaring at Matt. "Don't let Adam trick you like he always does."

Gabi darted off into the woods before Matt could respond. Matt watched him disappear, completely unsure of himself, and then ran off in the opposite direction while also veering off the path that would lead to the gunshots.

# Day 2,412 - Caves

*Thunk.* Eva jerked and snorted awake, dropping an oar.

*Splash!*

She scurried over to the side of the boat and thrust her arms into the water, feeling around for the floating wood. Her fingers found it, and she pulled the oar back into the boat, breathing heavily. Her body was exhausted, and even the smallest exertion was taking too rapid a toll. Eva needed to get off the water, eat something, and light a fire.

*Thunk.*

The boat collided with a rocky surface again. Eva's whole body tensed at the noise. She didn't want whatever had taken Jacob to find her. She wanted to do the finding. In this cave, she was the weaker species and desperately needed the element of surprise.

She stretched her arms out onto the rocky surface, measuring it by feel. It was even with the water and maybe wide enough for her and the boat. With one hand gripping the edge of her boat, she climbed out onto the rocky surface. She clutched the bow with both hands and threw her whole weight backward. The hull dragging against the stone echoed down the river. Eva winced, knowing that she was most likely leading those flying predators right to her. When the boat's stern was secure on rocky land, Eva dropped her end with a bang and collapsed to the ground, chest heaving.

As her breaths came easier, Eva pulled herself up, listening for the sound of wings, but was met only with the soft lapping of water. She pushed herself off the cool stone and rose, taking a few shaky steps toward the boat. She grabbed its edge, followed it to the center, and found her bag. She rummaged through it clumsily until her fingers touched the waterproof rectangle plastic container filled with matches. She pulled the matches out of her bag and shoved them in her parka pocket where she swore to keep them from now on in case she was suddenly and without ceremony pulled from her vessel like Jacob. She collected a handful of sticks and leaves along with a small log from the center of the boat. She would run out of fire materials in three more camps, then she would be lost to the cold and the dark.

Eva measured out five large paces from the boat and set the log down on the stone floor. She put the leaves and small twigs around it, securing them under it. She slid one of the matchboxes from her waterproof container. Her hands shook as she blindly looked around the cave. She needed fire, but she also knew the fire would expose her, possibly seal her fate to whatever had befallen Jacob. When the trembling of her hands had finally begun to subside, she opened the matchbox and pulled out a single dry match. She scratched it several times against the box's edge before a sizzle and a spark gave life to a small flame. That flame kissed a leaf, which curled, its edges glowing, and leaf after leaf followed the first. Eva lit the leaves in several other areas, dropping the match as she gently blew on the fragile flames, stoking their newborn embers. The flickering tendrils' shadows danced on the walls, filling Eva with a primal warmth and something else, a fury. She was angry and grew angrier, and she nursed those baby flames into a small burning inferno.

Her boat was on a large smooth ledge, the largest one she had seen in the cave so far. The river was six feet at its widest and flowed beneath a low and jagged ceiling, maybe ten feet at its highest. There were about six different landings along the river before it disappeared around the turn into the next unknown chamber. Eva searched every inch of the illuminated ceiling for any potential threats. The water's surface was like glass, and nothing glowed beneath it, not even the tiniest of flatworms. She exhaled, relieved that she was alone, but by the time she inhaled again, she was devastated by the same fact.

She shook off the hopelessness chipping away at her protective armor as she walked back over to the boat and carefully removed one of the flaky cooked fish. She wanted to warm it on the fire but didn't want to burn her flames faster, so she sat down, back to the cave wall, feet by the fire, watching its light bring the stone walls to life and picked away at the cold fish until only its bones remained. The fire was dimming, and its flames lowered, licking the white charred edges of the blackening log. Its center glowed red. Eva knew the comfort of light and sight were going to be gone much too soon. She couldn't afford to burn through anymore of her wood at this stop. She scooted as close to the log as she could without getting burnt and squinted across the river at the opposite wall, searching for something new, something different, something to give her hope. Her eyes didn't land on anything but more rock and more water as she slowly began to admit the truth to herself, admit that she knew the voice that had accompanied the flapping wings that had silenced her friend. The voice she had heard had made her laugh hundreds if not thousands of times, comforted her when she was sad, chided her when she was whining, teased her when she was being too serious. She would know that voice if a thousand years passed. She had been there when that voice first spoke. She had helped create that voice.

*Marin. Marin had taken Jacob.*

*Marin had flown away with Jacob?*

*No, Marin can't fly. Whoever Marin was with must be the one who flew.*

*But, who? Who would Marin team up with against me?*

A dark thought jumped into her head without intention and too fast for her conscious self to stop it. Eva hated herself the minute she thought it, but once it was thought, she couldn't stop thinking it. There was only one person that Marin would work with against her.

*Iris.*

But Iris couldn't fly either. *None of this made sense.*

The fire died and darkness slowly swallowed the cave up until its lips closed, leaving one very small puckering red circle glowing near Eva's face. Her cheek pressed against the stone floor, staring past the last glowing embers, eyelids drooping, too tired to keep them open no matter what was coming after her. Her last thought before sleep was a question.

*If not Iris, who?*

# Day 2,412 – Island - Cabin

Adam stood in front of the cabin. Awestruck and somewhat terrified, Mari, Dezi, Matt, Jake, and Lena faced him, the lake in the distance behind them.

"Didn't I always tell you? I would find a place we could be safe?"

Dezi whispered to Mari, letting their arms touch. "I can't believe there's an actual house out here. We can really stay, for good."

Mari couldn't help but think, *Eva's house.*

Lena smiled and nodded, lazily holding her rifle, and leaning on Jake. Jake's arm wrapped around her waist.

"This island is beautiful, Adam," Lena spoke, reverently.

"There's more. Come on."

Adam walked up the steps of the porch of the two-story log cabin with its plexiglass window. He smiled as he pushed open the front door and his little white goat stumbled out, still a bit unsure of his footing. Its tiny misshapen hooves hit the wooden steps awkwardly as it tumbled down them into the sand.

"Is this your goat? From the cabin?" Dezi bent down and pet the white fluff on its head. Dezi waved for Mari to join her. "He's so soft, Mari. Touch him." Dezi's fingers landed on the front hoof of the baby goat.

Mari remained still, surveying the little creature, the house, and Adam. Adam's jaw clenched as he watched Dezi touch the goat's deformed hoof. His body tensed as he slinked down the stairs closing the short space between him and Dezi, reptilian. Mari inhaled. She sensed the all too familiar shift in his stance and his mood. Adam fixated on the deformed black tips of the goat's feet, his expression darkening, the curve of his smile flattening to a line.

He shoved Dezi out of the way. Mari flinched.

"What the hell, Adam?" Dezi glared up at him from the sand, kicking his ankles and knocking him to the ground. Adam lay still for a moment, catching his breath, and then started laughing. He flicked sand at Dezi and got back to his feet. Those two had always rough-housed—it was part of their relationship—but tonight, their violent dance filled Mari with dread.

Adam gathered up his goat and snuggled it close to his face, keeping his eyes trained on Mari. "I'm hungry. How about you all?"

Adam scratched the little goat's ears tenderly.

*Baa-bleat. Baa-bleat. Baa-bleat.*

"Mari, what do you think of all of this?"

Mari glanced around and focused back on Adam, avoiding his eyes. "It's perfect. I always knew you'd do it."

Adam scowled at the goat and dropped it back in the sand. "Perfect, huh?" He stalked toward the lake. "I'll show you just how perfect it will be. Everyone, come on!"

Lena and Jake rushed after Adam. Mari took a few steps toward Dezi and put her hand out for her. Dezi took it and pulled herself up. "Dezi, if Adam finds Gab—"

"Not right now, Mari." Dezi tore her hand from Mari's and kept her eyes lowered. Mari felt the new bond between them lose its form as Dezi plodded past her toward Adam. Mari hoped that Dezi would not retreat to her silent role as Adam's second, that the island's promise of something more than basic survival would disrupt that dynamic. Mari sighed and trudged after Dezi toward Adam who was now splashing in the shallow waters.

Adam hovered his hand above the water, eyes gleaming like an evangelical minister reaching for a deadly snake. Mari stopped about five feet from the others.

"Eva's not the only one who can make life anymore." Adam sank his hand into the shallow waters. He swished his fingers until he formed a fist around a glob of the flatworms. He lifted them out of the water and set them on the sand.

"It took me a while to figure it out with them wiggling like that, but it's all about concentration, a focusing of the mind, a meditation kind of."

Adam picked a few pieces up and folded them together. They twisted and slowly fused to make one piece. He set it on his hand and the others started jumping and forming with the first two, mostly white and brown pieces. Adam scooted a bit closer to the water as more pieces swarmed toward his hand, growing, and glomming. Adam set them down on the wet sand, and the pieces formed four little hooves. Skinny bony legs followed, then a body, and a short little tail and a long nose and ears with two little horns atop its head. Adam kept his hands in the wet sand, always touching some of the wriggling worms that inched toward the almost formed goat. This time the legs were all the same length. The eyes grew in even and perfect. As the final worm completed the tuft of hair atop the goat's head, the bright orange of the setting sun shone off the lake into their eyes. They squinted and covered their faces.

*Bleat.*

They turned back, and another tiny, little goat moved its lips around, trying to chew the grass that was not in its mouth. Its side-slanted eyes with rectangular pupils blinked up at them. It wobbled around the sand, knees buckling and straightening, as it acclimated to its legs. Adam frowned when he spotted its hooves, still imperfect, still a strange black toenail.

Lena giggled.

"How is it possible?" Mari whispered.

"It's the island. There's a power out here. I don't know what it is, but it chose me, like it chose Eva. I can create life now. I can make food. We don't need her anymore."

Jake shot Adam a wary look. "What exactly happened out here? With you? And Eva?"

"You might have known, if you looked for me a little harder." Adam's expression darkened. Jake's left foot took a small step back. Lena strode overconfident, putting herself between Jake and Adam.

"We looked as best we could, Adam. Matt nearly capsized the boat and sent Jake into the lake like the idiot he always is. We had to get dry clothes, or he'd have frozen to death. We figured you could handle Eva on your own until we came back."

Adam scowled, and his expression went flat. He watched his goat run toward the grass by the cabin. He pulled out his gun. Jake put his hand out. "Adam, don't!"

Lena gripped her rifle but didn't dare raise it to Adam.

"Adam, they're telling the truth. They came right back to get us," Dezi said softly but firmly. Adam snarled as he stomped toward Jake. Jake stumbled back and fell backwards into the sand.

"Adam, we didn't think—"

"None of you ever think. That's why I have to do all the thinking for everyone."

Adam raised his pistol. "Eva tried to kill me that night. You assholes know that?" Adam's barrel turned and lined up with Mari's forehead. "I think she had some help. Don't you, Mari?" He glared and pulled the trigger.

*Click.*

Mari's eyes twitched and watered but she kept her lips stiff, eyes lowered.

"What the hell, Adam!" Dezi stepped toward him. Adam smirked as he lowered his gun. The goat stumbled back toward the group, bleating.

"Relax, I knew it wasn't loaded. Anyway, you all are right about one thing, I can handle Eva." Adam smirked down at the cowering Jake. He stuck his hand out for Jake to grab. Jake grimaced and took it. As Adam pulled him to his feet, he tugged him in closer. "You freeze to death before leaving me behind again." He let him go and smacked him on the back.

"Lena! You and Jake get a fire started already. You all are so undisciplined. Wouldn't last a week without me."

The small goat nuzzled Adam's pant leg. Adam leaned down and scooped it up. He scratched its head and whispered into its ear. "I'm hungry, aren't you little guy?"

*Baa-bleat. Baa-bleat. Baa-bleat.*

Adam's arm jerked ever-so-slightly. A sickening snap came from within the goat. Adam released the small creature's head. Its neck went limp against his arm. Its pink and black tongue hung from its mouth.

Matt released a pained groan.

Adam strolled right up to Mari, cradling the goat. He held its lifeless body out to her. "I made it and killed it. You clean and cook it."

Mari reached out, focusing on stopping her hands from shaking and took the goat from Adam. Its body was still warm in her hands. She clenched her jaw, keeping her eyes flat, dull, and emotionless. Adam leaned close to Mari's cheek and hissed.

"We'll discuss Gabi later."

Mari nodded, lowering her gaze. One of the goat's little eyes pointed right at her own. Its life had been short and fleeting, sweet for a moment and then cruel the next. Mari fought against her fear that Gabi would turn out like this goat. She said a silent prayer that Gabi found a good hiding place just like Matt had told him.

Adam didn't turn back as he headed to the cabin. Tears trickled down Mari's face. Dezi reached out to touch her shoulder then pulled her hands back and placed them at her side. The goat's unseeing crystal irises and rectangular black pupils stared over the lake. Mari brushed her fingers over its face bringing down its furry eyelids.

"He wanted to make a goat so badly. How could he just kill it like that?" Matt whispered. Mari and Dezi didn't answer. It wasn't necessary. It wasn't really a question. They all knew the answer. Adam just wanted to conquer things.

Mari cradled the goat, petting its head. Silently, she turned and walked toward their new home. Dezi and Matt walked beside her, holding vigil for the little beast that only had a few minutes of life before another creature decided its hunger mattered most and for the better life they had lived for a few fleeting moments earlier that day.

# Day 2,413 – Cave

*Swat. Rustle-Rustle. Plop.*

Eva's eyes shot open. It was just as dark out there as it had been behind her eyelids. Exhausted, her lids lowered—

*Swat. Rustle-Rustle. Plop.*

She pushed her body up, and her hand slid through the cooling ashes left from her fire. She scrambled to her feet.

*Swat. Rustle-Rustle. Plop.*

The sound was coming from up ahead, maybe at the end of the cavern or maybe past the turn.

*Swat. Rustle-Rustle. Plop.*

It might be coming from behind her. The origin of a sound traveling in this zigzagging cavern could not be precisely discerned, having bounced off several different surfaces before it finally hit Eva's ear. Eva listened for several minutes. The sound continued. There wasn't a consistency to it, no true cadence to the intervals. Part of the sound remained consistent—once the swat sounded, it would be followed by a rustle-rustle and a final plop. Eva crept to the bow of the boat again and threw her weight against the boat until it slipped into the water. She jumped in and listened as the boat ceased sloshing water back and forth. Nothing. She floated down the river, hitting the edges with her oars and occasionally with the bow or stern of the boat. Her heart sank. The noise still hadn't returned as she rounded the final turn of the cavern to face the tunnel into the next segment of the river. A very faint blue light emitted from the ground on the far side of the new cavern. The light reminded her of a far-off comet in the sky. If she squinted too much or not enough, it seemed to disappear, but if she focused just right, she could see the patch of light filling the darkness.

Eva slipped the oars in and out of the water quietly and gently, keeping one eye on the faint patch of light and both ears searching for the sound that had echoed throughout the cavern moments before. As Eva's boat closed in on the light, she saw that patches of tiny blue powdery, glimmering creatures lined the rocky wall beneath the water, a swarm of lichen-like beings forming what looked like an underwater field of plumbago. They glowed but so faintly that one had to focus on the light, or it would fade back into the darkness. This light was different from the leviathan and the fish, something other and new.

*Swat. Rustle. Rustle. Plop.*

And with the return of the sound, Eva felt the boat vibrate. She slipped her fingers in the water and felt faint ripples against her skin.

*Swat. Rustle. Rustle. Plop.*

There it was. Louder this time. She was certain she was closer to it now. There were the ripples again, following the sound, responding to it maybe. Eva resumed rowing toward the sound.

*Swat. Rustle. Rustle. Plop.*

Eva reached out to the ledge of the nearest landing. It was encased in barely visible wisps of glowing light. A stream trickled through a powdery web creating a film on the stone floor that led to a small tunnel several feet in front of her. She gripped the edge. There was not enough room to pull up her boat, and she could not see into the tunnel from her current position. Even though there was little to no current in this section of the river, she feared losing her boat. She couldn't leave it.

*Swat. Rustle. Rustle. Plop.*

Eva pulled herself up on the edge, keeping one foot in the boat as she spread out as far as she could from her vessel toward the tunnel. Eva squinted toward it.

*Swat.*

Eva gasped. She saw something thin fly up out of the ground, hit the ground, then disappear below.

*Rustle. Rustle. Plop.*

Eva held her breath until she heard the sounds again and watched the tentacle fly up from the ground and then fall back down below. It happened again and again. With each swat, the glowing microscopic creatures hummed, responding to the sound or the contact.

Eva shimmied back to the boat. Once back in, she ripped off her parka. She tied one arm tightly around the tiller of the motor and tied the other around the two oars, setting them on the stone floor as far from the water's edge as possible. She stepped back out of the boat carefully and sat by the oars, waiting to see if they would hold the boat to the shore.

It took a few minutes for the boat to tug on the oars. The oars slid a bit, but her parka provided enough friction, so combined with their weight, they tugged back. The boat slowly floated back to the edge. This sequence occurred several more times. Each time the boat would pull the oars a little bit closer to the water. It was slow enough to give Eva about two minutes to go see what was making the sound at the end of this ghostly tunnel. She pulled the oars as far away from the water as possible and steadied the boat. She shot the set-up one last look, nodded, and rushed toward the tunnel.

*Swat. Rustle. Rustle. Plop.*

The thin tentacle flying out of a hole in the ground, flopping in the air, and then swatting against the floor looked like an ancient demon rising from the depths to pull victims down to some unknown terror. Walking toward it was one of the hardest things Eva had ever done, and she had done many hard things.

*Swat. Rustle. Rustle. Plop.*

As Eva got closer, she heard something else— murmuring voices.

*Swat. Rustle. Rustle. Plop.*

With each step, the faint murmurs became louder, but not clearer.

Her oars scraped against the stone behind her. Eva started. She glanced back. She could just make out the red of her parka in the darkness. The oars were still on shore. She still had more time.

*Swat. Rustle. Rustle. Plop.*

Right as the tentacle disappeared beneath the surface, Eva willed herself to run forward and peer down the hole.

The voices stopped.

Eva spotted what looked like a pile of tentacles piled together. She squinted and could just make out another form reaching up toward her.

"Eva?"

Eva swayed, almost fainting. She had not expected that voice to come up from the hole. She took a step away from the hole. She must be hallucinating. She had finally cracked.

"Eva? Are you really up there?"

Eva stepped back toward the hole and dropped to her knees. She carefully leaned over the hole and peered down.

"Iris?"

"Eva! It's Eva! It's Cain and me. We're stuck down here."

"Iris? Cain?"

"Yes, it's us!"

Relief crashed through all Eva's internal dams and filled up her heart. She had found her sister.

The oars scraped against the rocks behind her and fell into the water with a splash. Eva's eyes widened, and she ran back toward the boat.

"Wait, Eva! Don't leave!"

Iris's face was covered in dirt. Her legs were wrapped around Cain's neck. He swayed, leaning against the wall, holding her ankles.

"She just ran off!"

Cain bent down and grabbed the coiled root. He tugged it back from the vines that were trying to pull it back, wrapping it around his arm into a lasso. He handed it up to Iris.

"Did you really see her?"

Iris frowned and lightly whacked his shoulder. "I *saw* her. She was just there . . ."

Iris lifted the root lasso and placed it firmly on her shoulder, watching the hole, willing her sister to return. Cain steadied one foot against the wall and dug the other into the vines, leaning back, pulling the root up, fighting the constant tightening of the plant below them, pulling against the part of the root they had untangled and coaxed out of the mass.

Iris heard splashing and wood hitting stone. A few moments passed, and Eva's head reappeared, smiling down at her.

"You're really down there, aren't you?"

Iris beamed. "We are! I just hope you're really up there."

"I am. How did you get down there?"

"I want to get out of this hole before I tell you the very long story. I'm going to throw this root up to you. I need you to catch it and pull it as far as you can and secure it to something."

"Okay, toss it up."

The white root came flying out of the hole. Eva thrust her hands toward it. It slipped right through her fingertips.

*Swat. Rustle. Rustle. Plop.*

"Sorry!"

Cain grabbed a bit of the root as it fell to the ground. He rolled it back up again, secured himself and handed it to Iris.

She grabbed the root. "Okay, be ready on three. One. Two. Three!"

Iris tossed up the root. Eva missed it. This happened many more times. Eva secured her boat for a second time and ran back to the hole. Cain huffed to Iris. "We aren't very good at this."

Iris shushed him and flung the vine upward. It whipped through the air and popped up out of the hole. Eva reached out. This time, both her hands clasped around it. She yelped as the root fell downward and dragged her toward the edge. She kept her grip as the root burned her palms. She tossed her body away from the hole onto the floor on top of the root. It continued to pull her toward the hole. Her feet dangled over the edge, but she didn't let go. She kicked one foot into the side of the hole and then another, holding on for dear life as the root tightened. She stopped moving, her butt a few inches from the ledge.

"I got it!"

Iris and Cain whooped from below. Cain lowered Iris from his shoulders. Iris shouted up to Eva. "Wrap it around your waist, and I'll try to climb up!"

Cain shot a wary glance up to Eva as he struggled against the force of the giant plant below, constantly tugging the root, trying to pull it back into its place. "Iris, if I don't make it up there, I am sorry about the motor."

Iris turned to Cain. Her face scrunched up into a frown. "You are your own person and had your own reasons."

Eva carefully stepped back from the hole, turning as she went, wrapping the root around her waist. She continued until it wrapped around her three times and there was no more give. She tugged the root, and it was as tight as it could be.

"Okay, I'm ready! Iris, you come up first."

Iris tugged on her end of the root.

Cain struggled against the plant. "Still, I should have trusted you both about Jacob."

"I didn't trust the others when they were trying to heal Jacob and . . . We've all made mistakes that put the group in danger." She turned her back to him and pulled on the root rope. "It's normal to trust yourself more than others, but this time, please trust us more."

"About what?"

"About being able to pull you up. Don't try any martyr stuff."

"I will try." Cain nodded for her to go up as he tugged against the vine.

"I'm serious. We need you, Cain. You are more important to us than you realize." She gripped his arm. "I will never forgive you if you don't make it out of here."

Cain shot her a wry smile which she returned. She released his arm and gripped the vine. She quickly put one hand over the other, swaying her legs as she ascended the root.

Eva felt the added weight squeeze the vine around her waist. She held tight to the end of it. It was taking all her strength to hold the extra weight.

Iris's head popped up, and she pulled herself up. Eva stumbled back a few steps when Iris's weight came off the root. She held on as the line went taut again. Iris quickly scrambled to her feet and rushed over to Eva.

"Do you have a knife with you?"

"Yeah, in my bag with my fishing gear in the boat."

Iris rushed to the boat.

"Wait, where are you going? I can't hold this that much longer."

"We need a knife, or this isn't going to work."

A few moments passed as Iris rustled through Eva's belongings. Eva listened as Iris scraped the oars against the rock, pulling the boat back closer to the edge. Iris ran past her again and looked down the hole.

"Cain. I'm going to drop a knife. When I say so, cut the root free and hold on tight!"

Iris held Eva's knife over the hole and dropped it down.

Cain shouted from below. "Got it!"

Iris positioned herself between Eva and the hole and gripped the root.

"Okay, Cain, start cutting it!" Iris glanced over her shoulder to Eva. "Lean back as far as you can. When he cuts the root free, I hope it'll release enough force to help us get him up here."

The root tugged against Eva as a raspy screech flew up the hole into the tunnel. The dim glow of the tunnel brightened. Eva felt the large snap. She and Iris stumbled backward. The root shot up through the hole faster than they could have pulled it on its own. There was still some resistance which Eva hoped was Cain's weight. She landed with a thud next to the boat, and Iris fell after her. Iris jumped up and dashed to the edge of the hole.

"Cain!"

Cain's hand gripped the ledge. His other dangled behind him. He flung it upward, and it slapped the stone. Iris grabbed his arm as his fingers slid across the smooth rock. Cain pulled himself up with one hand while Iris pulled his other. He flopped an elbow up on the stone and then shoved the tip of his boot into the rocky wall and lifted his other leg up, straining every muscle in his body as he started the awkward and tough climb toward the top. Eva sprinted over and joined Iris in dragging Cain upward. He kicked his body out of the hole until he finally collapsed on the ground next to the girls. They all lay in a pile for a long while, breathing heavily, until a splash sounded behind them.

"The boat!" Eva shot up, limping back to the edge of the river. The oars were floating in the water, and the boat was floating away. Eva lay down onto her stomach, reached her arms out, and grabbed the oars. Cain and Iris dropped down next to her and helped her pull the oars out of the water, dragging the boat back toward the shore. They flopped the oars down on the stone, and Eva dropped her burning arms on her soaking wet parka. Iris and Cain collapsed on the ground next to her. After several more excruciating moments, the giant plant stopped screeching. After a few more moments of silence, Iris placed her hand on Eva's arm, squeezing it softly.

"There's so much more down here than we ever thought."

"Yes." Eva pulled Iris closer, resting her forehead on hers. "More dangerous that we thought, too."

They all remained quiet and rested, listening to the water lapping against the boat and watching the blue ghostly glimmering fade in and out across the walls and ceiling. They stayed like this for a long time until the faint sounds of flapping wings and muffled laughter in the far distance broke the silence. Cain shot up. "What's that?"

"I think . . ." Eva trailed off as she pulled herself up, listening for sounds in the darkness. The source of the sound wasn't in this section. It was farther away.

"Yes, I feel them." Iris stood up, also searching but seeing nothing. The sound seemed to be travelling away from them, so quiet now, they could hardly hear it.

"They took Jacob."

"Who?" Cain asked.

"Marin and at least one more. It doesn't make any sense. They can fly now, I think. They didn't even try to talk to us, just took him and left me. Why would they do that?"

"We found the Source, Eva, and there is a power there that is very hard to resist, maybe impossible," Iris answered.

# Day 2,414 – Island - Woods

A thundering roar transformed to a series of huffing grunts as Matt crept up, concealed by a large shrub. Eva's mighty bear staggered on its hind legs in the small clearing. The fur on its massive chest wet with blue blood where several holes had been blasted into it. Dezi held a large stick behind the bear. It circled around and took a swipe at Jake. He jumped back. The bear fell to its front paws and roared at him.

"Shoot it again, Lena!"

Jake danced away from the bear.

"I can't. I'm out of ammo."

Lena dropped her gun and grabbed another fallen stick from the ground while the bear's back was turned.

"I told you this was a stupid idea!" Jake followed Lena's lead. "Dezi! Stick it! Before it stands back up!"

The bear turned back toward Lena. She held a stick out in front of her, spear-like.

Dezi let out a primal yell and jabbed her stick into the bear's left flank. The bear howled and raised up onto its back legs again, turning toward its attacker.

Matt searched the ground and spotted another stick. He scooped it up. It was the size of a baton, not anywhere near as big as he would like it to be, but it had a pointy end. He gripped it and watched the others, moving behind a nearby tree. He didn't want to help them kill this bear, but he didn't want to watch any of them get torn apart by it either.

Lena didn't hesitate. She never did. She lunged and jabbed her stick into one of the bullet wounds on the side of the bear's belly. She released her hold on the stick and rolled away as the bear swiped in her direction. It twisted its body around with more agility than expected, faster than Lena anticipated, and landed on its front paws right in front of her, galloping toward her, teeth out, grunting. Lena scuttled across the ground, kicking herself away from the bear's jaws. Jake dashed forward and jumped, his stick above him, bringing it down into the bear's backside. The bear's back leg folded underneath it, and its belly slammed to the ground. Lena jumped up and darted into the trees, right next to Matt. They made eye contact.

"Get in there and stick it, Matt!"

The bear pushed itself up, but its left leg and right arm were both bleeding, struggling beneath its massive weight. It staggered up, swaying, but roared, still ready for a fight. Lena shoved Matt out into the clearing. He stumbled and almost fell to the ground.

"Kill it, Matt!"

Jake spotted Matt. "Yeah, get it, Matt!"

"Matt, hurry!" Dezi stumbled away from the towering bear.

"Kill it! Kill it! Kill it!" Lena and Jake started chanting. The bear huffed and grunted, stretching up on its haunches, finally making eye contact with Matt who clutched a three-foot long stick, more kindling for a fire than a weapon.

"Kill it. Kill it. Kill it."

The bear staggered toward Matt and roared, its hair vibrating. Matt gazed into its throat and then over at its massive claw that was rising outward.

The chanting continued as Matt's vision blurred.

"Kill it. Kill it. Kill it."

Matt's knuckles lightened as he raised his stick. The bear raised its claw. Matt spotted something just beyond the bear in the woods. He saw Gabi bent down, arm around a small cub, holding its mouth closed.

Matt froze.

The bear's claw began to drop.

A gunshot rang.

And then another. And another. Four more plunged into the bear's chest sending its left shoulder back and then its right, then its hind leg and its front staggered, and its massive chest and head started falling toward Matt who was still clutching his stick. Jake lunged and knocked him out of the way just as the bear landed with a thud.

"You're gonna get us all killed one of these days." Jake whacked him in the head as he got up. Matt turned to see the bear's mouth open, tongue hanging out, eyes staring at him as it huffed a few last breathes. Matt rolled away and checked the spot where he had seen Gabi, but Gabi was no longer there. Neither was the bear cub. Matt rose to his feet and turned to face Adam, shotgun barrel on his shoulder, a wicked smirk half-concealed by his long black hair. Mari stood behind him, stoic.

Everyone but Lena was silent. Lena ran toward Adam, smiling. "That's one problem solved. Next, we got to get those wolves."

Adam's smirk disappeared, and his green eyes flashed deadly.

"We got bigger problems than some wolves." Adam's eyes rested on Matt, looking past him for the missing member of the group. "Eva's out here. Jacob too, and they have my guns. None of us are safe until we find them. Is that clear?"

The others nodded. Lena surveyed the woods. Matt moved his eyes to one of the bear's wounds, watching the gushing blood cascade down its fur onto the ground.

"Good. Now, let's get this meat back to camp." Jake pulled out a large blade and nudged the bear with his foot.

Lena searched the forest until she saw some plants with large green fronds. "Mari, cut down some vines. I'll grab some of those big leaves. We can wrap up the meat."

Mari trudged toward a tree with vine-like branches hanging down. "You guys couldn't have gone after something just a little bit smaller?"

Adam stalked over to Matt and putt both hands on his shoulders. "The bear was a threat to our camp. We had to kill him. Matt, you can't freeze like that. I won't be around forever. I definitely won't allow it that long." Adam looked over Matt's shoulder into the forest. "Still no Gabi?"

Matt was careful not to make eye contact with Adam. "I can't find him."

Adam gave Matt a shove toward the bear. "Go on, help them with the bear. I want you neck deep in that thing's entrails, get you ready to actually kill something, earn your keep around here." Adam stepped toward the woods where

Gabi had been hidden. Matt's eyes locked with Mari's for a moment. She glanced toward the forest as Dezi watched, silently. Gabi had been absent for two nights. She knew Adam wouldn't wait much longer.

Matt scrubbed his hands at the lake's edge, sitting in the water. He was covered in layers of blood. The water cooled the rawness of his hands, but he still felt the warmth of the bear, smelled earth, metal, dung, acid, all the odors that assaulted him as they cut up the animal. As he and Lena skinned the bear and Dezi and Jake cut pieces out of it and handed them to Mari to wrap, his eyes stung from the overpowering stench of death, yet it was worse when he closed them.

When they were shut, he saw the little bear cub and the horror in Gabi's eyes. The whole time, his stomach turned with both nausea and hunger. He wanted to take a bite out of the flesh as much as he wanted to vomit all over it.

# Day 2,414 - Caves

Iris held one oar up above the water and the other just atop the surface as the crowded boat turned a craggy corner. Eva watched Iris rest her hand on the oar, her breaths shallow. She frowned.

"You both are still tired, why? You're never tired. Are you injured?"

Cain leaned forward. "The cavern we told you about was filled with strange glowing plants. It changed me from within. Did you feel the same way, Iris?"

Iris shot Cain a worried look. "Yes, I noticed its effects on you."

"It didn't make moving and breathing harder for you?"

Iris shifted the oars as the boat drifted into a large cavern. "It probably did, but I couldn't be sure if it was that place or my interaction with the queen."

Iris slipped her hand under her hair to rub the nape of her neck, an action Eva could not see in the darkness.

"What did she do to you?"

"She opened me up, like she wanted to pull something out of me."

"Did it hurt?"

"Not exactly. It aches."

"Still?"

Iris nodded her head, another action Eva couldn't see.

"Let me row for a while." Cain tapped Iris's shoulder. "I feel stronger than yesterday. I am hoping the side effects of that place are temporary."

Iris shook her head. "No, I want to row a little longer. I know where we need to go."

Eva yelped. "It's back." She pointed to the far end of the thin passageway the boat had just entered. The leviathan emitted a green glow at the far end. "That thing is stalking me."

"I know that beast." Iris spat, a bit bitterly. "It took part of my toe."

"It took your toe?"

Iris raised her foot toward Eva. Eva reached toward the silhouette of her foot. She gasped when her fingers landed in the empty space that should have been her sister's big toe. "How?"

"It's made of the worms like everything we make, like me, but it's different somehow. I can feel the smaller beings that make me what I am yearn to return to the beast. That yearning gets stronger the closer I get to it. That's what happened, part of me unraveled and returned to it."

"Then we need to turn back, you can't get any closer to it."

Iris dropped her foot and reached for the oars.

"We don't have another choice. We must go back to where I saw the others. We can't leave them."

Eva returned her gaze toward the leviathan that was now glowing a dark purple with flashes of indigo and teal along its sides. A humming filled the cave, reverberating off the walls, and a golden light shone from the tunnel behind the leviathan. The humming began to separate and become more distinct. Eva could hear individual sounds coming together like an orchestra. It was the most beautiful and devastating sound she had ever heard. Eva reached up into the air as if she could pull a string and join the band. The harmony wrapped around her like a giant hug. "What is it?"

Iris also stared into the air, rapt. "You hear it?"

"Is that what you've always been hearing?"

"Yes, but not as strong."

Cain scowled and scratched his arm.

"Can you hear it, Cain?"

"Not exactly. I can feel it. It's itchy."

Iris turned to Eva and grabbed her arm.

"You know what this means, don't you?"

Eva's stomach turned. Her brain buzzed, every bit of her skull tingled as it responded to the song in the air. Her hair rose as if static electricity was flowing through her. Golden wisps of light travelled across the water, reaching out from the queen, a siren's call that, once heard, burrowed a hole into your brain, creating a craving to unite with the source of that song. Eva couldn't say what she thought it meant. Iris glanced over at Cain and back to Eva, excited, clasping her hands around hers.

"We're the same. Something in you is like me, and something in me is like you. We really are sisters."

Eva jerked back a bit. That last sentence stung. Her eyes lowered, staring at their hands.

"Iris, it's moving toward us, fast. Eva, start the motor. Regardless of where we may have to go, I don't want to be dragged there by this thing."

Eva watched as the leviathan pulsed toward them. She fumbled with the motor until it roared to life. Iris and Cain held on as the boat sped to the left, swerving just in time to avoid the rocky shore. The leviathan flapped its body against the surface sending a large wave to crash into the boat. Eva turned the boat into the waves the creature continued to create with its massive body. The bow of the boat pointed up to the ceiling of the cave as it climbed a three-foot wave. The motor sputtered but came back to life as they slid down the wave, gas fumes stinging Eva's eyes and filling her nose. They cut through the waves, carefully circling the beast.

"I'm back where I started," Iris whispered. "I knew we were going in circles down there."

"We're close to the Source?" Eva asked.

Iris pointed at a narrow strip of water between the creature and the rocky walls that lead toward the tunnel that would take them into the queen's chamber.

"Head that way. Once you get into the tunnel, it won't be able to reach you."

"How do you know that?"

Another wave slammed into the boat.

"It's how I escaped it the first time."

Eva struggled to keep control of the boat as the beast dove under water. Cain grabbed an oar as a weapon and kept careful watch of the descending threat. He shouted, "Go, now! It's under us."

Eva cranked the motor, using everything it had, shooting the boat across the surface, which skipped dangerously over the waves, its sides slamming into other waves. Iris flew off her seat and landed on the floor of the boat next to Cain's knees. The leviathan's pulsing body was rising rapidly directly underneath them.

"Faster!" Cain yelled. "It's gonna knock us out of the water."

"It doesn't go any faster." The boat's bottom slammed against another wave as it approached the tunnel. Eva fixed her attention on the golden light, the song filling her heart, brain, every cell of her body, calling her toward the tunnel while the fear of the ascending leviathan chased her into the tunnel with the same intensity. There was a small voice in her head that warned her of these two forces with the same agenda. The voice sounded a bit like her mother. Eva wanted to heed it, but there was nowhere else to go.

The leviathan's back breached the surface and hit the boat. Eva screamed as they catapulted into the air, flying fast and out of control toward the tunnel. Her eyes widened. They were dangerously close to hitting the rocky wall next to the tunnel's entrance.

"Hold on!"

The boat landed hard against the water with a crack. Eva flew back and slammed against the transom and slid into the bottom of the boat. As she struggled to catch her breath, water began filling the hull. One of the boards had busted in half and was letting in water and the light of the sea beast. She grabbed her satchel and struggled to pull herself up. Cain had been flung from the boat and fought to keep his head above the waves right inside the tunnel. Iris wasn't in the boat either. Eva scanned the waves for her, finally spotting her swimming for her life away from the mammoth leviathan. The beast rolled along the bottom just below her.

"Iris!"

Eva flung herself out of the sinking boat, plunging into the icy waters. She opened her eyes. At first, all she could see was blurred light through murky water. She blinked several times until the beast that had been stalking her through the caves came into crisp focus.

It shone bright green. The millions of miniature marine worms that constructed its enormous diamond-shaped body moved together in exact unison, creating a spectral murmuration. Its two pectoral fins spanned like wings at least five times her height. Its three fins forming a tail whipped back and forth, turning a deep indigo at its tip. The color change slowly crept toward the body. It was one of the most beautiful things she had ever seen even if it was trying to kill them all. The queen's buzzing melody vibrated through the water and lulled Eva. She felt her eyelids droop. A gold light filled the corners of her eyes as if it was coming from inside her skull. She shook her head, cursing. It was difficult to stay in control so close to the queen's song. Despite the burning in her lungs, she felt her body relax again, succumbing. Through partially closed eyes, she watched tentacles grow out of the beast's sides. The worms manipulated their bodies to create these new appendages, and they were all reaching for and clawing at Iris. Iris locked eyes with her and screamed. "Help me!"

Iris's fear snapped Eva out of her trance. She kicked toward her sister as Iris fought off one of the creature's tentacles. Eva grabbed onto one of the tentacles, and it whipped her violently away. Another tentacle twirled around Iris's leg. Eva tried to swim back to her sister, but she was no match for this thing's size and strength. Iris reached her arms toward the surface as she was ripped deeper into the water away from Eva. The leviathan flipped around, dragging Iris like a ragdoll doing a quick one-eighty. It torpedoed directly toward Eva, diving below her right before they collided, dragging Iris toward the tunnel, glowing pieces peeling off it. The worms transformed into small fish that darted behind it. Eva shot up to the surface and took in several hungry gulps of air before she swam after her sister. The stingray shaped monster shrank as the worms shed off it in fish form, making it small enough to enter the narrower tunnel.

Cain dove after Iris. Eva kicked after them into the tunnel toward the golden light and the pulsing leviathan, now half indigo, half green. Something else inside her screamed to turn back. This something was not her mother or her father but something new, revealing itself as separate from her for the first time, and it was very afraid.

Eva kept kicking forward, flailing a bit. She wasn't the best swimmer. She had gone swimming for the first time on her sixteenth birthday, which had been only weeks ago.

The next time she went swimming, she was pulling Jacob into the water, nearly killing them both.

The last time, she had lunged after Adam and been knocked out cold and kidnapped.

And now. She made a silent oath to never swim again if she survived. She paddled along as the light from the leviathan disappeared completely. Only the golden point of light at the end of the tunnel guided her through the darkness.

The waves stilled after a few minutes.

The humming and buzzing ceased.

Cain was still underwater, nowhere to be seen. Eva was alone, again. Her teeth chattered. The water was cold, too cold for her to swim all the way back to the beginning, and her boat was destroyed. She was going to have to confront whatever was at the end of this tunnel and hope that there was a way to return home alive.

# Day 2,414 – The Hive

Eva crept along the edge of the passageway, keeping a constant lookout for the light of the leviathan. She was certain it waited beneath her in the dark waters, waiting to pull her off to wherever it had taken Iris. She prayed that it wasn't unravelling the rest of her sister as she treaded water in the dark.

Something splashed up ahead. Eva froze as the splashing got closer.

"Eva?" a voice whispered. Eva released a relieved breath, kicking toward the voice. "Yes, it's me."

Cain grabbed her hand. "You're freezing."

"I-I-I'm fine. Have you seen Iris?"

"No. Jump on my back." Cain flipped around and Eva crawled up on his back, partially out of the water, which just made her colder but being close to his body helped. He gracefully maneuvered the waters toward the glowing light at the end, which grew brighter with each stroke. Eva focused on getting her teeth to stop chattering.

"Do you think it's going to kill her?"

"I don't think so. It wants to transform her against her will."

Again, Eva could feel the scream from within her. She held onto Cain's neck and back tighter, trembling.

As they swam further through the tunnel, the golden light took up more and more of the darkness until Eva didn't feel cold or afraid anymore—she was so full of light. The crashing sound of water grew deafening as they approached the large cavern. Cain grabbed her arm to get her attention, shouting above the roar of water. "Don't let them touch you!"

"What?" Eva moved closer to him, straining to hear. Cain leaned in, putting his mouth right next to her ear. "When we enter this place, do not let any of the creatures touch you. They are dangerous in there."

Eva nodded as they paddled forward, entering the cavern. The giant waterfall pouring into a large pool came into view. Millions of multi-colored flatworms swarmed the waters, coming together and separating constantly, molding and unmolding, a beautiful primordial stew. Cain tensed as the creatures touched his skin.

"Get out of the water."

He quickly darted to the stony edge and pulled himself up and then helped Eva. Eva flinched when she felt his hand. It was slimy. She glanced up at him and for a moment, his skin oozed and shifted before it tightened back up.

"What was that?" She pulled her hand away from him, recoiling.

"I don't know." His eyes widened in horror as he scanned the cavern for Iris. She was nowhere to be seen. "We have to find Iris and fast."

Eva gazed up at a giant shifting icosahedron, its twenty sides morphing and changing colors to the faint humming of that magical song Eva had heard right before the leviathan attacked them. It had returned, or it had always been there, and she just tapped back into its frequency. Eva felt two forces inside of her shifting in and out of sync as the music filled her mind, heart, and body again. She glanced over at Cain who was watching her in wonder and terror.

"What?" Eva touched her face, self-consciously. He was looking at her as if she were a monster.

Cain shook his head. "Your face, it was, it just, for a minute, it looked like it was shifting along with that thing."

Eva nodded and slowly slid her hand off her face. This place was going to transform them all if they stayed too long. She stepped closer to the large geometric shape, squinting at its many sides. She could make out smaller compartments inside. Plastic worms went in and out of the chambers. As she got closer, she saw that several of the compartments had been busted out of, their walls pushed out and torn apart. She pointed up at them.

"What do you think did that?"

Cain shook his head. He peered up at the ceiling, and his mouth dropped open. Eva followed his gaze and saw a giant golden creature with a round plump thorax and abdomen with large sparkling wings. It was bigger than any creature she had seen on Earth, easily eight times the size of her bear. It lay flat and upside down on the ceiling, its wings resting against its rippling body.

"Is that creature the Source?" Eva whispered, in awe, as she turned and took in the whole room.

"It's part of it for sure. I don't think it's all of it. I don't even know what the Source really is, now that we're here, seeing all of this," Cain stammered. "Do you see Iris?"

"Iris is here." A calm, familiar voice of one of Eva's aunties spoke from behind them. Eva turned around to find Rhea and Dee standing before her, taller and their faces even more beautiful, their skin different. "We all are, just as we should be."

Eva rushed to Rhea and hugged her. She released her and hugged Dee. "We've missed you so much—" She jerked away when she felt Dee's skin on hers. It was hard and smooth, like a shell, but still flexible and soft. "What happened to your skin?"

"We transformed to our mature forms here. What you and Iris created was an infant stage, one we had to emerge from, here, in this place."

A gleeful holler from atop the waterfall filled the chamber. Brigid cascaded over the falls. As she shot out over the pool, her back bulged, and large translucent wings unfolded, slowing her descent as she flitted across the chamber toward Eva and Cain. Marin whooped as he came barreling down the falls behind her, but he dove into the pool, plunging into a swarm of worms that shot out in all directions when he entered the water.

Brigid crashed into Eva and Cain, hugging them both tightly. "You're both finally here!" She squeezed them even tighter. "Marin, they're here!"

Marin's head had emerged, and he swam to the stony edge and pulled himself up. He walked toward Eva for a hug, but she stepped back.

"Where's Jacob? You took him. You and—"

"Me." Brigid raised her hand, giggling.

"Yes, and Iris, too. Where are they?"

Cain scowled at his family and their joy in this strange reunion.

"Iris has been screaming in pain ever since she left this place," Rhea said. "We've been searching for her, but she disappeared where we couldn't hear her. The minute she returned, we went after her. She needed help or she was going to die." Rhea gazed at Eva and Cain so earnestly that it was impossible not to believe her.

"Why was she in pain?" Eva asked.

"She had started a transformation before she ran away, one that cannot be reversed. She must either complete it or it will kill her."

Cain stepped closer to Rhea. He looked at her with love but also suspicion. "No one asked Iris if she wanted to transform, Rhea. Did they ask you?"

Rhea laughed. It sounded like a babbling brook. "This is not the type of thing you have a choice in. Does a caterpillar choose to become a butterfly? The same with all creatures who experience metamorphosis. We are these kinds of creatures. We cannot remain in our original form, or we will die."

Rhea surveyed Cain and placed a gentle hand on his cheek. Eva detected a hint of pity in the look Rhea was giving him. Her heart started beating faster.

"Where is Iris?" Cain repeated, gently removing her hand from his cheek.

Rhea gazed up at the ceiling toward the golden creature. "She is in the light."

Eva and Cain craned their necks upward. Eva spotted a little bulge in the golden ripples of the creature's body.

"No! Let her go!" Eva yelled, shooting angry glares at all of them. "You have to let her go!"

A deep, comforting voice came from behind the icosahedron. "Eva, they're not hurting her, they're helping her." Jacob stepped out from around the giant hive structure. Like Rhea and the others, he also looked stronger, healthier, even more handsome than before. He radiated a force that pulled Eva toward him, a warmth that seemed to remove the last chill from her bones.

"Jacob! You're okay." Eva rushed toward him. As she got closer, she felt warmer, and the world narrowed to include only the two of them. She reached out toward him and fell into his open arms. She hugged him tightly, but he didn't hold her in his normal way. His arms didn't wrap around her as tightly as in the past. She pulled back, searching his eyes, and she saw something she had not seen in him before. She stumbled back a few steps, dizzy. Jacob's eyes were different. They were no longer the ones she had gazed into so many times before. They were a gleaming green, gorgeous emerald, supernatural, nearly iridescent. They were a color she had seen before, the color of an old, dear friend.

"Abel?" Eva's voice was shaking, her arms trembling as she backed away from him. "What have you done with him? Where's Jacob?"

"I didn't do anything to him. Jacob's right here." Jacob tapped his head.

"What have you done?"

"Exactly what I am supposed to do. Do you remember that day we first met? When you discovered our kind? You were fishing on top of the rocks?"

"Yes, that day changed everything."

"It did. But, not exactly for the reasons you think. You slipped and hit your head. Do you remember that?"

Eva shook her head. "No, I don't."

"You sank into the sludgy black water, and . . ." Jacob's lips quivered with Abel's emotion, and their fist clenched. "And they jumped on top of you, submerged into the bleeding wound on your head, and disappeared inside of you."

Abel reached out and gripped Eva's wrist firmly but gently. "You died for a minute that day, Eva, and when you were brought back, you weren't alone. They were in there with you. I could feel them, but couldn't see them, touch them, meld with them. I could only feel them vibrate inside of you."

Something inside of Eva buzzed as Abel pulled her closer to him. His green eyes gazed past Eva and searched deeper inside of her.

"I love you very much. You must come back to me."

Eva shuddered. He was looking into her soul, but he was not speaking to her. She felt love and repulsion pulse through her body.

"You can't stay in there like this. She will die and when she does, you will die with her."

"Jacob? Are you still in there?"

Eva placed a hand on Jacob's cheek. He leaned into the touch for a moment and then pulled away.

"Jacob is not present like that anymore. You can't talk to him or be with him. I am sorry for that, Eva. If it could be done differently so he remained as well, I would have done it that way. He or I are now and forever who you call Abel."

"How?" Tears rolled down Eva's cheek as she pulled her hand away from Abel.

"After you had nearly killed Jacob with your gun, we were healing him, but hatred somehow crept into Iris. She intervened and poisoned him. She was killing him. I had to act rashly. I saved Jacob's life that night but lost control of my own."

Eva's eyes widened in horror. "Iris would never—" Eva stopped, knowing the words did not ring true. In that moment and on that night, Iris would have killed Jacob. Eva loved Jacob, and even she had shot him that same night.

"You did save his life."

Abel nodded. "I know what it feels like to lose someone I love deeply." His expression darkened. "There's more to it than that. I melded with him in a way that cannot be undone. We are one creature. Kind of like our kind is with each other, all connected, always communicating."

He looked past Eva again, now talking to the being inside of her.

"You did it. You connected us with humans."

Abel gestured at his body, grimacing.

"You were right. We do need them if we want to leave the island to expand our work, but we are supposed to play the dominant role. You are refusing the next step."

Eva heard a scream inside her head again. Her brain became foggy with frustration as something burrowed deeper into the core of her brain. Abel grabbed Eva's face.

"Why are you doing this?"

They both stared at each other for a long time, shaking, emotional, lost, and confused. Eva trembled as a voice both her own and not her own spoke. "I wanted to say goodbye. You could have waited and let me say goodbye to him."

Abel's hands released her face, and he stepped away from her again. "That would have made it harder."

"For who?" Eva spat.

Abel didn't look back to her. "For all of us."

Cain glared at Abel, once Jacob, and then to Rhea and the others.

"So, what's the plan from here? Is it to kill Eva?"

Rhea stepped toward him. "Of course not, Cain. She will still be alive."

Marin and Brigid shared uncertain looks. Dee did not meet Cain's eyes.

"Like Jacob?" Cain scoffed and glanced up at the ceiling. "No wonder you took Iris by force. You know she would never agree to this."

"Iris will agree once she fully understands. Her primary goal is fixing the planet. They made her that way. She will want to do it the only way it can be done." Rhea gestured at Eva reverently.

"Eva made her that way." Cain glared back at Abel.

"You're thinking like a child because you can become no more than a child, Cain." Abel walked over to Cain and placed a gentle hand on his shoulder. Cain ripped his shoulder away. "You do not hear the song, no?"

"I feel it," Cain growled.

Abel peered over at Eva. "Eva, you can hear the music, yes?"

Eva did not answer him.

"That frequency connects us all. It is part of the Source. All our kind can hear it."

Abel returned his gaze to Cain.

"You can't transform because you were created by Iris alone before she went through her metamorphosis. You don't have an architect inside you, just many builders. Iris wasn't ready to create larger lifeforms that would last on their own. Many of her creations will eventually break down and die, including you. They require a slightly different lifeform, something Eva knows instinctively because they are inside her, guiding her."

Eva's cheeks flushed. She felt angry, sad, and hopeless all at once. She knew what Abel said was true because she had always felt that Cain was different, strange. At first, she hated that about him, but now, now it was the thing she loved most about him, in his vulnerability was great strength. Iris built him exactly right. She was a master at creation, one of the best. Eva was furious, and so was the something inside of her. It did not agree with Abel.

"We all will die, eventually," Eva whispered.

"No, we don't. Our kind returns and becomes something else. We don't die. We transform. You will rot if you don't live the life you are supposed to live." Abel glared at Eva but was speaking to the creature deep within her.

Eva shook her head, tears rolling down her cheeks. She was experiencing two sets of emotions and did not have the strength to control either of them.

"That's where you are wrong, Abel. Every creature returns. We all just do it differently."

"Maybe. I am not as good at figuring this all out without you. I need you to do this right." Abel stepped toward Eva and took her hands in his. She did not pull away as he touched his forehead to hers and spoke softly so only she could hear. "Won't you please come back to me?"

His quiet voice was the calm before a storm, brimming with tension. In response, her heart raced and her mind fogged. A strong part of her wanted desperately to meld into him, go back home. Tranced, she pressed her body against his, moved her hands up his chest and around his neck, raising her head to kiss his lips. For the first time in her life, Eva was a passenger in her own body. She pulled Abel as close to her as she could. He squeezed her even tighter than she held him. Eva felt disconnected from this embrace, like in a dream where she watched some version of her act from within herself. After a very long time, Abel pulled out of the kiss and gazed down at her. "You will return then?" His words became garbled as Eva felt a wave of deep sadness sweep over her. Involuntarily, she pulled away from Abel as her head shook.

Abel staggered back a few steps, gulping down the hurt. He trembled when he spoke. "I will not force you to return to me. I just hope that you will one day."

He glanced up at the ceiling. "She will not be so patient."

Abel turned to the others. "Marin and Brigid, please come with me."

Cain took a few steps closer. He reached out to touch her but then pulled his hand back, deciding to wait. She did not look ready to be touched. She did not look herself. "Eva?"

Eva's breaths were ragged, her thoughts still jumbled, but she was starting to feel in control of her body once again. She couldn't speak, not yet. She reached over and squeezed Cain's large hand. He clasped onto hers and did not let go.

Abel glanced at the swirling pool waters. The green, purple, and blue flatworms were coming together, slowly melding to form the sea beast. Abel grabbed Eva, ripping her hand from Cain's. He nodded at Marin who grabbed Cain from behind.

"Let me go, Marin, or I will crush you!"

Marin held tight and whispered. "I'm stronger than you remember, old friend. We're trying to help, I promise."

"We must get you both back to the surface."

"I'm not leaving Iris!"

"You have no choice. If either of you stay down here, you will either transform or die. It will simply happen. This place has its own power."

"Why should I believe you? You took Jacob from me." Eva ripped away from Abel and glared at the rest of them.

Abel stared back at her compassionately. "I gave Jacob the time to be with you, make things right. It was more than he had without me. He is only returning the favor."

"Willingly?"

"It was no longer his choice to make, and it was never your choice. We must go."

Rhea walked over to Eva and put her hands on her shoulder. "Please, trust us, Eva, as we have always trusted you."

Eva's eyes welled up with tears. She wanted to trust Rhea like she always had, but she shook her head. "None of you even gave me a chance to say goodbye to him." Eva glanced over at Cain who still struggled against Marin. His skin looked strange again, like it might pull apart at the seams. She blinked, and it was normal again.

Abel put his hand out to Eva. "This place will destroy Cain, and Iris will not forgive any of us for that. You know that is true."

She looked her two oldest friends in the eye and never felt less confident in either of them, but she grabbed his hand. Abel jumped into the water with Eva. Cain glanced up at the bulge that was Iris as Marin wrapped his wings around him, sealing Cain into a protective cocoon, and flung them both into the water.

Once underneath the surface layer of worms and the rapidly forming leviathan, Abel pulled Eva toward the waterfall. Marin released Cain once they were below the worms, and they both followed. As Eva swam closer, she felt the pressure of the water falling on top of the surface push down on them. As that pressure dissipated and they moved closer to the craggy wall under the falls, Abel pointed to a large hole, and pushed Eva toward it. A strong current pulled her toward the hole, one she could no longer fight against. It sucked her up into a narrow vent. Her lungs were burning, her ears popping and her brain bulging as she swiftly traveled up. As the vent flattened, the current continued to pull her along, but the water was shallower, so she could catch gulps of air in the tiny raging underwater tunnel. The sound was deafening, and the tiny space narrowed at times to the point that Eva was sure she would not make it through. She kept her eyes closed and lost all sense of time as the water carried her quickly away from the hive and her sister. Right as she started losing consciousness, she heard a loud suction sound, and the force and pressure disappeared. She forced open her eyes, trying to stay awake, hoping it had all been a terrible nightmare, but instead, she found herself suspended above a giant bed of seaweed, breathing in way too much water. Abel, then Cain, and finally Marin popped up behind her as her vision began to fade again. Abel grabbed her waist and kicked upward toward the light at the surface.

Her head popped up out of the lake, about forty yards offshore of the island. Eva gulped the fresh air desperately as Abel held her above water. She examined the area and realized this was the spot where she and Jacob had their deadly confrontation out on the boat. This is how Abel had returned to save them both. She had been so grateful for him that night. Now, she knew he didn't do it for her at all. He did it for whatever was inside her.

*They?*

Eva detangled herself from Abel, pushing him away. "Let go of me."

Cain swam over to her and touched her arm.

"Are you okay?"

"Not at all." Eva shook her head, treading water. "Are you?"

"Better than the last time I was out here."

Eva laughed a little despite the situation. Cain smiled. Abel shot him a dangerous look. Marin was diving and swimming circles around the group.

"Wasn't that amazing?"

"That was horrible." Cain scowled at him. "What was that?"

"A series of tunnels carved out by our kind to travel to and from the lake faster. It relies on a lot of gravity and water, air, and static pressure."

"It's not for humans. I almost died," Eva spat.

"You are not exactly human which is why you lived." Abel spoke very softly. Eva had no response to those words. She turned and started kicking toward shore, needing to get as far from Abel as possible, eager to get on the beach, gather some supplies, and go get her sister with the other boat.

A gunshot rang from the island. Eva stopped swimming and turned back to Abel, panicking. "What was that?"

Cain squinted toward the island. He couldn't see anybody, but there was smoke in the distance. "You're sure you killed Adam?"

Abel frowned. "Let's just say, Eva, to her credit, is not very good at killing people."

Eva's eyes narrowed at Abel.

"What did you do?"

"I didn't do anything. Jacob put him in the water."

Another gunshot went off.

"So, what?"

"So, as I explained, just like with you, things don't always stay dead in the water out here."

"So, I did kill him, and your kind brought him back to life?" Eva glared at Abel.

"Yes, I suppose you did succeed in killing him, just not keeping him dead."

Eva fixed her gaze on Cain. He looked as terrified as she felt, neither thought they would ever have to face Adam again.

# Day 2,414 – Island - Lake

A noxious haze blew in over the island, a painful and smelly reminder that the rest of the planet was still polluted, still toxic, and still dying. Eva glanced up at the sky, wondering if it would indeed be better if she transformed, letting whatever was inside her take over. They might have an easier chance at survival if she surrendered. She frowned, shook off those thoughts, and did what she always did when life on this planet got complicated. She put one foot in front of the other. Eva plodded through the shallow waters, her whole body shaking. The frigid temperature was dropping rapidly as more clouds rolled in. Her nostrils and throat already burning from breathing, eyes watering. She wished she had brought her goggles and mask from the cabin to her cave. The night air was brown, rather than her preferred black. Every breath in caused a cough, one that went deeper into her lungs with each inhalation. She was the only one in the group that wouldn't make it through the night if they didn't take shelter, the only weak link up on the surface.

Marin moved his tongue around in his mouth and contorted his face into disgusted grimaces. "I hate when the air tastes like this."

"Let's hope the winds pick up and it blows over tonight," Eva whispered. The last time the haze visited the region, the winds had grown stagnant, and she had been forced to stay inside for a week. Eva craned her neck toward the distant voices. An orange glow flickered up through the trees. She trudged across the sand toward the cave, away from the yelling echoing across the beach.

"I should go check the cabin now. We need to know how many there are." Abel's voice was soft yet resolved.

Eva flipped around and shoved her finger into his chest. "The last time you scouted something, we never saw you again, not in the way that we knew you. Then, you lured everyone into that thing's hive or whatever it is and changed everything. So, no, don't go check the cabin without the rest of us."

"I didn't lure them to the cave, and their transformation was predestined."

Eva's trembling from the cold was now uncontrollable and travelling deep into her heart and lungs. "Did you even ask them if they wanted it?"

"It is beyond any of us. Deep down, I think you understand it better than all of us. What we do about Adam is not. We can't be caught off guard by him again."

"You better go back underground then because this is a small island, and it's only a matter of time before he catches us off guard."

"I'm going to go see how many there are."

"I'll go with you," Marin chimed in.

"I want to wait with Eva." Brigid shook her wings, flinching as another gunshot boomed in the distance, followed by angry shouting. Brigid moved toward Eva, wrapping her arm around her arm. It took all of Eva's willpower not to jerk away from Brigid's scaly snake-like skin.

"I am staying, too," Cain said. "They have guns, Abel. You saw what those things can do, even to us." He put his hand on Abel's chest.

Abel glared down at the hand on his chest but didn't remove it. He met Cain's gaze. "In the dark, he is no match for this many of our kind. Even with guns."

"Can we please decide this in the cave before I freeze to death?" Eva shot an exasperated glare at Abel before stomping off.

Cain removed his hand from Abel's chest, but Abel grabbed it and pulled him closer.

"You know as well as I do, if not better, we need to deal with Adam sooner rather than later."

Cain removed his hand from Abel's grip and turned his attention toward the fire glow down the shore. "Kill or be killed? Is that our relationship with humans now?"

"I don't want to kill the humans, Cain."

Cain returned his gaze to Eva who stumbled in front of the cave's entrance.

"No. Just make them disappear." Cain sighed and jogged toward Eva, leaving an expressionless Abel standing in the wet sand.

# Day 2,414 – The Hive

So much light again. There was no shaded tree to hide beneath, no darkness to disappear into. Even when her eyes were shut, Iris could see the light, feel the lives of all the *polylilakes* that had been there before her. No, not just feel, she was becoming even more connected to them, fused with the light. *Polylilakes.* That is what the creatures called themselves. *Polylilakes.* That name was her name too. She recognized it right away even though she had never spoken it. Of course, that is what she was called, what she had always been called. They were all filled with such a powerful light, a collective light that drew a dormant seed through your flesh, a light that melted your insides, separated all the smaller lights within you, rearranged the spirits and melded them into a new stronger, larger one, ready to take its first breath. This time, Iris felt no fear in the face of this light. As it tore her apart, she opened her eyes wide, letting the light fill every crevice, every nook. She felt her body tighten. She burned like when she sat too close to the campfire, and then felt a soft pop. Her body deflated, and she felt her old path merge into another as the light restructured every piece of her.

*Slurp. Squish. Slurp. Squish.*

Iris felt a million tiny explosions within her at once. She watched as the light rebuilt her cells, reformed her arms and legs. This light was millions of tiny polylilakes reacting and fusing and bursting out, transforming everything they touched. They had one plan that required millions of individual and small actions. Everything they encountered was transformed in one way or another.

Iris remembered Eva telling her that in the beginning there was light, and whether it was named goddess or god, it began creating and destroying in a never-ending cycle. It filled up the darkness of the world and brought forth life. Now, there was something new bringing forth life. The polylilakes. As they rebuilt, some life was made new, some life was left behind. Polylilakes found and lost themselves in others, just as others lost themselves in the polylilakes.

*Slurp. Squish. Slurp. Squish.*

Iris couldn't squeeze her eyes shut because she didn't have eyes at the moment or a face or a neck. Her chest was forming. Small breasts rose where there had been none before. Polylilakes linked, braided, and knotted together to form her arms from the marrow to the skin. Her fingers began knitting themselves together. They were much longer than they had been before. A young woman was sprouting from the globular pile of polylilakes that had once been Iris the child.

*Slurp. Squish. Slurp. Squish.*

The light pulled something through her from the center of her chest, a molten thread that travelled to her neck down to her hips. Two nubs rose out of her back as her chest cavity closed and her hips and legs came into shape. As her feet formed and the toe that had been stolen from her regrew, Iris could not deny this light, nor did she desire to stop it, but somewhere deep, she grieved the loss of the child Eva had built, said goodbye to the brief paradise they had shared together.

# Day 2,414 - Cave

Eva slid out from the three-foot gap under the slick rocky barrier that separated the mouth of the cave from its first chamber. The low hum of the queen's music vibrated through her, beckoning, tugging at a thread in her brain. She could hear the song clearly, unlike before when she had travelled to the hive, when it had eluded her, just like Cain. She could hear her sister's voice rise occasionally in the cacophony of frequency and pitches. In those moments, she swore she could hear the other being inside of her sing out, answer the song. It was difficult not to plunge into the water and swim toward it. She longed to return to the source of that song and felt a deep sadness that she could not, not if she hoped to remain herself. She realized that the longing was probably not hers but belonged to the other.

*Where do I begin, and where do they end? Would it be any different if we switched places?*

The image of Cain's body losing solidity back in the hive flashed into her mind. She felt a small bit of agony for him. He would never be fully one of these new creatures. He could not even be in the hive without it trying to break him down, correct the anomaly. Eva shook her head. She and Cain would still exist as complete beings, just different from the others; maybe they were the others now. She looked back down toward the gap, simultaneously annoyed about how difficult it made getting into the cave and grateful that it helped conceal it. She could hear Cain's knees slide against the loose rock of the sandy floor and his back scratch against the rough top of the gap.

As Eva pulled herself up off the ground, she spotted a faint orange flickering dance across the far wall. She took a sharp inhalation and held it. The music had been lulling her so deeply with the idea of another version of her world, she hadn't noticed that someone else was in this cavern. Every muscle in her shivering body tensed, her fear fighting against her need for warmth. There was a very small fire burning just behind the column in the center of the cave. A humanoid shadow hit the far wall above the pool of dark water. Cain's head and shoulders emerged from the gap. Eva placed a hand on his shoulder as he sat up, pointing to the light. His eyes opened wider, and he rose to his feet quietly. A few pebbles rolled down his legs to the ground. The shadow rose, its head almost touching the cavern's ceiling. Deftly, Eva crept toward the figure who had helped himself to her few remaining supplies.

The shadow stepped out of the light of the fire, disappearing into the dark frame of the fire's light. Eva stopped moving, and so did Cain, both listening for the tiniest of sounds. Cain slipped into the shadows and slunk around the column. Eva dashed forward, heart racing as she remembered Adam squashing the little heartbeat of her tiny yellow frog, smearing its guts all over his face, taking pleasure in killing, taking pleasure in causing her pain. She would never forget the menacing gleam in his eyes. She would also never forget the look in his eyes moments later when the poison collided with his central nervous system, how wide they had gone, full of horror and surprise.

As she crept closer to the light, fear rose in her throat. If Adam had been brought back to life by the same type of creature that had brought her back, he would remember what she did to him. After all, she remembered all the details of her life before that moment when she hit her head on the rock while she was fishing, that moment before she died briefly, at least according to Abel.

*Had she fallen that day? Had she really died and then come back to life?* None of that seemed possible, yet she had seen the same thing happen with Jacob, and now maybe with Adam.

"Let me go!" Feet shuffled on pebbles and stone. Cain appeared in front of the orange glow, clutching Gabi's arm. Eva felt warm relief fill her body. She jogged toward them.

"Gabi!"

"Eva! I knew you were alive!" He squirmed and wiggled. Cain released his arm, and the boy rushed into Eva's arms, hugging her tightly.

"I'm so glad you're okay." Eva pulled back from him and bent down to his eye level. "What are you doing in here?"

Gabi glanced over toward Cain, suspiciously.

"You can trust him. He's my friend. Cain, this is Gabi. Gabi, this is Cain."

Cain nodded at Gabi, wearing a stern face to mask his concern.

"Gabi helped me back on the mainland."

"So, he was with Adam?" Cain bristled, scanning the cavern.

Gabi frowned at Cain. "I'm not *with* Adam."

"Gabi, is Adam here?"

"Not here in the cave, but he's back on the island, alive. So, are the others. Mari too."

Through the gap, muffled footsteps echoed. Gabi grabbed onto Eva's arms and shot the entryway a fearful glance.

"Don't worry. There are others with us. Who else knows you are here?"

"Just Matt. Probably Mari," Gabi whispered, watching the entryway where scuffling and kicking sounded.

Eva hugged him and whispered very quietly. "The people with me are not bad, but you can't trust them. Only Cain." Eva glanced up at Cain and stood. They watched quietly as Abel pulled himself into the cavern.

Small, padded footfalls tramped across the floor behind them. Eva released a spontaneous laugh when she spotted her furry bear cub chortling and tripping, then rolling toward her, clumsy like its father. She ran her fingers through the soft fur under its chin when it reached her, smiling for a moment before remembering the last time she had seen the cub. Adam had tried to kill it, kill them all. She had lost her mind to rage, lost control, and attacked Adam which almost ended up being a fatal mistake. Papa bear had charged that day, protecting this brand new little one.

"Gabi, it's dangerous to play with this cub. Where is its father?'"

Gabi stared down at the ground. Several pairs of footsteps came from behind Eva. Jacob's face with Abel's eyes emerged out of the darkness into the glow.

"Adam and some of the others killed him." Tears fell down Gabi's face as he scooped up the cub, squeezing it tight. The cub licked his salty cheeks. Eva's eyes narrowed as she rose back to her feet, her rage threatening to make her lose control again. Marin helped Brigid up off the ground.

Eva met Abel's eyes. They were also steely and resolved. He wasn't the same partner he'd been the last time they were in this cave together, constantly at her side all these years, guiding her, loving her or whatever was inside of her, but they were on the same side, at least in this moment.

"He killed our bear." Abel spoke softly, dangerously.

Eva wiped a small tear forming at the corner of her eye. "He'll kill everything."

The shadows and light cast by the fire's flame danced across Gabi's solemn face. Abel stood near the edge of the pool, staring deep into the cave, his back to the group. Marin and Brigid leaned in toward Gabi, intrigued by the little human. Eva sat close to the fire, her red parka drying beside her.

"He's been standing over there a long time," Gabi whispered to Eva. "Isn't Jacob cold?"

Eva glanced over at Abel. "I don't think so. He's not exactly himself." She shot Gabi a tense smile and gazed back into the fire, her eyelids drooping. Even if Adam charged into the cave at this very moment, she wasn't sure she would be able to withstand a fight. She needed sleep. She also knew once she fell asleep, Abel may go looking for the weapons, maybe make all the important decisions before she woke again.

"We are staying here for the night?" Gabi continued to stare at Abel's back. Eva nodded.

Gabi abruptly turned back to the fire and the others. "Do you all like stories?"

Marin perked up at the word story. "Yes, please tell a story." Marin scooted closer to Gabi as Gabi scooted closer to the fire. Eva smiled over at them. She was glad to see that Marin was still himself even with wings and new skin. He had always loved stories of all kinds, was fascinated by the human desire to tell them, fascinated by their twists and turns, and disappointed by their endings, usually.

She turned her attention to Cain who kept a constant watch on Abel. He hadn't moved, even shifted his weight since he sat down an hour ago. Where Eva had once felt anger and jealousy over Iris making Cain, now all she felt was grateful and relieved. She could sleep tonight knowing Cain was on guard. Gabi scooped up the cub and placed it in his lap. The cub wiggled and curled up, resting its chin on his leg, brown eyes wide and curious, following the movement of the fire.

"This is a story that happened after the first shutdown. The events occurred long before any of us were born when my mom's mom was a child. It is a story she told Mari and me, a story her family had told her after they settled near the large river in the southern part of the state. It's a story about the river and its many dangers. The river was toxic and deadly even way back then."

Gabi raised his small hands to the flames and began his mother's story. His tone changed, and he grew animated as his mother came to life in his face.

*For the last five of his twenty-eight years, the nomad had lived right off the shore of the polluted river in the center of a small thicket of shrub* trees, a few miles outside of the city. He was the oldest surviving member of his pod. When the first shutdown occurred, he was only an infant, a preemie no one thought would survive the elements. The whole country had been ordered to stay in their homes. No one was allowed to drive, to have things shipped, or travel across their county lines. The government promised to deliver food, but in a short time it became clear that there wasn't enough for everyone, not even close. Many families stayed indoors and waited, waited until it was too late. Not the nomad's family. His family had packed their car the week before the official shutdown. His mother had worked at the highest level in the city. She had heard a conversation she wasn't supposed to hear, making it very clear how even the current state of terrible was about to get a lot worse. She gathered her family, and they took to the road and never returned.

The nomad grew into an old man. He and a few of the younger remaining members of the family had lived in isolation for decades, most of the group long gone, taken by what they soon started calling The Wasting, each member dying younger and younger. He had stopped speaking to the others a decade before, maybe hadn't chanted or mumbled actual words to himself in five years, a vow of silence in a way. They lived off the scraps and supplies they scavenged in the city late in the night when the cold kept the remaining survivors inside their homes. He did his moving around at night, when the cool, dry, chemical-laced air made his cough unbearable if he lied down.

On one particularly frigid morning, as the sun was just beginning to rise, the nomad had gone closer to the shore than he normally wandered. The other members of his group were huddled together in their tent, still sleeping. He had wandered far from the campsite that night, chasing a scurrying creature into the darkness, hoping for a rare rodent kill to roast up for breakfast. The chase had been wild, and all he got for his effort was a cold campsite. His fire had died while he was away, and sometime during the erratic evening hunt, he had dropped the lens he used as a fire starter. He insisted on keeping the fire-starting equipment, not trusting the others to keep track of it, but this time he was the careless one, the one who had put their survival in danger. They had run out of matches a long time ago. Daily, along with food, water, and other essential items, they searched for flint or a Ferrell rod with no luck for years. They had been using this lens they had found from an old telescope until this morning. The nomad knew if he couldn't find it, he would have to risk the trip into town to scavenge for a new one, hopefully two. The chill hadn't woken the others yet. He hoped once the sun came up, he would be able to track it down, but for now, he was out of luck and freezing and would have to try an old trick. He hoped the sun would be bright enough that morning. It was impossible to tell during the blue hour, dawn still a little while off. The sky was mostly gray, and blue skies were very rare indeed. The nomad clutched an empty plastic bottle. His plan was to fill it up with the clearest lake water he could and try to set some old newspapers on fire by reflecting the sunlight through the water onto the darker print. That method took a very long time and was unreliable, so he also kept an eye out for some old glasses, something that would work faster.

He stopped steps from the sludgy stagnant river searching for the cleanest section of brown water closest to the shore. A few feet out, a couple air bubbles rose, pushing the almost solid, muddy surface layer up.

Plop! Pop!

The nomad unscrewed the cap of his plastic bottle with his gloved hands and hunched over by the water's edge, every bone aching and a few creaking. He lowered the bottle and another air bubble rose to the thick, muddy surface.

Pop! Plop!

A chilly breeze hit the man's arm as he slowly dipped the mouth of the bottle into the water, careful not to let it touch him.

Pop! Plop!

Slurp.

*Air bubbles weren't that odd, but the nomad stiffened at the new sound. It sounded like something was breathing in the muddy water. It sounded like life. Life was rare on the river.*

*Pop! Plop!*

*Slurp.*

*Splash.*

*He dropped the bottle and rose to his feet, squinting out across the sludge. Something weaved just under the surface, big and snakelike.*

*A whispering chant moved toward him with the creature, sounding like a faint chirp of a cricket at almost an undetectable level . . . almost. The song mesmerized the nomad. He swayed, tranced before the river, his temperature rising a few degrees each second until he became uncomfortably hot. He swore his insides were burning. Sweat dripped down his face and neck. His shirt was soaked with perspiration.*

*The creature stopped a foot away from him.*

*Slurp!*

*The figure sank back down, and the muddy bulge slowly lowered until it rested mostly flat with the rest of the surface. The man's hands shook, an icy chill hitting his sweaty flesh, causing his body to shudder violently. He fell back, kicking away from the shore, trembling. Struggling to catch his breath, he stared at the spot the creature had sunk into, waiting for it to reemerge.*

*Plop!*

*A mud bubble expanded from the spot.*

*Pop!*

*The bubble exploded.*

*Plop. Pop. Plop. Pop. Plop. Pop.*

*The nomad's eyes widened in terror. The mud settled and the shore became silent again. Minutes slowly went by, and the man never moved, never took his eyes off the spot.*

*Squish. Scrunch. Squish. Scrunch.*

*Those sounds came from further down the shore.*

*The nomad knew he should not look. He had heard stories of a creature that lived near the river, one that took the form of a beautiful woman and was always hungry. They were all very hungry, but unlike the rest of them, this creature refused to starve or to let its belly rumble.*

*Squish. Scrunch. Squish. Scrunch.*

*It was close now. He could hear it breathing, a faint gurgle with each inhalation and tiny gasp with each exhalation—an underwater creature taking its first gulps of oxygen.*

*Gurgle. Gasp.*

*Gurgle. Gasp.*

*Gurgle. Gasp.*

*The creature hacked several times before its breathing turned normal. It was only a few feet from him now.*

*Squish. Scrunch. Squish. Scrunch.*

*The nomad closed his eyes as a wet hand brushed across his shoulder. A cool mist hit his cheeks, followed by the rotting smell of wet leaves and algae. Five fingers clasped the skin by his collar bone and squeezed. The fingers kneaded into his flesh, tenderizing the area. He didn't dare move or open his eyes. He knew what happened if you let a rakshasa in—that's what his father had called the shapeshifting demon. A rakshasa would devour your flesh or worse.*

*A familiar voice croaked at him from down the shore.*

*"Uncle, what are you doing so close to the water's edge?"*

*The nomad tensed. The voice was that of his favorite niece. She always had a joke and a smile, no matter if her belly was empty or the air black with ash. She was the ray of light in every day. He opened his eyes but kept them on the water, watching as the sun peeked out just a sliver above the horizon. Dawn was here. The sun would be bright enough to relight the fire. Maybe his niece had scared away the dark beast.*

*He turned his gaze toward the figure beside him. His niece stood beside him, clothes soaking wet, feet muddy, toenails and fingernails perfectly cut. The sun glowed off her face as she smiled. Her teeth seemed sharper than normal. She held out his water bottle filled with semi-transparent brown water in one hand and his telescope lens in another.*

*"You dropped these."*

*His hands shook as he took the items. He looked up and locked eyes with hers. Her eyes were gleaming a light brown, almost amber in the morning sun.*

*"Come, we need to get back to the fire. You'll freeze out here."* *Even though she was soaking wet, her color was good, and her lips did not tremble. Her body did not shiver. She turned and walked toward the camp, leaving the nomad clutching his lost items.*

*Whatever she was, she was not his niece.*

*His niece had blue eyes.*

*The nomad screamed.*

*Thud.*

*His body slammed against the sand.*

*Crack.*

*His skull hit a rock.*

*Squish. Scrunch. Squish. Scrunch.*

*His niece dragged his limp body back toward the water.*

*Plop. Pop.*

*Gurgle. Gasp.*

*They slipped beneath the surface, leaving a plastic bottle and telescope lens at the edge of the water.*

Marin and Brigid's eyes were wide.

"Is that the whole story?" Marin leaned in. "What happened? Did she eat him?"

Brigid scrunched up her face, disgusted. "Why would she eat him?"

"He said she devoured people. Maybe some people eat people in this world. I feel like that is something Eva might not tell us." Marin shot Eva an accusatory look, but it was not an angry one. She ignored him. He was right. She wouldn't and didn't tell him about those kinds of things.

Gabi stared down at the ground, thinking quietly. Finally, he looked up, very serious.

"It's an old story Mari told me. She likes to tell scary stories. So did my parents, at least that's what she tells me. That one is from my mother's side of the family."

Abel finally turned from the underground pool of water and walked over to the group.

"Why did you tell us that story, Gabi?"

"I thought those creatures weren't real, just monsters from a story."

"So, you think we are monsters?" The shadows of the fire slowly moved across Abel's face, distorting it. Gabi tilted his face, so his serious gaze met Abel's. "I think Adam should be dead, but he's not. I think you are not Jacob anymore, not exactly. Your eyes are different."

Gabi studied the new green color of his eyes. "I don't know what you are."

"Did the uncle die?"

Gabi turned to Brigid who had asked the question.

"They never found him. The story goes that the rest of the camp disappeared one-by-one until only the niece was left. She started travelling from town to town again, and whatever town she stayed in, people went missing."

"What do you think the girl was, Abel?" Marin asked.

"I think the girl was a way for Mari to explain bad things people do to each other without having to be totally honest with you. Nothing more." Abel shifted his weight and shot a glance toward Eva, frowning.

Eva remained quiet and stared back at Abel, not so certain. Could there be other water creatures like him in other parts of the world? Creatures that possessed humans? Creatures that didn't want to fix the world, only devour it? There were many humans like that, so it didn't seem that far-fetched. She rubbed her arms as she glanced into the fire, leaning on Cain's arm, keeping one eye on Abel. His expression was blank, his jaw clenched. After a while, his jaw relaxed, and he sat down on the ground across from her and Cain, crossing his legs.

"Monster, human, whatever he is. Adam is too dangerous to stay on the island."

"What if you could change him? What if you did to him what you did to Jacob?" Eva asked, piecing together another possible solution.

Abel cocked his head, listening to the other being inside of Eva. He paled and shook his head. "He's too unstable for that."

"Will that matter? If he's no longer at the helm? Couldn't he be changed for the better?" Eva continued, getting more excited by her idea. "He'd be one of your own."

"No, it's not right," Cain growled. "It is not our place to decide that fate for him. For anyone. That kind of choice should be made willingly."

"Killing him is better?" Abel snapped. A storm brewed from deep within him, gray clouding his green eyes. Eva glimpsed conflict but it was gone as soon as it appeared. Looking into his eyes was like staring into the lake's waters, she never knew what would emerge from their depths. She never fully understood Jacob or Abel, but now, there was no chance.

"It might be," Cain whispered. "We don't know what it's like for Jacob."

Eva pushed thoughts of Jacob deep down. She didn't want to kill again, even if it was Adam. She wanted a second chance, and she could feel that the being inside of her wanted it too. His murder weighed heavy on them. Eva had prayed for redemption and now, she felt whatever was driving life on her world had delivered it to her. It must mean something.

Eva stoked the fire with a stick. Gabi leaned against her, the bear cub sleeping in his lap. Before he fell asleep, he whispered faintly, so only she could hear.

"Adam's not going to forget what we did, no matter what you do to him."

Despite the large log Cain dropped on the fire, the cave felt cooler and darker.

# Day 2,415 – Island - Cabin

Mari jolted when the door of the cabin slammed behind her. She blinked her eyes and plunged her hands into the sand. She had slid off the log she had been sitting on. She pulled herself up and glanced behind her. She cursed softly when she saw Adam stumbling down the stairs of the cabin, his shirt still covered in blood from the hunt. He was usually the last to sleep and the earliest to rise, probably to assure that every waking moment was difficult and tense for those around him.

He jogged from the porch and hunched in front of the fire, watching the bear meat smoke over the crackling embers. His shirt would need washing once the sun rose when it was warm enough for him to go without it for a bit. Mari stared up at the cloudy sky, shaking off the never-ending list of chores she made, searching for the evening stars that remained elusive.

The noxious brown haze had blown over the island and out across the lake a few hours ago. The moon was still new, leaving the sky dark and moody, a void to get lost in. Mari shivered as she shot a side glance at Adam, then quickly returned her eyes to the sky, hoping the darkness would blanket her little brother as well. The others had all gone inside hours ago, stuffed with bear meat and exhausted from the hunt.

"I thought I told you all to stay inside? The air is shit tonight." Adam asked, not looking at her. Mari remained quiet for a beat longer than Adam liked.

"Mari! You deaf?" Adam jeered.

"I only came out a little bit ago, after the poison blew over. Someone needed to check the fire." Mari spoke loudly enough for him to hear her but not so loud that she seemed confrontational.

"I suppose so." Adam put his hands over the embers, rubbing them together.

"I'm surprised how easy it was," he murmured, staring over the fire into the trees, eyes gleaming, calculating, hungry for something that he would eventually find and kill. Mari wanted to ignore him but knew better not to leave too much silence for him to fill with his own paranoia and suspicion.

"What was easy?"

"For our system to fall apart."

"One bad apple can spoil the bunch," Mari forced her voice not to tremble.

"Bad apple?"

"Jacob. I always worried about him."

"You did?" Adam's voice chilled the air around the fire. He sounded amused but Mari knew better. "You never told me that."

"I didn't know how to tell you or what to tell you. He never did anything exactly. It just seemed like . . ." Mari stopped, searching for the right words. She couldn't say what she was thinking. She couldn't say that it seemed like Jacob would overpower Adam and take over the group one day. Adam wouldn't respond well to that statement, even if it was the reason he had kept Jacob so close to his side, never letting him get too far from him, never giving him space to remember a world without him.

"You thought he was stronger than me." Adam kicked sand toward the burning embers. Mari's hand shook a bit, and she grabbed it with her other. She switched her gaze from the sky to the fire. She sighed. "No, Adam. Jacob is not stronger than you."

"Smarter then?" Adam sneered.

"No. Neither of those things." *Yes, both of those things.* "Jacob never seemed like he had found a home in the group, not like the rest of us. It felt like he was still searching."

"For Eva," Adam sighed, releasing the tension from his body. His face softened as he let go of the anger that had been building inside of him. "We're all searching for her in a way."

Mari's brows knit, and she turned to look Adam right in the eye, something she always avoided. She was so startled by his strange statement she had to see his eyes, discern his meaning. His black, greasy hair hung over his left cheek, covered in very light freckles. He gazed back at her in a way he never had before. He looked thoughtful, earnest even. For once she didn't feel like a mouse in a cat's presence, waiting to be toyed with or worse. She squinted, searching deeper in his eyes, as the fire's light danced across his face.

"Do you know where Eva is, Mari?" A crooked grin grew between his cheeks like a flower opening with the sunset. Just like that, the cat was back.

"No. We haven't seen anyone since we got here," she replied.

"You saw me."

Adam tossed a log from a small pile that Jake and Lena had dragged over from Cain's neatly stacked log pile by the house.

"Did Gabi stay back at the cabin?"

"No. He came out with us."

"Where is he then?"

"I don't know."

Adam picked up a long stick and stood up. Mari's eyelid twitched. She gripped the log she was sitting on, forcing herself not to move away from him. Adam stoked the embers and sparks flew up and circled the flames like tiny fireflies.

"You don't seem very worried about him."

"I am very worried about him."

"Yet, you haven't asked me to form a search party or even so much as brought it up."

Mari swallowed. Her fingers flit atop the log and back to her lap. "I thought he would have returned by now. If he doesn't return by morning, we should send everyone out looking for him."

Adam stoked the fire again surrounded by sparks, smoke, and flying ash, peering into the face of the giant roasting bear's head. A few of the large sharp teeth had slipped from the gums, consumed by the fire, sinking below the hot embers. Its eyes had melted away, leaving dark charred and smoky caverns facing back.

Adam winced as if something sliced him, and he jerked back, stumbling in the sand a bit. He steadied himself, breathed in deeply, and coughed out the smoky air before he finally tossed the stick underneath the roasting chunks of Eva's bear. Mari felt her fear slip to the back of her mind, trying to puzzle together his odd behavior.

Mari squinted and found herself scooting across her log to the very edge, getting as close to Adam as she could without standing up or drawing attention to herself. She studied his face and brought her hand over her mouth.

Tears were falling down his cheeks as he lifted his gaze to meet the bear's hollow eyes again. He didn't look up from the sand near the edge of the fire when he spoke so softly Mari barely could make out his words.

"It's different . . . killing an animal." He turned away so half his back faced Mari. He sniffled a few times, loudly cleared his throat, and released a loud huff of air. "You think Gabi's okay?"

Mari waited a moment to answer as her gaze penetrated Adam's back, uncertain.

"I hope so," she answered truthfully.

"Something has changed in you, Mari. You're different."

He was right. She had glimpsed a different way, a better way.

Without turning his back, Adam released a low and familiar gravelly threat. "I'll find him."

Adam took a few steps away from the fire toward the woods.

"Right now?" Mari quickly rose, her voice a bit higher than she had meant. Adam stopped.

"If he's hurt or in danger, it's better I find him tonight than wait for morning. Don't be stupid, Mari. You're not being stupid, are you?"

Mari sank back down onto the log, deflating. "No, of course, you're right. Thanks for doing it."

Adam's back was tense. She saw him clench and unclench his fist before he relaxed and strolled toward the forest. "If he's out there, I'll find him. No one knows this island better in the dark than I do."

# Day 2,415 – Island - Woods

Gabi kneeled in the dew-covered grass, sucking the water off a few of the larger blades before popping them in his mouth. It was an hour before dawn, the grass was soaked with fresh cool water. Gabi chewed as he glanced back at the cave. He zigzagged through the forest, stepping over fallen branches and dried leaves, checking his surroundings constantly.

The wind blew through the trees behind him, rustling the leaves. A twig snapped as a small animal scurried off to his left. Gabi jumped. He heard Adam behind every skittering creature in the darkness. He quickened his pace.

As he disappeared into a thicket of shorter trees, a shadow rose behind him. The shadow stayed still as Gabi put distance between them, and then it slowly crept into the thicket after the small boy.

Gabi glanced over his shoulder as he approached the hollowed-out tree, slowing his pace. The tree was several hundred yards ahead. The forest silenced completely with his soggy footfalls when he came to a complete stop. Nothing moved in or around the clearing. As Gabi stood, listening, the black sky slowly turned blue then gray. Dawn was closing in on him.

"I know you're out there," Gabi hissed and turned to peer into the woods behind him. The shadows and leaves morphed into imaginary figures, darting from trunk to trunk; the long branch arms lowering down and blowing forward revealed a tall familiar figure. They blew back, and the figure was gone again. Gabi blinked his eyes, his heart in his throat making it impossible for him to call out again.

Gabi jumped when the first bird chimed. A few early morning risers chirped in the branches above, starting like popcorn on the stove, slow and infrequent at first, then another, and another, and another, until the forest was a cacophony of birds chattering away, and Gabi no longer felt alone.

He released the breath he was holding and moved closer to the tree. The birds silenced themselves, and the sound of many wings beating in the sky above filled the quiet.

Gabi shot another wary look into the trees; the gray light of dawn had chased away the shadows. Gabi turned and travelled another fifty yards toward the tree in the center of the clearing.

Footsteps pounded through the forest a short distance off to Gabi's left, grass and branches swatting a body, getting louder the closer they got to Gabi.

Gabi remained still, watching the green brush. A little further off, he heard a different set of footsteps attached to a different body rushing through the brush. Gabi found himself praying that it was only the wild pack of wolves heading home from a long night of prowling and howling.

Matt flew out of the brush beside him, out of breath and red in the face, holding a chunk of bear meat wrapped in a greasy leaf and a bottle of water.

Gabi released a loud breath he had been holding, relief covering his face. Matt shook his shoulder good-naturedly, smiling. "I'm glad I found you first."

Matt shoved the wrapped meat and water into Gabi's hands and chest. "Here, you must be starving. I brought you some breakfast."

Gabi tried to give the meat back. "I don't want that."

"I didn't want the bear to die either, Gabi, but it's dead, and that's all we have to eat. So, eat." Matt shoved the meat in his hand.

Gabi reluctantly took the meat and then unscrewed the water bottle. He took a long, thirsty swig. He swallowed and watched as Matt removed a pistol from his waistband and began searching the area.

"Adam's been looking for you since last night. Hasn't come back, yet. At least not since I left. I was sure he'd found you by now."

Gabi glanced into the part of the forest he had come from.

"Why? I'm a great hider."

"This island is small, Gabi. Adam's a great tracker."

"Adam's great at scaring people, not sure about tracking. He never found Eva all those years he was looking for her. He didn't find her this time. He didn't find me last night or the night before."

"Maybe he has found Eva. Maybe that's why he hasn't found you."

Gabi's expression darkened as he shot a look in the direction of the cave.

"I don't think so."

Matt eye's followed Gabi's gaze. Frowning, he grabbed his arm. "Come on, let's move them, and get you back." They moved to the trunk of the tree.

"You said I shouldn't go back. Not with Adam there."

"You have to go back now. It's gonna be worse if you don't and he finds you."

"What changed?"

"Everything. Adam's really different and the same all at once. He's got Mari really freaked. He can make animals, Gabi, which is creepy when he does it."

Gabi froze when Matt spoke those words. "Adam made an animal?"

"I couldn't believe it either, but I watched him do it and then kill the poor thing right after."

"He created something and then just killed it?" Gabi's eyebrows knitted, and he glared back toward the shadows in the forest.

"He's obsessed with finding you, talking to you."

"Because I helped Eva. You really think he won't hurt me?"

"Of course, he's going to hurt you. I just think he might hurt you less if you come back. Face him like a man and maybe he doesn't kill you."

Gabi placed the water and meat atop an exposed twisted root. Matt carefully placed his pistol next to the items. "Should I climb up with you or can you pull them out on your own?"

"Matt—"

Crack.

The sound came from behind them. Matt moved first, leaning down and grabbing his gun. He adjusted his grip on the handle a few times. Before he rose again, he whispered to Gabi, "G-get behind me and stay there no matter what."

Matt pushed Gabi behind him as he turned around. The color drained from Matt's face. A dirty and disheveled Adam stared at them, lips thin, eyes gleaming. Matt didn't point the pistol at him, but he didn't lower it either.

"Gabi, get out from behind Matt. You really think he can protect you? What the hell were you thinking? Staying out in the woods? You should have frozen to death or at least be halfway to it by now, but you seem fine. You find shelter somewhere or what?"

Adam shot a suspicious look in the direction of the cave. Gabi stepped out from behind Matt but kept close to his side. He remained silent, transforming his glare into a casual look of indifference.

"I got lost."

Adam's sharp laugh echoed across the clearing.

"Used to think you were a terrible liar. I don't think that anymore, little guy."

Adam's attention shifted to Matt's hand clutching the pistol.

"So, Gabi got lost, and you . . .?"

"Mari sent me out looking for you both, sent some food and water for you to share, if I found you."

Matt nodded at the wrapped-up meat and bottle of water.

"She did, did she?"

Adam took a few steps toward the two boys, then stopped and tilted his head, gazing up at the dead tree behind them. "That was thoughtful of her."

"You better raise that gun all the way and shoot me, Matt, or set it down before I take it and shoot you myself. I can't tolerate a man who points a gun and doesn't pull the trigger, you know that."

Matt's arm trembled as he raised the pistol and aimed it square at Adam's chest, meeting the older boy's eyes for one of the only times in his life. "I can't let you hurt Gabi."

# Day 2,415 – Island - Cave

The golden rays of the sun glistened across the lake's smooth water. An orangish glow bounced off the rock as Eva crept into the forest to the place where she had buried Adam's guns. She stood over the patch of earth, frowning. The dirt was disturbed, sunken down where it used to bulge. She dropped to the ground and dug her hands into the damp, icy soil. She kept digging and found nothing. She frantically crawled around, glancing from bush to bush, hoping she was wrong about the spot, but finally she sank onto her knees and hit the ground with her arms, hissing one of her father's more shocking phrases.

"I haven't heard you say that before," Cain said carefully. "What's wrong?"

"Everything is wrong. We've lost Jacob. The others are all different. We probably have lost Iris or when she comes back to us, she won't be the same. Adam's back and . . ." Eva's gaze fell on the disrupted soil as she rose to her feet.

"I take it we've lost something else as well."

"Adam brought a bunch of guns over to the island, and I buried them. Right here." Eva's lip trembled, and her words muddied into choked sobs. Tears cascaded down her cheeks.

"What happened with him? You haven't spoken of it." Cain placed a hand on her shoulder. She grabbed a couple of his fingers but didn't turn around to look at him as she stood.

"He hurt the kids who followed him if they didn't do exactly what he told them to do. They were all so scared of him. It was so awful. Adam thought this one boy, Levi, had betrayed him with Jacob. He broke his arm and threw him in the lake to drown. He beat me so bad my first week over there, I didn't think I would walk again. His violence changed me, made me do something terrible, something I had never done before." Eva sobbed quietly, turning into Cain's chest. He wrapped his arms around her, enveloping her small frame.

"Whatever you did, I'm sure you had to do it. You had to escape that place and get back to us. He would have killed you if you hadn't, that I know for sure."

Eva wanted to believe that there was no other way, that she had had to kill Adam the way she did. The only other person who knew exactly what she had done was an eight-year-old little boy who was now in grave danger because of her failure to destroy Adam completely.

She pulled back and gazed up at Cain, rubbing tears from her eyes. "I planned it out and everything. I created a living creature, knowing that its only purpose was to act as my weapon against him. No, I created two living creatures for that purpose. I made a beautiful beetle and an exotic tiny frog, both extremely toxic. I knew when we got close to the island, they would come to life along with my other creatures. I knew that the horrible goat that Adam had tried to create would fall apart. I knew how mad he would be, especially when I told him a tiny child had been able to create life when he could not. It worked. The frog ate the beetle, and then Adam smashed the frog which would have killed him, but he went one step further and ate it. It stopped his heart. He was dead, absolutely dead. I killed him, Cain. Something I wanted to take back the moment I had done it."

"So, Adam being alive gives you the chance to do things differently."

Eva's tears had dried up, leaving dirt smudges on her cheeks. She shook her head and spotted Abel stepping out of the cave and taking in the morning sun that had risen a bit over the horizon. "It's a selfish desire. He will kill Gabi if we let him live."

"We won't let him kill Gabi."

"How will we protect him when he's not with us? I came out here looking for him. He wasn't in the cave when I woke up. And the guns are not where I left them."

"And you think Gabi took them."

A gunshot rang from the forest. Eva jumped, eyes panicked. "I know he did! Come on." Eva sprinted into the forest.

"Eva, stop! What are you going to do against guns?"

"I'm not staying here while Adam kills Gabi because of me."

Abel rushed over and stood shoulder to shoulder with Cain, frowning. Cain moved to follow her when Abel's hand clamped down on his arm, pulling him backwards.

Through gritted teeth, Cain growled, "You need to stop touching me."

"Yes, but first, we need to agree on something." Abel tightened his grip on Cain's arm. "This world doesn't work without her. She's our only priority."

Cain ripped his arm away from Abel. "I don't need you to tell me how important Eva is."

Cain dashed off after Eva, Abel following close behind.

# Day 2,415 – Island - Woods

The barrel of the pistol smoked as Matt opened his eyes. Adam yowled. The flesh on his shoulder was torn apart, blood oozing down his arm. He staggered back from the bullet's impact.

"You actually shot me," Adam straightened and took a few unsteady steps toward them, gasping. "If it didn't hurt so freaking much, I'd be kind of proud of you. Finally manned up."

Gabi gripped Matt's shirt, tugging it, terrified. "Shoot him again!"

"Killing me once wasn't enough for you?!" Adam charged toward them. Gabi jumped away just as Matt pulled the trigger and Adam collided with his chest, grabbing his arm and thrusting it into the air.

The gun dropped to the ground. Matt grabbed Adam's wounded shoulder with his other hand and shoved him backward, throwing his entire weight against Adam's chest. "Gabi get out of here! Get Mari!"

Gabi was sprawled out on the ground, holding his arm, frozen, watching Matt and Adam fight. Adam screamed as he landed on the forest floor with a thud, Matt falling on top of him.

"Get the hell off me!" Adam grabbed Matt's face. Matt pushed his fingers into Adam's wound. Adam released a squeal, not unlike the boar piglets when you caught one by the leg. Adam jammed his knee into Matt's crotch. Matt doubled over and released his grip on Adam's shoulder. Adam punched Matt in the jaw with his good arm and wriggled out from under him, kicking him in the face. Adam's eyes darted around at the trees, the sky, Matt, and finally Gabi. He growled. "You're gonna wish you killed me, assholes."

Gabi scrambled to his feet and half-ran, half-crawled toward the pistol. Adam stumbled toward the small boy and the gun. He landed on Gabi's back. Something cracked and Gabi screamed. Adam was on top of him, clawing at his sides, trying to get at the gun underneath him.

Matt pulled himself to his feet and lunged at Adam, landing on his back, arms around his neck. Adam thrashed, not letting go of Gabi. Matt's weight made Gabi scream again.

*Boom!*

Another gunshot thundered from beneath. Adam fell to the ground, screaming, holding his side, fresh blood coming out of the wound. Matt fell off him and rolled onto the ground.

Gabi remained motionless.

"Gabi?" Matt gasped, reaching out toward him.

Eva jumped over a fallen log, Cain now a few yards ahead of her and Abel passing her. She spotted Adam, bleeding and writhing on the ground, nearly foaming at the mouth. Matt scuttled toward Gabi's limp body. Gabi lay face down in the grass, a pool of blood appearing from under his chest around his sides. Blood also dripped out of a small hole in his back. Matt put his hand on the hole and flipped Gabi over. Blood gushed out of another hole in his chest. Matt placed his other hand tightly over the second wound. The pistol rested in the pool of Gabi's blood.

"Help! He's dying!" Snot and tears fell down Matt's face, but he kept his hold on Gabi. Gabi's eyes fluttered open, and he tried to speak, but then they closed again. Eva fell to the ground next to Matt, looking over Gabi's small body, helpless. The blood was coming too fast, and his body was too small. Adam peered over. Even he had tears running down his face. He kept repeating. "I did not shoot him. I didn't."

Abel fell to his knees next to Gabi, looking stricken. Somewhere inside of him Jacob must be screaming out in agony. Cain placed himself in between Adam and the others. Abel leaned close to Matt and touched his arm.

"Matt, I need to lift him up. Can you keep pressure on his chest? Eva will hold his back. Right, Eva?"

Eva's eyes flitted up toward Abel. "I don't think we should move him."

"If he stays here, he dies. We need to get him to the water."

Eva hesitated, processing what Abel was suggesting. They might be able to save Gabi, but he wouldn't be human anymore. He'd be something else. Something like Eva. Something like Adam. Maybe something like the monster from his story. She didn't want to change anyone without giving them a choice, but that's not how this transformation worked. There wasn't time for a choice. Eva nodded and put her hand on Matt's bloody hand covering the hole in Gabi's back. She gazed into Matt's frantic and grief-stricken eyes. "We can do this, Matt. We can save him. You just have to do exactly what I say, okay?"

Matt nodded as he choked back another sob.

"On three, slide your hand away. One. Two. Three."

Matt slid his hand as Eva pushed hers down over the wound, sealing it up. Abel lifted the small boy, Eva on one side and Matt on the other. Eva met Cain's eyes, motioning with a tilt of her neck toward the gun on the ground. He dashed over to scoop it up.

Eva glanced down at Adam as they rushed by him. Other voices could be heard shouting in the near distance. The other kids had heard the gunshots and would find them. Mari would be here soon enough, see Adam and find Gabi bleeding out in her arms. Mari would know exactly who to blame for Gabi being hurt. Brigid and Marin were probably already watching from the trees, staying hidden. She hoped they stayed hidden anyway. Their new forms would frighten the human children, and Eva knew the kids were frightened enough this morning.

Matt stumbled over a root as they awkwardly maneuvered through the branches and brush. Eva and Abel adjusted as Gabi's body lurched. All three of them steadied, functioning as one, and continued toward the lake, peeking through the gaps in the trees. Eva tried to ignore the sticky, wet blood oozing out from under her hand and focus on forging a steady path through the wild woods.

Only a few years ago, this entire forest was dead, the branches were bare, almost black and white against a gray landscape. Nothing grew in this forest, and Eva was afraid of the trees and the possible spirits that dwelled in them. She had never thought the older trees would bloom again, but these ancient creatures had protected the life deep inside of them, outlasting the polluted elements in a type of hibernation, waiting for a time when conditions would be right to bear leaves and fruit again. That time eventually came when Eva's abilities awakened, or more accurately, when Eva hit her head, fell into the sludgy lake, took her last breath as the self she'd been born as, and awoke again with something else inside of her, woke as her new self. She hadn't realized there was another creature co-existing with her for all these years. She had thought her ability to shape these strange plastic creatures into other life was entirely her own. She had believed it was her talents and her creatures that had healed the island's ecosystem, made way for green shoots and blooms to grow from the decay and toxic rot. In a way, that was true. It was her hands, her body, that had done the work, the building, but it was also the creature that had saved her life, the quiet and powerful entity with which she shared her body. It was them, together, that had unlocked the life on the island, and set the healing of their planet in motion. Whatever they were, Eva had needed to become what she was to survive, for any of this to be possible. She would be in bed dying of the wasting right now if she hadn't changed. She needed to evolve into this other creature. She just would have liked the choice, but when you're dead, you don't get to choose what fills you back up with life. Maybe her species, without these worms, was facing extinction. Maybe any human who wants to survive will have to evolve. She pressed against Gabi's wound harder, a tear slid down her cheek, as she studied his tiny, ashen face. Life was leaving him. It may have already. Eva sniffed and clenched her jaw. Her eyes filled with steely resolve.

"Matt, we need to go a little faster. Can you manage?" Matt nodded and picked up the pace. Abel stared straight ahead, his expression a question mark. Eva could not read him at all right now, and she didn't feel like trying. She knew why they were going to the lake and that's all she needed to understand at this moment.

# Day 2,415 – Island - Woods

"Argh!" Adam writhed on the ground, glaring at Cain, clutching his side tightly with his good hand, keeping the wound from bleeding. Blood covered his shoulder as well, but it wasn't gushing out. The bullet had only grazed him.

Faraway voices travelled through the forest from several directions. Cain gripped the pistol, sticky with blood. "Maybe you'll think twice before shooting another person after this." Cain shot Adam a disdainful look. "I doubt it though." Cain studied the weapon's mechanics.

"You don't even know how to use one of those, do you?" Adam asked as he attempted to stand, but fell back to the ground, woozy.

"It seems pretty self-explanatory. Point and pull this?" Cain aimed the gun's barrel at Adam and moved his finger over the trigger.

"I hope you're ready to pull that trigger. Where I'm from, you don't point a gun at a man unless you're ready to kill him."

Cain's expression remained blank as he kept the pistol trained on Adam. "I'm from here, and we don't point guns at each other at all."

Adam eyed the gun, his bravado faltering, but just a little.

"Why did you shoot Gabi?" Cain cocked the gun. Adam flinched at the sound, a detail not lost on Cain.

A few of the voices grew louder as they get closer, a girl and a boy, maybe two girls.

"I didn't shoot him. I said that already."

"Then who shot him? We were all here. You were the only one near the gun."

"Gabi was trying to shoot me, and when I landed on him, the gun went off and it got us both."

"So, you are saying he shot himself?"

"Not on purpose, but yeah." Adam appeared vulnerable for once, shaken by the morning's events, the loss of Gabi, his own wounds. "Just do it already."

"I am not emotional the same way your kind is. I am sad that you shot Gabi and am angry that you hurt Eva, and everyone else I care about, but that is not why I am going to kill you."

Cain took one step closer to Adam, a strange fury painting his face. "I'm going to kill you so that Eva doesn't change you into one of us."

"What? I don't want to be one of you."

"But you are halfway there. Your true self already died. Surely, you remember the moment with the frog?"

Adam paled as he searched through his vague recollections, darkening when he finally spoke. "I remember being on the boat. I remember a frog then a lot of pain. More pain than I've ever felt. I could hardly breath. My heart exploded or at least it felt like it. I remember Eva watching as it happened."

"And for some reason, she felt sad about that moment. Sad that she did what was necessary to survive. Blaming herself for having to take out a rabid animal." Cain pointed the gun at Adam with a clear purpose. "I won't feel any of those regrets."

"Jake! Hurry up! I think someone was here. There's a broken branch." Lena's voice cut clearly through the forest, not too far from the clearing. Cain clenched his jaw and lunged toward Adam.

Adam bellowed out before Cain could stop him. "Lena! Jake! Over here! Hurry!" Cain kneeled next to Adam, gun right at his chest. Adam stuck his chin out, daring Cain to shoot him.

"You gonna kill them all, are you? It's not just me you'll have to kill now. You'll have to kill them, too, definitely Jake and Lena. Eva will forgive you about me, but how many others can you kill without losing her trust?"

Cain scowled, his finger twitched, ready to shoot. "I shoot you now, you die. I run. Only you will die."

"Then do it."

Adam's piercing green eyes gleamed back at him, and Cain locked spirits with the other being he had to kill to be rid of Adam. Cain searched deeper for the creature that dwelled inside of Adam, listening for some answer to this dilemma. If he killed Adam, what of the other creature inside of him? Was he capable of sacrificing this other life to be rid of Adam? Or did he have to take Adam to face the queen like Jacob had done, have whatever existed dormant inside of him awaken and transform this horrible human being completely?

Something deep within Adam answered. Cain paled and his grip on the pistol loosened. He shoved Adam in the chest so that he fell back to the ground hard.

"Adam! You okay? We're coming!" Jake shouted, very close now. Cain glanced back into the woods. He still couldn't see them. He turned to walk away in the other direction.

"I knew you weren't man enough to pull that trigger," Adam hissed, baiting Cain to stay, to act.

"I'm not a man, Adam, and neither are you anymore. With those wounds, without our help, you're already dead. Again." Cain disappeared into the wood long before Jake, Lena, and Dezi finally ran into the clearing.

Jake paled when he spotted Adam. "Oh man, you are messed up." He turned to Lena who looked like she might barf. "Come on, we got to get him back to the house. Mari's got to fix him up fast."

Adam searched the area. "Where is Mari?"

Dezi stepped forward. "She said she heard something by the water and went that way."

"Find her, Dezi. I need her back at the house."

Dezi stood over the pile of blood, studying it. She shot Adam a worried look, one that grew more perplexed when she examined his actual wounds a bit closer. "That's a lot of blood. Is it all yours?"

"No. Some of its Gabi's."

Dezi looked like someone slapped her. "Gabi's? Where is he?"

"Eva. She and a bunch of her weirdo friends took Gabi."

"Eva's alive?"

"Enough questions, Dezi. Go find Mari, now!" Adam barked.

Dezi nodded her head but didn't move. Jake grabbed Adam around the side and helped drag him to his feet. "We got to stop the bleeding before we head back."

Lena ripped off her jacket and pulled her blade out. She cut a length of her shirt off, sheathed her knife and stalked over to Adam. "I can stop the flow of blood on your shoulder but you're gonna have to keep pressure on your side. Is it deep?"

"Deep enough."

Adam glared at Dezi who still stood motionless, studying the clearing and the puddle of blood below the hollow tree.

"What are you waiting for, Dezi? Go get Mari!"

Dezi glared at Adam. Before she dashed into the forest toward the lake, she hissed, "You better not have done this, Adam."

# Day 2,415 – Island - Lake

The crisp, cool lake water lapped against Eva's arms like icy
jabs. Her legs cramped up within moments from the frigid
temperature. Her lips turned blue, and her teeth chattered.
Abel lowered Gabi into the water, two red rivers flowing out
of the young child, clouding the water around him. A swarm
of multi-colored flatworms twirled and swirled around them.
Matt jerked a bit as they slid against his legs and arms.

"Is this going to work?" Eva locked eyes with Abel. The
sun's bright morning rays flashed off the bright green of his
eyes.

"I don't know. This is new to me too," Abel spoke softly
and turned his focus to the water around Gabi. "One of our
kind must enter his wound. They must choose to do it. I can't
make them."

"Just like you chose to help Jacob."

"Yes, like that."

Footsteps pounding onto the sand sounded behind them.

"Gabi!" Mari yelled. She sprinted toward the water, dropping the gun she was holding.

Matt released his hold on Gabi and rushed toward the shore. Splashes followed shortly after as Mari dashed into the water. "Mari, stop!"

"Matt, what's happened? Is that Gabi?" Matt grabbed Mari into a bear hug, and she struggled against him.

"Gabi's hurt bad, Mari. So bad, there's nothing we can do, not even you. Eva's trying to help him," Matt choked. Mari hit him in the chest and wiggled out of his grip. "You were supposed to protect him!" She tripped on the rocks as she pushed against the water toward her brother. She saw the water surrounding Gabi was red and Jacob, his shirt crimson and wet. Her eyes landed on her little brother's still and angelic face, Eva's hand pressing on the wound in his chest.

"Stop it! What are you doing to him?"

Mari grabbed Eva's shoulder and pulled on it but stopped when she saw how lifeless Gabi's body truly was, floating in the lake, a red halo rippling out from around him. The large school of the island's ever-present flatworms spun around him, several of the larger of the worms joined. Eva held Mari as she slumped, and Matt returned to her side.

"I died out here once, Mari."

Mari didn't take her eyes off her brother.

"These creatures brought me back. They saved me."

Mari reached out to Gabi, but Abel, Jacob to her, put his arm out to block her. "You can't. If you disturb them, this might not work." Mari's eyes flashed daggers at him. "My brother is bleeding to death, and you put him in a lake because you think some worms will fix him? You've all killed him."

"He drew his last breath on shore. This is our only hope," Abel stated.

"What hope! These creatures are trying to eat him!" Mari's body trembled.

The worms were starting to glom onto Gabi's arms and face.

"Matt, help me get Gabi out of the water now."

Mari lunged toward her brother but was scooped up by Abel. He held her arms and body firm against his chest as she kicked in the water toward the worms.

"Let me go! He's my—" Mari's words were sucked back down her throat. Her eyes widened, fixed on the wound on her brother's chest. A large, long teal flatworm slid forward, stretching its body to its maximum length, wavy and wide. Its color was an exact match to Iris's eyes. The worm scrunched up and stretched out again. It did this action twice before its sides explored the edges of Gabi's wound, bright red blood flowing over its body. Mari had lost the ability to speak or maybe just to form a thought, mesmerized by this strange creature's dance across Gabi's chest. The worm stretched its body long again, crossing over the gunshot wound. It flattened and spread out, completely covering the hole. The hope that Abel had mentioned snuck into Mari's eyes as she leaned forward, tears still falling down her cheeks.

Eva also leaned in. She had seen this moment when Abel had entered Jacob. That act had healed Jacob, saved his life. This teal worm was making its choice right now, choosing whether it would join with this human and evolve into something new with him. Eva wondered if it was a choice like Abel said or if it was more of a drive, an instinct, or a call of nature that one cannot resist.

Eva noticed now that the teal worm had a lightly speckled back. Flecks of yellow glimmered among the swirl of teal and red. The flecks began to glow first, followed by a teal shine that blinded the group, forcing them to shut their eyes. Eva tried to force hers open but had to look away. She stared at Jacob's body holding Mari and saw Abel, eyes wide, watching the miracle that the rest of them could not witness. The teal light shown off his face and basked him in a glow that reminded Eva of a warm safe place she had been, once in a dream, maybe in a time right before she came into this world. The water felt warmer as the sun rose higher. The teal light disappeared, and Eva was able to turn back toward Gabi. Blood stopped flowing from his chest. He remained still as a teal light shown out from under the water below his chest. It pulsed out through the water, blasting past their legs before it disappeared completely. Gabi's chest pulled up and in, remaining concave for a moment. His eyes opened, and he struggled against an Adam who was no longer on top of him, pushing up into the air. He coughed and sank into the water. Mari found her voice again.

"Gabi!"

Abel released her, and she dove into the water toward her brother. Matt, shaken and pale, couldn't quite form a smile but his eyes lit up as he rushed over toward Gabi. Mari examined every part of her brother, checking for wounds, wiping the blood off with the water and her hands. The wounds were gone, and Gabi's skin was whole again. A slow, cautious smile crossed Eva's face. She stole another glance at Abel who looked pleased but wary and exhausted.

Gabi's eyes fluttered open, and Mari hugged him so tightly that he struggled to pull his first breaths. "Mari, I can't breathe. Let me go!"

Eva laughed, relieved and ecstatic. She smiled over to Abel who smiled back. Gabi was okay, maybe more than okay. After all, he wanted nothing more than to make creatures and now he would be able to do it. He would be able to help build more life out on the island, something he was destined to do. Eva strongly felt that's why the flatworm had chosen to save him. She just had no idea why another worm would have chosen to do the same for Adam.

"Adam will never hurt you again, Gabi. I promise." She loosened her hug but just a little.

"Mari!" Dezi's voice travelled across the surface of the lake. Eva turned to the shore and saw that Dezi waved at them, a bit frantically, fearful. "Is that Gabi? Is he okay?"

Mari waved back and nodded. "Yes, he's okay."

"Oh, thank God. There was so much blood . . ."

Eva searched the shore for the others, Jake and Lena, but they weren't with her. Her smile disappeared as she ran toward the sand.

"Eva, where are you going?" Abel shouted after her.

"I have to make sure Cain is okay. Take them back to the cave. We can't go back to the house, not yet."

Eva ran as fast as she could over the rocks, stumbling only a few times before her feet hit the sand. She stopped to catch her breath by Dezi.

"Eva! You're okay. And Jacob too—"

"Where's Jake? Lena?"

"They're taking Adam back to the cabin. He's hurt pretty bad. Can someone tell me what is going on!"

"Was there anyone else there with him?"

Dezi frowned. "No. Who else would be there?"

"Matt will explain." Eva scanned the beach and found what she was looking for, the gun Mari had dropped. She scooped it up, heart pounding, hoping Cain had chosen to be non-confrontational, and raced into the woods.

# Day 2,415 – Island - Woods

"Cain?" Eva slowed to a jog as she entered the empty clearing. She examined the two blood spots on the grass and crept toward the one closest to the tree. The pistol was gone, and so were Cain and the others. She flinched, seeing a flash of Gabi's small frame face-down in the grass, hearing the crack of his arm.

*Why was Gabi out here?*

She approached the dead tree where she had found Matt and Gabi struggling with Adam. She gazed upward at its flaking and chipping branches. This tree hadn't stored any life for another season. It never grew leaves or nuts again like its brothers and sisters. A few of its dry, brittle branches lay on the ground, along with a few smaller twigs. Eva touched a spot where the bark had been kicked away, exposing the bare wood beneath. Someone had been climbing up this tree.

Eva tested the lowest branch before she pulled herself up, lodging her foot in a ballooned knot. After a few more precarious steps on some weaker branches, Eva was perched atop the fork, peering inside one of the hollowed-out branches. She leaned down and brushed the leaves aside, revealing Adam's canvas back. A wave of relief flooded her body. She grabbed the bag and pulled it up out of the trunk. She leapt down, landing with thud right next to a twisted exposed root. She needed to be the one to stop Adam and the others. She was the reason they were out here, why the others were in so much danger. She took a few reluctant steps in the direction of the cabin, not quite ready for another fight.

Buzzing wings sounded from the canopy of one of the taller trees. Brigid lowered herself slowly to the ground in front of Eva, arms crossed.

"The cave's the other way."

Eva turned. "Brigid, go back with the others."

Brigid put her hand on Eva's hand, the one grasping the canvas bag. "So you can get yourself killed for no reason? I don't think so."

Brigid tugged on the bag, but Eva tightened her grip.

"This is all my fault."

Brigid worked on loosening Eva's fingers clutching the bag. "This is not your fault, Eva. You aren't responsible for everything that happens."

Eva released the bag, and it fell to the ground. She sobbed, tears falling down her cheeks. Brigid wrapped her arms around her as her wings folded into her back, almost disappearing completely. "There, there, girl. Got to hug this messed-up morning out, it's the only way."

Eva pulled back. "Did you see everything that happened?"

"Enough of it. You don't have to worry. Marin is keeping an eye on that awful Adam boy and his two friends." Brigid gazed at Eva with big sympathetic eyes. "I'm sorry you were trapped with him for so long."

"Where'd Cain go?"

"Cain went back to the cave. I think he's a bit upset he didn't kill Adam. I was sure he was going to do it."

"You think Adam will live?"

"Maybe, but he's wounded pretty badly."

Eva frowned and wiped the tears from her cheeks. Even after everything Adam had done, Eva really didn't want to kill him all over again, especially now that she knew Cain had chosen to let him live.

"I don't think we need to worry about him, not right now." Brigid picked up the canvas bag and walked away from the tree in the direction of the cave. Eva followed, examining the faint outline of folded wings under Brigid's skin. Her skin had transformed into millions of tiny iridescent scales. She wasn't wearing clothes exactly, but the scales acted as a shimmering body suit. The scales glimmered when the sunlight hit them. Pale shades of blue, green, purple, gold, and orange blended to form a gorgeous surface.

"Wow, Brigid, your skin, it's amazing in the sun, so different from before."

Brigid grinned and ran her hand across her arm. "I'm still getting used to it. You really like it?"

"I love it." Eva held Brigid's gaze for a moment. Her eyes were the same old Brigid eyes, which was comforting. "Did it hurt?"

"Did what hurt?"

"When you changed, did it hurt?"

"It didn't feel good, but I don't know if I really remember pain exactly or much of it at all. It felt like a dream, like it was happening to someone else. I think most of me died and then was reborn, really. It was mind-blowing. I don't think any creature is meant to consciously experience that kind of brutal transformation."

*Brutal.*

Eva imagined that changing from a creature who walked to one with giant wings would be brutal. She had read a great deal about metamorphosis in insects. The entomologists all seemed to agree that the caterpillars don't feel any pain. They don't have pain receptors as humans do. The phrase "a deathlike intermission" stuck in her head. She imagined Iris turning to mush, her organs melting, every cell in her body dying, and then regrowing from that sludge.

"Do you feel the same?" she whispered and stopped.

Brigid tilted her neck, her eyes looking up into the sky, searching for the right answer. "No, I don't."

Eva's shoulders slumped, and she bit her lip.

"Well, don't look so sad, Eva. I'm not the same but I'm still me, at least at my core. I'm just driven by different impulses, drawn to other outcomes, and probably other things I haven't discovered yet. It's a little scary but not bad. It's exciting."

Eva started walking again, focusing mostly on the forest ground to avoid eye contact with Brigid. She jumped over a few fallen branches and side-stepped a puddle, shifting the weight of the canvas bag to her other shoulder.

"So, do you still . . . care for me?"

"Of course, I do!"

Brigid tossed her arm around Eva's shoulder and pulled her to her side as the cave came into view.

"Do you care for the other being inside of me more?"

"I think I care for you both the same. I don't really know you as different creatures. I guess, I would prefer you stayed this you since that's who I talk to and have loved my whole life. If the creature like me came to the surface, I might like her just as much, maybe more, but that's an unknown."

"Something you haven't discovered yet."

"Yeah . . ."

Brigid's face scrunched up, puzzled at first and then hurt. "Eva, we're not like that. We don't want to leave you behind."

"I didn't say . . ." Brigid was right, that's what she had meant. She feared being left behind or worse, erased completely. Eva squeezed Brigid's hand. "Thanks."

Thunder rumbled in the distance and icy gusts of wind shot through the forest, sending the girls' hair flying. A gray cloud half-covered the slowly rising sun. A flash rainstorm was coming in from the east, already raging out on the open lake.

Abel strode up to the cave carrying Gabi. Mari walked beside Abel, holding Gabi's hand. Matt and Dezi followed a short distance behind, the wind blasting leaves across the sand at their backs. Eva and Abel's eyes met. The tension between them was dissipating for now, but it would rise again. He wanted his friend back, even if it meant her destruction. Their entire friendship was built on Abel loving the being inside of her, not him caring for her. Eva forced herself to think about that every time she looked at him. She could never let her guard down again, knowing that he would destroy her like he did Jacob when the time was right.

Gabi wiggled in Abel's arm. "I can walk on my own. Let me down!"

Eva rushed over to him, ruffling his hair, smiling. "You weren't supposed to go after Adam without me. I thought we were a team."

"I didn't go after him. I'm not crazy like you." Gabi grinned up at her, pushing at Abel's arms, trying to get loose.

Cain ducked out of the cave entrance and studied the healed Gabi. "I'm glad you are feeling better, but it will be a while until you will be yourself after those gunshot wounds. Take it from me."

"I don't think I'm going to be myself ever again."

Abel finally loosened his grip on Gabi. Gabi slipped his hand out of Mari's grasp as well. His feet sank in the sand when he landed. "Did Adam . . . is he dead?"

"No. He's not."

Gabi's lip trembled, his expression darkening. "He's going to come for us."

"Not if we go after him first," Cain said firmly with a quiet brewing conviction. Eva raised her eyes to meet Cain's, but he avoided looking at her as he walked by Abel to stand in front of Gabi. He didn't look to her for assurance that she agreed like normal. He kneeled so that he was eye-level with Gabi and hesitantly placed his hand on the boy's shoulder. He examined his small completely healed chest.

"You are very lucky to be alive, just like me. Like us all. Adam has nearly killed all of us in one way or another. We all know what it is to fear him, but we will not let him win, not if we stick together. I promise."

Gabi nodded his head.

Eva and the others watched, waiting for more from Cain, wanting to hear a plan.

"You were very brave today. I know how scary it is to get shot."

Gabi lunged and hugged Cain, surprising everyone, but Cain most of all. Cain put an arm around him. Gabi whispered something in Cain's ear, and Cain nodded his head. Eva watched this intimacy, curious at their connection and Gabi's newfound trust in him. *What was he possibly saying to Cain?* Eva felt shame for feeling a pang of jealously and suspicion at a time she should just be grateful that everyone was still alive.

Dezi rubbed Mari's arms, trying to warm her up. Eva was surprised that Mari didn't push her away but leaned into her instead. She was shivering and her teeth were chattering.

Dezi's eyes flashed. "Can we light a fire and get warm, then talk about how we are going to defy certain death? Mari's a popsicle."

Mari blushed, unaccustomed to others attending to her needs. "I-I'm okay."

Now that the chemical effects of fight and flight were wearing off, Eva's skin tingled, numb against her wet clothes. The trembling wasn't adrenaline and shock, but her body was fighting off mild hyperthermia. Several billowing gray clouds blew across the lake as the strong winds created white caps on the waves. The storm was coming in fast, and the temperature was still dropping.

"Dezi's right. We need to get inside before the rain."

# Day 2,415 – Island - Cabin

Adam floated in the lake, bobbing violently atop the thrashing water, trying to keep his head above the waves, which were only growing bigger and choppier by the minute. His blood seeped slowly from his wounds, though it should have been gushing. The plastic flatworms crashed against the rocks and flew back out to the deeper waters with the waves, again and again, swirling in the turbulent lake. None of the small creatures attempted to approach Adam.

"Argh!" Adam struggled to his feet.

Jake and Lena watched as he trudged into shore. With dark clouds above and rumbling thunder, Adam took on the appearance of a lake monster emerging from an angry tempest.

"He's not acting right, even for him," Lena whispered.

Jake nodded but didn't say anything, just watched as Adam's feet sank into the mud, charging toward them. Blood mixed with lake water dripped down Adam's arm and his waist. The corner of Jake's mouth twitched before he opened his mouth to speak.

"We got some medical supplies. We should sterilize those wounds now that you've soaked in the lake," Jake spoke a little louder than he intended.

"Where the hell is Mari!" Adam bellowed and shoved Jake as he limped past him. "Where's Dezi? Matt? Gabi?"

Jake stumbled but didn't fall. He watched as Adam staggered through the sand toward the house.

"I want them back here, now!"

"Does he want us to go find them?" Lena tensed, watching the violent storm brewing across the lake toward them.

Jake shook his head. "We can't be out in the rain once it starts, it's toxic. Damn it. If they don't get back soon, it's gonna come out of my ass."

"Both our asses. Do you think he's going to make it? He's lost a lot of blood."

"It's not gonna happen. Adam's got nine lives and a will that can't be stopped. As far as I'm concerned, he's invincible."

"Yeah, I really thought he was dead this time." Lena sounded wistful.

Jake squeezed her arm. A large boom shook the lake. Moments later lightning flashed across the sky. A couple of fat raindrops landed on his face, followed by several on the sand around them. Soon, hundreds of giant raindrops splashed down around them. Lightning flashed again, and the thunder cracked. The two put their hands over their heads and rushed after Adam, not knowing any other compass to follow.

The front door of the house slammed. Jake and Lena followed the trail of Adam's blood into the home that was not their own. Outside, next to the window, stood a boy with wings peering in at them. Lena gasped and pointed, shaking Jake's arm. By the time he looked, the figure she'd seen had disappeared.

"What? What is it?"

"I saw, I saw—I don't know what it was. A really big bird, maybe. It just looked . . ." Lena scowled and shook her head as her cheeks reddened. "Let's just get Adam fixed up."

The two shook off the rain and stomped their boots in the doorway. Lena slipped her boots off first and peeked into the next room. In the living room, on top of Eva's rug with a red, black, and white animal totem, Adam lay motionless covering the bear and the fox of the design, blood smeared across the raven near him.

"Is he out?" Lena hissed.

Jake slid his boots off quietly. "Let's hope. We'll bandage him up best we can and hope Mari gets back soon. Go get Mari's kit, and I'll grab a blanket from upstairs."

# Day 2,415 - Cave

Brigid stood up, moving away from the blazing fire in the middle of the cavern, talking in hushed tones with Abel. The others rested around the fire, long dry, the storm still raging outside. Gabi dozed on Mari. She had one arm wrapped around his shoulder holding his head in her lap. Cain kept a constant eye on Abel.

Brigid whispered to Abel. "The sun's setting. He should be back." Her wings rippled under the skin of her back.

Eva moved to the middle of the group, carrying Adam's canvas bag. She placed it on the stone ground in front of them.

"I took this bag from Adam, when we came out here, after I . . ."

"She killed Adam with a poison frog. I helped her." Gabi muttered, flashing a lazy, proud grin.

Mari smacked him. "Killing is not something to brag about." She turned to glare at Eva. "I told you that you would get Gabi killed, and you did."

"I am sorry. I should never, never have involved him." Mari released an angry hiss through her pierced lips and crossed her arms. "Sorry is not good enough."

Eva nodded as Mari's red-hot gaze burned into her. There was nothing she could say to fix what had transpired. Her actions had gotten Gabi killed. "You are right," she sighed as she turned away to face Cain. "I buried the bag so no one could find it."

Gabi rose, rubbing his sleepy eyes. "Hardly buried the bag. I found it after an hour of poking around the cave. I moved them to the tree."

"The important thing is that Adam doesn't have them. We do," Eva said.

Abel nodded. "Eva's right. Nightfall is almost here. Brigid should go to the house, find Marin."

"We need to stick together," Eva argued.

"Brigid is less likely to be detected and sees well in the dark. Abel and I will follow behind, just in case." Cain rose and turned to Matt and Dezi.

"Do you know where all the guns are back at the house?"

Dezi shook her head. "I'm not telling you where all our guns are."

Matt rose from his place on the ground. "I know where some of them are." Dezi elbowed him. "Ow! Dezi, you didn't see Adam out there. He was worse than he's ever been. I'm not going back to the way things were. It's a death sentence."

"I don't want to go back to the way things were. Just don't want to jump into something new either." Dezi shot a suspicious look at the newcomers.

Matt walked over to Cain, stretching himself as tall as he could. "We didn't bring that many guns out this time. Jake and Lena share the room upstairs. They'll have four guns, two rifles and two pistols. Dezi, where's your gun?"

Dezi didn't answer, face flushed and defiant. Mari let her arm brush Dezi's and whispered something in her ear. Dezi scowled, still refusing to tell.

"My pistol is in the front room, on top of the bookshelf," Mari said. She frowned, struggling with an internal debate. "I also have one hidden in my medical kit in the side room by the stairs," she whispered. Finally, she added, "It's a small handgun."

Gabi shot her a surprised look, followed by Matt and Dezi. "You have a hidden gun?"

"I've always had one," Mari answered. "It was father's gun."

"How did you keep it hidden from Adam?" Dezi asked, awed, her respect deepening.

Mari didn't answer, but her lips curled at their corners. "I need to keep a few secrets."

"That's all of the guns? Except Dezi's? It's important we don't miss any." Abel stepped closer to the group. The others nodded.

"Brigid, find Marin and then, if you can, collect all their guns and come back here."

Brigid's eyes gleamed. "Oh, like a scavenger hunt."

"A very dangerous scavenger hunt. You need to be careful," Cain snapped.

"I'm fast and hard to kill, Cain. I'll be fine," Brigid responded in her harshest tone.

"This is not a game. Only go for the guns if you can do so without anyone seeing you," Abel instructed.

He turned to Dezi. "You need to tell us where your gun is. I don't want Adam shooting Brigid because we missed it."

Dezi stepped toward Abel. "I'll get it myself."

"Dezi, no." Mari placed her hand on Dezi's arm.

Dezi glanced at Mari's hand on her arm before she pulled away. "I know Adam better than anyone here. I'm going."

"You can't go out in this rain, none of us can, Dezi, you know that," Eva whispered. "Can't Brigid wait for the storm to calm down, until more of us can go?"

"I'm not giving him extra time. Like Cain said, we'll follow behind."

Brigid stepped between Eva and Dezi. "This needs to happen tonight. Marin and I can do it. Trust me, please?"

"Won't the rain hurt you?" Dezi asked.

"The rain doesn't bother me."

Thunder shook the world outside. "And the storm is perfect cover."

"It's more like a hurricane out there," Dezi tilted her head, listening, as the strong winds howled through the cave's entrance, whistling through the tunnel, its icy fingers reaching toward their cozy fire.

Gabi cuddled with his sister and leaned over her waist toward Dezi, shooting Eva a conspiratorial look. "Brigid's not exactly human. That's why she isn't bothered by the rain. Eva made her like her other creatures."

"Gabi, shoosh. That's rude," Mari wagged her head.

"It's okay," Brigid said, shooting Gabi a good-natured smirk. "You're not exactly human anymore either."

"I am too!"

"No, you're like Eva." She jabbed his nose gently. "Iris is going to have a playmate."

Eva groaned. "You better not let Iris hear you talk like that."

Mari shot Eva an accusatory glare. "What does that mean? He's not human. You're not human?"

"You saw what happened at the lake. Gabi died," Abel interjected. "The creature who entered him saved his life, but they are now forever connected. The creature lives inside of him."

"Like a parasite?" Mari grimaced.

Abel bristled. "Nothing like a parasite, at least not the way you think of parasites. After I entered Jacob—"

"Jacob? But you are Jacob," Dezi stammered. Her gaze darted from Mari to Abel to Gabi and finally landed on Eva. "That's Jacob, right?"

"Look at his eyes, Dezi," Mari whispered, shooting a quick glance at Abel, frightened. Dezi searched out Abel's eyes and gasped when she finally realized they were the wrong color.

"He is and he isn't." Eva spoke softly and slowly. "When I first discovered the worms out here, first realized I was able to make animals of them, I'd fallen and hit my head. When I awoke, I met a friend." She gazed at the body that was once her Jacob. "I met Abel."

Abel's intense green eyes burrowed into her.

"We made all this life you see together. We made Iris. Cain. Brigid. Marin. And others you haven't met yet. Abel was my best friend for a long time."

Abel took a few steps toward her then stopped. "I do care for both of you. That is possible, Eva." He turned to the others. "When Eva fell, my—I think humans would call them—my soulmate entered her just like the being entered Gabi today. My love became part of Eva forever. So, naturally, I stayed by Eva's side, every step of the way because I love them. I was meant to be with them and have no other way of existing but with them. Our kind is not exactly like humans. We are connected at a much more visceral level. We can connect with each other and other species in a much more intense way then humans can imagine."

"I'm still lost," Dezi stammered.

"Jacob is Abel now. He took him over," Gabi whispered. "Can that happen to me? To Eva?"

Cain coughed as he rose to his feet. "We aren't going to let that happen. What's important right now is that it can happen to Adam too."

Eva shook her head. "No, Cain. I was wrong about saving him."

"I thought so, too, but I saw the being that was inside him, the one like Abel. I could hear her. She chose him because . . . you told her to." Cain stepped close to Eva and stared deeply in her eyes, searching.

"Cain?" Eva's voice trembled as a lump formed in her throat. Cain was staring into her eyes, but for once he was not seeing her or speaking to her. He was speaking to the other inside her. "Don't do that," she rasped. "Please."

"I'm sorry, but I think it's the only way to do this. I can feel it deep down like I've never felt anything before. We need to take him where we left Iris."

Brigid stood up and stretched her arm. "We need to do this while he's badly hurt, or we won't be able to fly him there."

"We'll bring guns, just in case." Abel turned to Cain. Cain nodded.

Eva shook her head. "Wait until the storm stops. I want to go with you."

"No, Eva, I'm sorry. You need to stay here. You will only—" Abel stopped himself from completing his thought.

Eva opened her mouth to argue but then shut it.

*I would only slow them down.*

He was right. Her extreme exhaustion from the journey through the cave and the effects of the violent confrontation in the woods were no longer obstacles she could ignore. Even if she wanted to follow them to the house, she knew her body was not capable of making it long outside of the cave.

Abel pulled a shotgun out of the canvas. Eva inhaled sharply at the sight of it. It was her mother's gun. Adam must have taken it from the cabin. Abel handed the weapon to Cain who took it awkwardly, holding it out in front of him away from his body. Seeing the gun in his reluctant hands reminded her that killing was something that had nearly destroyed her mother, something that was destroying her too. She hoped Cain would never have to kill anything, that he would always stay who Iris had made him to be, a fierce protector with a kind heart.

# Day 2,415 – Island - Cabin

Brigid soared through the cloudy night sky. Thunder rumbled far out on the open lake to the west, now a low distant grumbling. A thin, jagged streak of lightning blazed and struck the water about fifty miles offshore. The storm had shifted direction and was now travelling away from the island. The rain drizzled less and less as the winds calmed. In total darkness, Abel and Cain circled a bend, boots sinking in the sand, as the home that Cain had built for Eva came into view several hundred yards ahead.

Cain held the empty canvas bag in one hand and the shotgun in the other. He dropped the bag on the wet sand. "We should wait here." He held the shotgun away from himself as if it were covered in a contagion.

Abel gripped a black revolver like he was born to hold one. Jacob's muscle memory must have been kicking in. "Why do they kill each other when so few of them are left?"

"Maybe it makes more sense when you must eat to survive, and food is running out."

"Yes, maybe."

Cain tilted his head toward the sky and pointed. Marin hovered outside of Eva's window on the second floor. Cain's brows scrunched together. Marin dodged off to the left of the window out of sight. "It looks like Marin's playing games. It feels like we are too. We have the advantage. We should just go in the front door."

"Someone would die that way."

Marin spotted Brigid above him, pushed off the wall with his feet, flapping his large wings as he flew up to her. They circled, talking to one another, occasionally pointing back to the house.

"Especially if Adam is able to fight." Abel crept a few yards closer to the house.

"He was struggling to stand when I left him earlier. He will have lost more blood since then, even if his wounds were not as bad as Gabi's," Cain muttered, following Abel, closing the distance.

"What was the real reason you didn't kill Adam when you had the chance?"

Cain halted and clutched the shotgun a little tighter. "I explained this already, I couldn't kill the other creature once I saw her within him. I no longer saw Adam, but the possibility of her, coming into her own, being reborn into something like you, someone we needed to rebuild this world."

"It has nothing to do with stopping me?" Abel's green eyes drilled into Cain. He wasn't angry but something sadder, melancholic.

"I'm going to stop you from destroying Eva, but my plan does not involve using Adam as a weapon to do that, if that is what you are implying. I can fight you just fine on my own." Cain glared at Abel who gave him a wry grin.

"Maybe I was wrong. Maybe Iris knew exactly what she was doing when she built you."

Cain turned his attention to Marin who darted down to check the first-floor window of the main room. He peered in and quickly flew back to Brigid, talking and gesturing to her. Brigid nodded and flew over the top of the house with him. Brigid and Marin landed softly on the porch, folding their wings into their backs. Marin opened the front door and slipped inside with Brigid right behind him.

"Adam must be in the living room," Abel murmured as Brigid disappeared inside, leaving the door wide open. Cain's skin crawled, and he focused on the open front door. He jerked when Marin shot out of the front door like a torpedo, wings out but folded back against his sides. Marin's one arm was wrapped around Jake's neck and terrified face, keeping his screams muffled. His other arm was wrapped around Jake's chest and rifle. The boy's legs dangled in the air as Marin's wings opened fully and thrust them into the sky. Jake stopped fighting against Marin and held on for dear life the higher they climbed. Brigid flew out of the door moments after him, holding Lena and her gun in the same way. Moments passed as they flew higher and higher into the air. They began to glide across the sky toward Cain and Abel. As they arrived above them, they swooped down and landed. Jake and Lena swayed, both looking ill. Lena started struggling, but Brigid easily held her tighter.

"Get off me! Let us go!"

Abel aimed his gun at Lena.

"If you make another sound, I will shoot you."

"Lena, listen to him!" Jake hissed, staring at the barrel of Abel's gun and glaring at Marin's hand on his arm. Lena sneered at Abel but stopped talking and struggling.

Abel shook his head and turned to Marin and Brigid. "This wasn't the plan."

"Well, the plan had to change because these two sleep with their guns," Marin said. He tossed Jake's rifle on the ground by Cain's feet. Brigid did the same with Lena's.

"We need to hurry back before the other one wakes up," Brigid said.

Abel nodded. Brigid and Marin handed Jake and Lena over to Cain and Abel and darted back up into the sky.

"You better kill him or he's going to kill you," Jake finally muttered, rubbing his face where Marin had held it.

"They're probably going to kill us too, Jake, you ever think of that?" Lena hissed, anger and horror carved into her face.

"Or just keep you outside in the toxic rain," Abel growled.

Cain's skin crawled and his stomach lurched. He stared at the house, his fist tightening on the shotgun. Worry etched deeper into his brow as he watched Brigid and Marin approach the cabin, wishing he had made a different choice earlier in the woods.

Marin tiptoed through the entryway. Brigid followed and gently closed the small crack she had slipped through, careful to keep the draft from blasting in. She squinted into the darkness. She could make most things out in the dark, but her depth perception wasn't perfect, so she moved cautiously. Marin pointed to the stairwell, thinking to her, *I'll get the other two guns upstairs.* Brigid nodded to him before he dashed up the stairs. She froze for a moment when she spotted Adam sprawled out on the rug in the next room, covered in blankets. She backed away in the opposite direction and slipped into a room filled with sleeping bags and packs. She searched the room but could not locate Mari's medical kit. Perplexed, Brigid frowned at Marin as he entered the room carrying two pistols. She thought to him, *I can't find the kit. See if you have better luck. I'll get the other guns.* He nodded as she exited the room.

She stayed close to the walls as she crept toward the room where Adam slept. His breaths were deep and his body still. She kept as far as she could from him, crossed the room toward the large bookshelves. She saw one of the guns on top and scooped it up, careful to avoid the trigger.

Brigid froze when she heard the floor creak; Adam was shifting his weight. She studied the revolver in her hand, gripping the handle, watching the pile of blankets moving up and down, finally settling as Adam groaned. Brigid stayed still for a long time, waiting for his breath to return to normal, for the restless movement of his legs and arms to stop. Finally, she resumed slinking along the bookshelf. She spotted the thin barrel of the rifle leaning against the far end of the shelves next to a chair by the window. Relieved, she rushed over to it. Her knee grazed something small and hard sticking out from the shelf. The haphazardly shelved book tumbled to the ground with a thud. Brigid tripped, just catching herself from crashing to the ground.

She listened for Adam's heavy breathing. When she heard he was still asleep, she quickly grabbed the rifle, careful not to hit the shelf or the chair.

Marin crept by the front door and moved toward her and the unmoving pile of blankets. She could see Adam's face, eyes closed, cheeks relaxed, and mouth open. He joined her over Adam.

*I don't like the way he feels. I want to leave him here.* Brigid handed the revolver to Marin.

He looked into her eyes, shook his head. *We must bring him back.*

Marin gracefully lowered himself down to Adam's level. He was reaching an arm around Adam's back when a fist smashed into his face. He dropped the revolver which Adam kicked across the room. Adam flipped up quickly and kicked Brigid's feet, sending her crashing down, the rifle clattering to the ground. He struggled backwards, kicking away from them, clutching a very small silver handgun—Mari's secret gun, the one Brigid couldn't find.

*He has a gun!*

*So do you!* Marin thought back at her as he rose to his feet and lunged at Adam. Adam pulled the trigger right as Brigid reached for the rifle.

*Boom!*

"Ugh!" Marin landed hard on the floor. The bullet had sliced through his cheek and grazed his ear. Blue blood flowed down his jaw and neck.

"Marin!" Brigid screamed and scurried across the floor toward her friend.

Adam struggled against the wall, pushing himself up to the standing position, his breathing ragged. The room was dark, too dark for him to make out Brigid and Marin.

Marin, trembling, holding his cheek, thought to Brigid. *I'm fine. Just be still. He can't see very well in the dark.*

Brigid nodded, touching Marin's ear. He gasped, and she pulled her hand back, tears falling down her face. She turned back toward Adam, glaring. She could see fresh blood gushing out his side, through his fingers, the fingers holding the small gun that had shot Marin. She spotted the revolver and rifle sitting next to the pile of blankets. She thought to Marin. *I'm going to try to shoot him.*

Marin held her hand tightly. *That's not who you are.*

She squeezed his hand. *I will pretend.*

Brigid pulled her hand from his and carefully and quietly crawled toward the pile of blankets. Another gunshot filled the room, hitting the wall behind them. Brigid stopped and flattened herself across the floor.

"Don't move! I'll shoot you if you move."

*You'll shoot us if we don't.* Brigid thought, scowling. She slid forward on her belly.

Adam shuffled away from the wall, limping a bit. He stood with the open door to his back, squinting across the room. His eyes adjusting to the darkness, just making out Marin's outline.

"You can't kill me. I don't die, don't you realize that?" Adam shouted, but his voice waivered. The gray sky was brighter, and it was no longer raining. A tall figure stood briefly in the doorway as Adam staggered toward Marin. Adam raised his gun.

Brigid's fingers touched the rifle's trigger. She was feeling the cold metal, struggling to make sense of it. She had never touched a gun before that day. The barrel pointed toward the wall, away from any target. Her fingers brushed the trigger and she applied pressure.

*Boom!*

The bullet slammed into the far wall, knocking Brigid back. Startled, she dropped the rifle and it discharged again.

*Boom!*

Another bullet lodged into another section of the wall.

"Stop shoot—"

A whooshing sound. Adam turned and saw the butt of a shotgun coming at his face.

*Crack.*

*Thud.*

Adam collapsed on the ground at Cain's feet, unconscious.

Brigid sobbed in the dark.

"It's okay, Brigid. I got him." Cain lowered the shotgun. He bent down and pulled the silver handgun out of Adam's grip.

Brigid rushed over to Marin, checking his face and ear.

"It's fine. It just burns," Marin gurgled. Blood had pooled in his mouth.

"It looks terrible. Let's get you to the lake." Brigid grabbed his arm and helped him to his feet. She walked by Cain and glared down at Adam.

"I don't want to keep him around either," Brigid spat.

Cain lowered his gaze and stared at the lump on the ground.

"We get him back to the cave like we planned," Marin gurgled.

"Will you stop talking until I fix you up," Brigid chided as she held his arm, walking Marin toward the door, leaving Cain to deal with the monster on the floor.

# Day 2,415 - Cave

Mari's face was ashen as she studied her brother, fixating on him. Gabi squirmed under her gaze.

"Stop staring at me, Mari. It's creeping me out."

"It's like the stories Mom used to tell us. What if it turns you into a monster?"

Gabi scowled and shook his head, standing up and walking away from his sister, frustrated. "It's not going to turn me into a monster. Eva's not a monster."

"What about Jacob? He's not even Jacob anymore. He's something else. Something with entirely different motivations and desires. That is right, is it not, Eva?"

Eva's lips thinned as she struggled to find some comforting words for Mari. Her own existence seemed in peril in an entirely new way, one she had not figured out how to confront just yet, let alone advise someone else on how to do it.

"For now, it should be enough that the creature saved his life. You would be mourning him tonight if he had not been changed."

"Yes, that is true, but now, he is no longer just Gabi. He's something else."

*Splash!*

Eva's head jerked toward the edge of the underground pool as one little splash became ten then hundreds, and finally a frenzy by the edge of the pool.

Dezi yelped and scuttled away in the opposite direction. "What in the hell?"

"What is that?" Mari whispered as Gabi darted to the edge. "Gabi, wait!"

Eva jumped up and rushed over with him. Thousands of the polylilakes swarmed along the edge, jumping up toward them, getting more excited as they approached. Eva was stunned. She hadn't seen them here before, and never this many, this excited.

Gabi reached his hand down and plucked up one glowing teal piece that matched the creature that had saved him exactly. He pinched it and pulled another of the same color out of the water and folded into the other. He set them on his hand. They fell naturally into his fold and wiggled into place, pulling and tugging until they became one creature.

"Woah," Gabi whispered, reverent.

The other creatures started jumping into his hand, slithering and layering together twisting and turning, slowly melding, some of them glowing, their light shimmering off the others.

Mari crept up behind them, keeping her distance.

"Are you doing that?" Eva asked, awed.

"Kind of. I'm thinking of something, and I can feel them humming back at me."

"That's really good, Gabi. It took me a long time to be able to do that. Keep going." Eva nudged him softly. "What are you thinking of?"

"A spotted wood owl. I saw a picture in one of your books," Gabi squeaked. He shifted his weight from foot to foot, bouncing, unable to stand still, his heart dancing as the tiny talons became legs that led up to a brown body, the pieces blinking on and off, slowly losing their bioluminescence as they became feathers on the owl's chest. The owl's head formed, a beak poked out, and adorable wide eyes grew into the head that was forming. Mari stepped closer, her face flushed and eyes blazing. As the polylilakes formed the feathers atop the owl's head, Mari smiled at her brother, and for the first time since Eva had met her, looked like she had let her troubles go, at least for a moment. The creatures in the pool started glowing more and more brightly until everyone watching had to look away. The splashing stopped and the room went dark again. Gabi opened his eyes first. The tiny little owl blinked its big, round, glowing, teal eyes at him and spun its head almost all the way around and back again, releasing a caw.

Eva laughed. "He's like nothing I've ever seen before."

Gabi pet the owl's head. It moved its talons from his hand to his wrist, clawing him. "Ouch. Watch out, little guy."

Dezi stood behind Mari. "Just like Eva and Adam. Are we all going to be able to do it?"

Mari just shook her head. She had no answer. The girls returned to the fire where Gabi had sat down, playing with his owl.

"Do you think he's hungry?"

Dezi stomach growled. "I'm starving."

"They should get back soon, then we can go get some food." Eva sat down next to Gabi. "Your owl doesn't need to eat. The creatures here don't eat because they have to, they taste things out of curiosity, at least as far as I have observed. They don't need food to survive, not like humans."

"Do you need to eat?"

"Yes. You, too. We're still mostly human."

"What about Abel?"

Eva's brows knitted. "I'm not sure. Jacob had to eat when he was like me, but if the same is true, now that Abel took over, I don't know."

Gabi scratched the neck of his owl. "I will ask him."

*Splash!*

Eva jumped that time. That splash had not come from something small. She rose to her feet and turned around. She had learned one thing for sure from her time in the cave: Anything could come out of those waters. Water dripped off a shadowy figure crawling out of the pool onto the stone floor.

"A *rakshasa*," Gabi whispered in horror.

Dezi stood up and got into a fighting stance—crouching, feet apart, arms raised, fists ready. Mari grabbed Gabi's arm and pulled him with her toward Dezi.

"Now what?" she hissed.

Eva shook her head, peering into the darkness as the figure slowly slinked toward them.

Eva wanted to yell but couldn't force any words out. Her mouth had gone dry. She glanced at the pile of guns at the center of the cave by her other boat. She turned back toward the pool.

The dancing firelight slowly revealed a shimmering, young woman with long, brown hair, a woman that Eva had never seen before. As the figure came into the light, Eva met her striking teal eyes, eyes she had known a long time. These eyes belonged to the girl she had built a whole new world with, but they were no longer in a child's body.

Iris was almost as tall as Eva now, just an inch shorter. She no longer wore the green dress Eva had recreated from her childhood for her. She wore nothing at all but was not naked. She was clothed in multicolored scaly armor.

"Iris!" Eva ran across the cave, barreling into Iris, nearly knocking her off her feet. Iris giggled and hugged Eva back. "You are safe!"

"You grew up? How did this happen? So fast?"

"It felt like a very long time to me. Time works differently deep in the cave, especially in the hive." A twinkle flew across her eyes as she smiled. She rolled her shoulders, and iridescent wings twice her size unfolded. "I can fly! Can you believe it? Me? I can't even make birds fly." Iris grabbed Eva's hands, excited, still childlike. "And the worm creatures—or all of us, I guess—we have our own name— Polylilakes."

"Polylilakes," Eva repeated, beaming back at her.

"Yes! I have so much more to tell you, and so much more to learn still . . . Rhea and Dee are going to kill me. I snuck away."

"Why?"

"Someone was calling me. Someone I could not ignore. It was so loud and powerful . . ."

Iris's gaze left Eva and landed on Gabi, petting his owl, watching her in wonderment. Iris kneeled so she was level with him. She stroked his owl. Their eyes locked, and, slowly,

Iris's pupils began radiating a soft blue light. "You were calling me."

"I was?"

"He was?" Eva's mouth fell agape.

"You were." Iris eyes dimmed back to normal.

"How? Why?"

Iris stood up and shrugged. "I'm not precisely sure."

"How would he have called you?" Mari stepped forward, hesitantly.

Iris shot Mari a perplexed look. "And who are you?" Iris turned to Dezi. "And you?"

Gabi crept up to her and reached out for Iris's hand. Iris took it. "I know you. Or I feel like I've known a part of you for a very long time."

"Yes, I feel that too," Iris squeezed his hand and held it.

"This all sounds so, so unnatural," Mari sputtered.

"It's perfectly natural. Nature has just grown in a way that you never imagined," Eva corrected. "Mari, this is my sister, Iris." Eva turned back to Iris. "Iris, this is Mari, Gabi's sister, and their friend, Dezi. They are some of the kids from the cabin."

Iris's expression darkened. "Friends of Adam."

"Not exactly friends," Eva was too tired to explain it further.

Scuffling sounded from under the tunnel leading into the cave. Cain stood up and brushed himself off. "Eva, we need to hur—" He stopped in his tracks and sucked in his breath when he spotted Iris. He approached her slowly, mesmerized by her transformation. "I worried we'd never see you again," he choked out. Iris ran up to him like the child she had always been and jumped into his arms. Cain staggered back at her extra heft.

"And you made it back in one piece! I was so worried."
She touched his cheek.

"I'm fine. I'm so glad you're back."

They stared at each other quietly for a long time. Iris
scowled, answering his thoughts. "Maybe . . . You really
think changing him is for the best?"

"So, he's still alive," Eva sighed.

Cain released Iris.

"Yes, but barely. I've half the mind to let him die, but I
fear the island would bring him back again, angrier, maybe
stronger."

Eva nodded. "I think you are right. They want him
alive."

She heard more scuffling and grunting in the gap leading
into the cave. "How many years of erosion will it take for
that gap to get bigger?"

Iris chuckled, eyes twinkling. "I don't think you want to
know."

"Cain, a little help." Abel's muffled voice came from the
tunnel.

Adam's pale face slid out from under the rocky wall as
Abel pushed him through from behind. Eva recoiled as his
bloody shoulder appeared next, then his chest. Cain wrapped
his arms under Adam's armpits and dragged him back,
setting him down gently as the blood oozed out of his
wounds.

"Those wounds look awful." Mari bent down to examine
Adam's shoulder, unable to stop herself from nursing a
member of the group. He moaned, and she jerked back. She
spotted Gabi, who cowered beside Dezi. She stiffened, stood
back up, and joined them.

Abel wiggled from beneath the low lip of the cave entrance and rose. Iris scowled at him when their eyes met. Abel stepped toward her, smiling.

"I'm so glad you were able to grow into the adult you were meant to become. That's all I want for us all, to complete our full life cycle."

"You aren't telling us the whole truth." Iris turned from him to Eva and searched her face like Cain had done last night, looking for someone different behind her eyes. Eva recoiled and reddened. Iris reached out and grabbed her hand. "I'm sorry, Eva, but the polylilake inside of you has been trying to tell us something, something Abel is trying to keep from us."

"It's not like that. We just don't agree on a few small things," Abel grumbled and glanced down at Adam. "Like him for one. I don't want to keep him around. I doubt I am the only one in the room who feels that way."

Eva avoided looking at Adam. "I felt so bad about killing him the first time that I really thought I wanted to keep him alive, but. . . now, I don't know, it does seem—"

"Stupid?" Dezi's voice rang through the cave. She had remained mostly silent the whole night, and her eyes darted from strange creature to strange creature, nervous and fearful, but her anger forced the words out of her mouth. "Adam eventually kills anyone who crosses him. Every single person that has ever stood up to him is dead. Except for the people in this room. And it is only a matter of time. It is stupid not to kill him."

Mari squeezed Dezi's arm, gazing at Adam, fearful he could hear.

"I know everyone is scared."

Eva watched as Iris commanded the room, this new creature, an adult now. Eva felt herself shrinking next to her. "But we have to bring Adam, or more importantly, the creature inside of Adam, to the queen."

Iris's teal eyes flashed at Abel. "It's what she wants. You know that. It's the way she thinks we evolve and survive. Together." Iris's voice rose, but she was not angry, just excited. "If we take Adam to the queen, the polylilake inside of him will take the helm. He will be buried."

"But not gone," Eva whispered.

"No, not gone, but not in control," Iris spoke cautiously, stepping around Eva's pain.

"And if we kill Adam?" Eva asked.

"Then we kill the other creature within him, and the one way for humanity to live on."

"What does that mean, Iris?"

"I absorbed a lot of information as my cells broke down and were rebuilt. I saw, or I felt, the plan for our kind and for humankind, an alliance in a way. Eva, I don't think humans can survive without the polylilakes. They will die out. You would die without the one in you. Eventually, all humans will need to combine with a polylilake for their DNA to live on. If not, all trace of humans will be gone and something new will take their place. At least . . ." Iris stepped closer to Eva, placing her hand gently on her cheek. Eva gazed back into her transformed sister's eyes, tears forming at the corner of her eyes but not falling. "You know this is true." Iris touched Eva's heart. "Deep down, that's what you both believe, why she chose you, why you were meant to be together."

Mari stood up; fists clenched. "None of this sounds right."

Gabi squeezed her hand. "I think it is right, Mari. I can feel it, inside of me."

Mari stared down at her little brother, stricken speechless and clamped her mouth shut as she squeezed his hand back.

Eva shot a wary glance at Adam. His body jerked and his fingers twitched. "Whatever we are going to do, we need to do it quickly before the decision is made for us."

Abel's green eyes lit up a bit, tiny flecks of bioluminescence flickered in his pupils. "I will take him back with Brigid and Marin. Drop him in the pool and let the colony decide. It is our way."

"Won't you slow them down?" Gabi asked.

Abel laughed. "Me, slow them down?" He chuckled a little bit more. "I am a pretty fast swimmer." Abel ruffled Gabi's hair. Gabi didn't pull away, but he frowned. His owl squawked at Abel.

"We need to move before he wakes up."

"Dezi, Mari, do you think you can talk Lena and Jake into not trying to kill everyone?" Cain asked earnestly.

Matt took a few steps forward. "Well, that depends. What exactly did you all do to them?" Dezi joined him and gestured at Adam. "Are they unconscious? Bleeding? Missing an arm?"

Cain shook his head. "They're just scared."

"They'll listen to you, Dezi," Mari said.

"Maybe," Dezi said, not sounding too sure.

Matt frowned and stood taller, stronger. "They have to listen. What choice do they have really?"

Dezi raised her eyebrows and patted Matt on the back. "That's what I am talking about, Matt. Look at you. Did some worm take you over too?"

Matt walked toward the tunnel, grinning. "It's just me."
Dezi followed. "Mari, you coming?"

Mari glanced down to Gabi. "Gabi?"

Gabi nodded. He turned to Eva and Iris. "Drop him in the lake if you have to."

Eva smiled as Gabi turned and followed the others toward the tunnel, the owl perched on his shoulder. He yelled back. "I hope you have to."

# Day 2,416 – The Hive

Brigid and Marin bobbed up and down as they flew into the hive, struggling with a limp and heavy Adam. Abel stood with Rhea and Dee watching as Brigid and Marin wobbled over the surface of the pool toward the stone edge where they waited. The large queen lay flat across the ceiling of the tall cavern, poking out like an art deco light feature, for once, radiating no light. In the corner, the iridescent side pool writhed with life, emitting light and colors that constantly changed from parts of the spectrum that most creatures had never seen. Abel gestured to the pool as he walked toward it.

"Drop him in here but be careful not to touch the liquid yourself." Abel stopped a few feet from the pool, also keeping his distance. "The pool is powerful, and I don't fully understand what would happen if either of you enter it or if I enter it again."

"Is it possible it will kill him?" Rhea asked as she crept closer to the pool.

"It's possible, but he's all but dead as it is." Abel frowned as Brigid and Marin held Adam over the pool, his boots inches from the surface.

"I hope it does." Brigid scowled down at him. "I never want to see that face again."

"Brigid, focus. I'm losing my grip here, and I don't want to get splashed," Marin hissed as Adam's arm slipped out of his grip. Brigid lowered with him, and Adam's boot dipped into the sludge. The much larger polylilakes slid up around his foot, changing colors as they pulled him down.

Brigid grimaced. "Ew."

"That's it. Very slowly, now—" Marin directed.

Adam's arm jerked and his foot kicked. His eyes shot open, flashing with fury. Brigid screamed and Marin cursed.

"What the hell are you doing?" He grabbed onto Brigid with his good arm as his feet sank into the sludge. She beat her wings desperately, pulling her body in the opposite direction. "Marin! Help!"

Marin darted over and clasped his hands around hers, pulling with his full force, beating his wings. Adam's grip slipped from her arm.

"You aren't taking this away from me," Adam wheezed as his hand slid down her leg, desperately searching for a hold as his leg descended into the sludge. His hand latched onto her foot as his chest submerged into the glowing rainbow sludge. The polylilakes were moving up his neck, covering his ears as he screamed. Brigid kicked at him until her foot finally struck his hand, knocking him loose.

*Plop. Pop. Slurp. Pop.*

Adam's head disappeared into the swarm. Brigid and Marin fell backward into the larger adjacent pool. Abel kept his eyes trained on the place where Adam had disappeared as Dee pulled Brigid back up onto the stone. Marin retracted his wings and kicked back away from the smaller pool.

"How long did it take with me?" Abel asked Rhea, who stood next to him.

"A few hours."

Water dripped down Brigid's water-repellent skin. "What if he's just as bad when he comes out? What if he's worse? And we just made him stronger?"

Abel remained silent. His eyes searched the pool. Rhea studied his face and sighed. "You believe that to be a possibility."

"Yes, I believe every scenario to be a possibility."

# Day 2,423 – Island - Lake

The damp sand was drying in the mid-morning sun, the air fresh and cool as Eva stepped out of the cabin. Iris soared high above the water, large fluffy white clouds behind her. A mallard drake flew low across the surface of the lake, calling out to the hens near the shoreline. His webbed foot skimmed the water. Gabi crouched in the shallow waters, grabbing at tiny polylilakes as he struggled to put a fish together, laughing as the little flatworms wiggled away from him. He spotted Eva and waved her over.

"This is impossible. I need help."

Eva walked toward him. "You're not trying to make the right animal. Listen to them." She spotted a red hawk lying lifeless on the sand. Grief crossed Eva's face at the sight of Jacob's favorite bird.

"What do you mean?" Gabi asked, holding a half-made fish up.

Eva crouched down next to him and gazed at the half-formed creature along with the bouncing and flopping polylilakes around it. "What fish are you trying to make?"

Gabi shrugged. "I don't know, just any old fish."

Eva shook her head and smiled at him. "You can't do it that way. Have you ever seen just any old fish swimming along?"

Gabi's brows knitted together as he tried to comprehend what she was telling him. "I've really only seen fish one time a few days ago."

Eva thought of the first fish she had made, a blue gill, and how hard it had been for her to create the second one out here on the island. She picked up the pieces from Gabi's hand. "Here, I'll show you. You have to think of a very specific fish. Not just a certain species either, but an individual member of that species. A one-of-a-kind fish but one with a lineage, a history on this planet. You can't just make a brand-new kind of fish."

As she explained, the polylilakes came together in her palm and formed a small blue gill, only three inches in length. With each bend and fold, they molded into a scale, a fin, a mouth, and then two eyes, and a tail.

Iris landed with a thud behind them. They both glanced over at her as the fish flopped its tail for the first time against Eva's palm and took a labored breath. Eva slid the flopping fish into Gabi's hand. "Study him before you let him go in the water. Then, make him a brother."

Gabi nodded and carefully held the fish in both hands, memorizing every curve, texture, and shade of its body. Eva rose, and Iris pulled her into a big hug.

"I want to take you up there. It's so beautiful."

Eva peered up into the blue skies. "Maybe tomorrow. Let me get used to you flying first."

"You've said that for a week now."

Iris linked her arm with Eva's and pulled her over to the hawk. "I still can't make birds fly. I don't get it." Iris fumed.

Eva laughed.

"It's not funny."

Eva squeezed Iris's arm. "It's a little funny."

"I was just flying. I know exactly what it feels like. I don't have to imagine it. Yet I can't make that bird fly."

"I'm sure you'll be able to do it at some point. Maybe Jac . . . Abel knows a way."

Eva and Iris stood above the hawk now. "Jacob's not gone, Eva. It's just different."

Eva didn't look at her sister. "It feels like he's gone."

Eva released Iris's arm and picked up a loose polylilake near the hawk. She flattened it out and smoothed it into the motionless hawk's wing. A shimmering light fluttered across its surface right before the bird ruffled its feather and hopped up on its talons, lifting one up and then another, feeling the strange texture of the sand for the first time. It tilted its head and gave them both a very serious stare. After a moment, it cawed, pushed off, and beat its wings, flying low just above the sand, picking up speed and height the further it got from them.

Eva caught Iris shooting her a jealous look. "Do not tell me you are still upset about this? You can actually fly, Iris."

"I know. I just want to be able to do it." She crossed her arms watching the hawk.

"Well, think of it like this, if you can do it, then what would you need me for?"

Iris frowned, getting very serious. "Do you really think that's all I need you for?"

"No . . . Sometimes." Eva sighed.

"Eva, you are so important to me. To all of us. Can't you see that?"

"Don't you think I'm going to disappear, just like Jacob, maybe Adam?"

"I hope not. I don't think so. I don't think the spirit inside of you wants that, not like Abel wanted it with Jacob. Not like it is necessary with Adam. Maybe each melding can be different."

"I just, I don't see why this world needs me when they could have the one who really made all this happen."

Iris's mouth dropped open. She looked like she might slap Eva.

"Do you actually believe that? That you had nothing to do with this? That you are just some vessel for a godlike being?"

When Iris put it that way, it sounded even more accurate. Eva nodded. She did feel insignificant as the picture of what was happening on this island got bigger and bigger.

"You are important to all of this, don't you see? You made an entirely different species, one with wings. One that did not exist before you connected with a polylilake. They didn't make flying creatures before you."

"I'm sure it was part of that queen's plan all along."

"Maybe, but she couldn't have done it without you making us."

"I couldn't have made any of this without a polylilake."

"Further proof that we need each other."

Iris folded her wings into her back and grabbed Eva's hand again. "You do still need me, don't you?"

"Always." Eva smiled, relieved that Iris still needed her. Iris could always fix things that were broken in her or at least make her forget them for a little bit.

"Good, because we were meant to do this together, and I can't figure out how to finish without you."

Iris plopped down on a dry spot on the sand and tugged Eva down with her. "I always wanted a little brother," Iris mused as she studied Gabi. Where he was just struggling, now he directed the polylilakes to their place with the ease of a seasoned maestro. "He's something special," Iris whispered. Eva had felt that too, that Gabi had a power that maybe none of them had, even when he was just a human boy.

"Yes, I think he is." Eva glanced toward the woods. "Do you think Cain's okay out there with others?"

Iris chuckled. "I think you meant, are the other kids okay out there with Cain?"

"Yes, that's what I mean." Eva laughed. "One thing for sure, this island was a lot less complicated without all these boys," Eva joked.

Iris cackled, shaking her head in agreement. The girls fell back in the sand, falling into a full-fledged giggle fit as only sisters can, hands clasped. Eva felt so grateful to have Iris back and was filled with joy that she had found a way to grow older. They all deserved the chance to age. Maybe they would all get it if they worked together. Eventually, their laughter subsided, and the girls stared up at the sun, relaxing for the first time since Eva's sixteenth birthday. Eva's eyes shut, and she began to drift off.

"Eva! Iris!" Gabi shouted from the shore, panicked, ripping her from her daydream.

The girls shot up.

"What is it, Gabi?" Iris yelled.

Gabi was jumping and pointing out across the lake. "Come here, quick! I see something!"

The girls scrambled up and ran over to him. He pointed out near the mouth of the bay.

"Do you see that?"

Eva squinted her eyes. The sun's rays reflected on the waves, making it hard to see, but slowly a large shape came into focus. It looked like a boat, but not like any boat Eva had ever seen before. This boat was big and official looking with a crane and other smaller boats attached to it. This giant boat was heading right for them.

# Epilogue

*A billowing smoke plume rose above the black cave, and the ground around it shook, sending several large rocks rolling onto the sand. Acres of flames raged on the other side of the island, just visible above the green foliage atop the crater.*

*A large ship maneuvered away from the shore into deeper, rougher waters. The ship was massive, dwarfing a small houseboat moored to a giant dead tree trunk by the shore. The large ship had the length and girth of an old icebreaker used for expeditions to Antarctica, but its top deck was covered in steel and solar panels with four sets of hydro turbines on the back, all designed to keep the toxic air and waters from breaching the inside but also to capture energy from the elements. A large crane stood at the center of the ship, next to a large cylindric water desalination unit surrounded by several submersibles.*

*A trench tore through the forest, and where the trees met the sand, molten lava sprayed up from the depths, large fiery bombs shooting across the beach toward the sea and the forest, setting the foliage on fire and frothing the waters. Writhing masses of shimmering polylilakes were shooting up from the trenches as well, landing in large piles on the brown sands of the beach. A raven-haired young man ran barefoot out of the forest, arm over his mouth, eyes watering from the smoke, deftly dodging the bombs and sprays as he crisscrossed the shore toward his boat.*

*He looked away from the sky for a moment as he leapt over a hot splattering molten glob. He glared out at the ship, resolved, and sprinted faster toward his small boat near the water's edge. The boy had become familiar with this ship over the last few weeks. They had tried to board it several times to no avail, lost several of their people trying.*

*A large shadow flew above him. He gazed upward again, just dodging another chunk of flaming rock. Searching the sky, his expression switched from anger to relief when his gaze landed on a winged figure darting around the scalding debris above him. The figure's long black braided hair flopped against a muscular brown back. He turned to the young man on the shore, his eyes a brilliant teal. The young man ran even faster toward the waters as the cave erupted, sending ash into the sky.*

*The trees and bushes shook at the edge of the beach and animals stampeded out of the forest, away from the heat, ash, and flames. Monkeys, rodents, birds, lizards, snakes, frogs, rabbits, and so many exotic insects ran, jumped, and crawled onto the sand, all creatures they had made together. The young man watched them as he stumbled toward his boat, tears running down his cheeks. There's nowhere for the animals to go, nowhere for any of them to go. One small bluish-gray langur charged and leapt ahead of the rest, screeching.*

*The young man pushed his houseboat into the choppy surf, glancing up at the winged man and back to the langur. The man nodded and flew back toward the mass of frantic animals. He swooped down and the langur leapt, gracefully, grabbing onto his back. They flew just over the top of the oncoming stampede, turning right as another blast of lava bursts out of the trench.*

*The boy glanced over his shoulder as he untied the boat from a large tree trunk, relief covering his face when he saw the man flying back, langur on his back. He tossed a rope into the boat, charged through the water, grabbed the back ladder, and hoisted himself up onto the vessel. He rushed by a makeshift sail directly to the steering wheel. He turned the key and pushed the throttle. It took a few failed attempts, but it finally started. The engine's roar was muffled by the explosions coming from the island. He pointed the bow toward the larger ship and slowly pushed the throttle control, increasing his speed.*

*As the boat moved further from the island, the flying man circled above, watching as the hoard of animals entered the water. Their entire island was erupting or already on fire. The sky was black. Gray ash rained down on the panicked creatures and the rough waters. The winged man lowered, just skimming the waters, flying side-by-side with the boy and the boat.*

*"We must not go to that ship."*

*The boy didn't look back. He wiped gray ash from his cheeks, keeping the boat pointed toward the larger ship. He pushed the throttle control as far as it would go, the boat's engine now working to its full capacity. "The volcano was dormant."*

*"Yes."*

*"They did this somehow." The boy flung his hand angrily toward the larger ship. "Now everyone we love, every creature we created, they're all going to die, all of them, and it's whoever is in that boat's fault."*

*The flying man stared helplessly back at the creatures floundering in the water and stomping on the shore, smaller ones already drowning. The langur cried out to the others like him trying to swim away from the inferno that was once their paradise.*

*"How could any creature have done that?"*

*"I don't know, but everything was just fine until they showed up." The boy tightened his grip on the steering wheel, willing the boat to go faster, on a collision course with the larger ship.*

*The winged man adjusted his wings and darted above the boat. The langur leapt off his back and jumped over to the boy's side. The man landed, wings folding and disappearing into his back. He flopped down on a worn cushion. "Going to that boat is death."*

*The boy jerked his head toward the winged man, eyes blazing. "Maybe it will be their death."*

*The winged man rubbed the creases in his eyelids with two fingers of one hand. "And after all this killing? Then what?"*

*"We fix our island."*

*The winged man brought his hand down his face and around his chin, looking back at their exploding island, flames reflected in his eyes. Smoke, ash, and mud raced down the slant of the crater toward the animals on shore. Bright red lava carved thin rivers through the green, fires erupting on both sides. Another loud blast sounded, and lava bubbled up from the cave's entrance and onto the dark sands as a black cloud grew, enveloping the island until it was no longer visible. Now the story of their paradise's destruction was being told only by the horrific sounds of earth cracking, animals yowling, and a volcano erupting.*

*"I'm not sure even we can fix this."*

# Acknowledgement

Writing *Plastic Girl* as a series caught me by surprise. I had only planned on it being a short story for my daughters. I should have known that characters inspired by them would keep me hard at work for years. Thank you to my daughters for everything they bring to my life. They are a daily inspiration. Thank you to my partner, Michael, to which this book is dedicated. There is no one who supports me more as a person and a writer. Thank you to the climate youth activists for giving me hope. As I watch forests burn, oceans acidify, and species go extinct, I find the strength to fight for the planet's future in their intensity and passion. Thanks to my mom who introduced me to science fiction and inspired me to write because she did. Thanks to my dad for always believing in me. Thanks to my grandparents who instilled in me a love for nature. Thanks to my siblings who made going outside more exciting. Thanks to my many cheerleaders with a special shout-out to Casandra for all her support, suggestions, and time. My copy editor, Trisha, has worked on every *Plastic Girl* book with me. The series would not be as strong without her. I appreciate every single one of her thoughtful notes and edits. Thanks to Katrina who saves me from all the terrifying typos. My cover artist, Leraynne, gets my weird ideas, and I love working with her. Finally, thank you to nature itself for allowing me to be part of it. Every day, I see something that seems like magic whether it be in a flower unfolding for the sun, a hawk soaring through the sky or a drop of dew on a leaf. Nature always tells the best stories. Nature's stories are full of never-ending mystery, conflict, and emotion. I am so pleased to be part of its canon.

# About the Author

An author, screenwriter, comic book writer and publisher, director, and founder of Wicked Tree Press, Jessica Maison grew up by the shores of Lake Michigan and currently lives in Los Angeles. Her sci-fi young adult series, *Plastic Girl*, addresses her fears and hopes for her daughters as the world faces a climate crisis.

Maison's novels, comics, and other work can be found at **www.wickedtreepress.com.**

Book One of the *Plastic Girl* series

PLASTIC GIRL

NATURE SELECTED HER
TO CHANGE EVERYTHING.

JESSICA MAISON

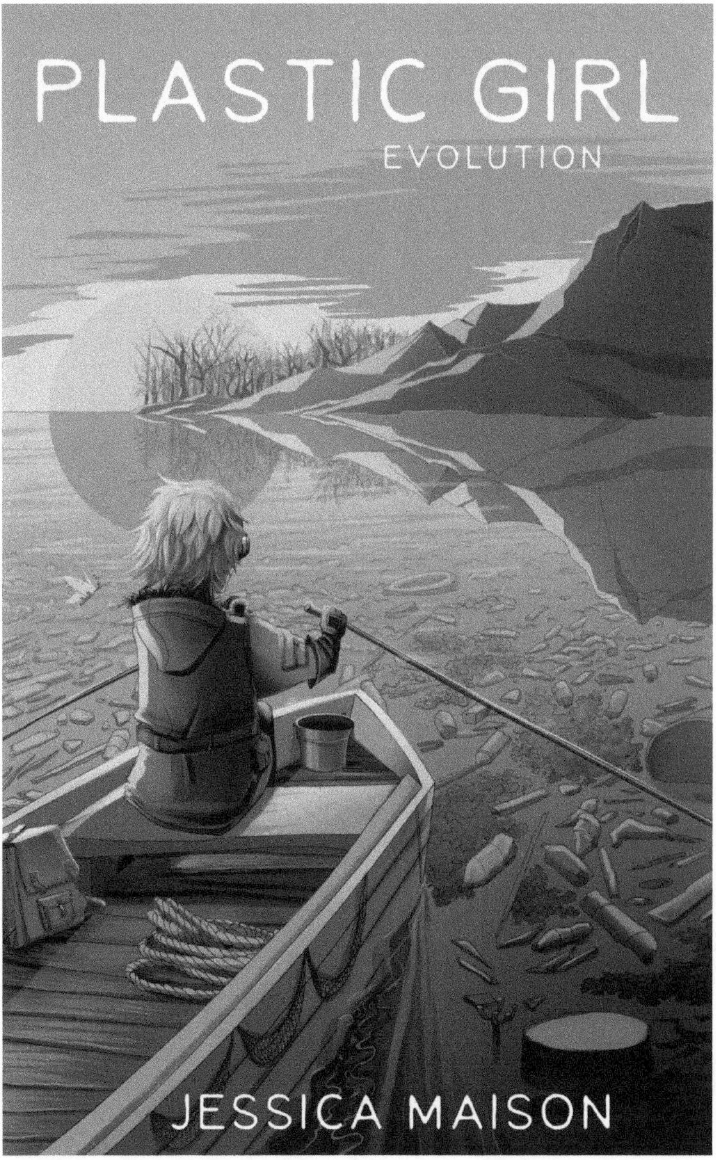
PLASTIC GIRL
EVOLUTION
JESSICA MAISON

# Excerpt from the Prequel Novella

## *Plastic Girl*

## *Evolution*

# Prologue

*Bullets blasted straight through a rusted tin can and into the concrete wall of an abandoned gas station. The can spun off an old milk crate and clanked to the ground.*

*Cheers and laughter filled up the empty station. Two near-feral boys sprinted along the gas station, slapping the faded adverts that hung like wraiths on the windows.*

*The larger boy kicked the can out of reach of the smaller boy who had leaned over to pick it up.*

*The smaller boy shoved the kicker hard.*

*"Don't do that!"*

*The larger boy shoved him back. "Or what?"*

*The smaller boy slugged the large one in the nose. Blood gushed from his nostrils down his lip and into his mouth. He howled and lunged at the smaller boy, taking him to the ground with a loud thud.*

*The smaller boy's head hit the corner of the sidewalk with a crack. He went limp. The larger boy was on top of him and pulled his arm back to punch him.*

*Boom.*

*A bullet hit the cement right next to the two boys.*

"Knock it off, jerkwads. We need to find food and shelter for the night," a gruff voice barked.

An older boy with long tangled black hair, green eyes and a dangerous smirk glared down at them, gripping a pistol, resting the barrel on his forearm while touching the trigger menacingly.

The larger boy smacked the smaller boy's shoulder as he stood up.

"Yeah, knock it off."

The smaller boy didn't move.

The larger boy glanced back. "Come on, Griff, stop playing."

A pool of blood expanded under the smaller boy's head.

"Griffin?" The larger boy ran back and leaned down.

"Come on, man, wake up."

The older boy holding the pistol laughed a mean laugh. "I guess that's one less mouth to feed tonight." He turned and stalked toward the small town about a quarter-mile in the distance.

The larger boy touched the smaller boy's face. He shook him, but the boy remained limp. The larger boy's bloody lip quivered, and tears created dirty streaks down his face.

"Let's move, Jake, or should I just put you out your misery now?" The older boy shouted.

Jake rubbed the blood, tears and dirt off his face with his sleeve. The smaller boy's fingers twitched a few times and then went limp completely. His eyes were open, lifeless. The large boy choked back a sob as he turned and hurried to catch up.

As the boys disappeared behind a hill, the door of the gas station creaked open. A small, completely covered figure stepped out, clutching a quart of motor oil. A red scarf and goggles concealed her face and head. She wore waterproof fishing boots, long rubber gloves and a bright red parka with a hood.

She approached the boy's body and knelt down, avoiding the expanding pool of his blood. The girl closed his eyelids. She spotted his satchel and carefully opened it.

Inside were a few cans of food, a bottle of water, a pocketknife and a photo of a family with two very little boys, one could be the dead boy before her, the other was probably the larger boy who had run off.

She took the two cans of food and shoved them in her bag along with the oil. She picked up the family photo again and gazed at it for a long time. She placed it on the little boy's chest, closed her eyes and whispered a prayer.

"I can't believe you forgot to grab his bag, do you want to starve? I tell ya, I have half the mind to leave you here-HEY! What the-stop! Get her, she's stealing our food!"

The small girl's eyes shot open, and her head jerked toward the voice. The older boy was pointing his pistol at her. She sprinted away as bullets started flying past her, barely missing.

She veered off the road into a neighborhood, hopping over a fence. She dodged through a couple of yards, zigzagging between houses with swift and familiar steps, quickly putting a few houses between her and the boys.

She crept into a garage and shut the door behind her. She stood perfectly still and quiet. The boys ran through the yard and past the garage and into the next yard. She peered out of a dirty windowpane and watched them search the adjacent yard for her as they kept jogging in the other direction.

When they were out of sight, she slipped out of the garage and retraced her steps back through the neighborhood until she arrived at a thicket. She glanced back toward the abandoned neighborhood. The boys were nowhere in sight. She ran quietly through the trees until she stepped onto the garbage-covered shoreline of a debris-filled lake. She shoved a fishing boat into the mucky waters.

The angry, but now muffled shouting of the older boy faded slowly as the boys searched for her deeper into the neighborhood. She gripped her oars and began the hard work of rowing her boat through the thick, tar-like water, putting as much distance between her and those *boys as possible. She stared down at the shotgun at the bottom of her boat and gagged, swallowing the bile back down that had risen up in her throat. It wasn't the first time she had seen someone killed, but it didn't make it any easier.*

Join the Wicked Tree Press mailing list and receive a free download of *Plastic Girl: Evolution,* the prequel novella to the *Plastic Girl* series.

The final book of the *Plastic Girl* trilogy, *Eradication,* coming in 2023.

More info at wickedtreepress.com.

# PLASTIC GIRL
## *ERADICATION*

IT'S A NEW WORLD.
SURVIVAL IS NOT ENOUGH.

JESSICA MAISON